To S.

Thank you for your support,
and may God continue to
bless and keep
you.

La'Ron Readus

7-9-06

LEGACY OF THE DARK WORLD

GENESIS FIRE

BY
LA RON S. READUS

Bloomington, IN   Milton Keynes, UK

AuthorHouse™
1663 Liberty Drive, Suite 200
Bloomington, IN 47403
www.authorhouse.com
Phone: 1-800-839-8640

AuthorHouse™ UK Ltd.
500 Avebury Boulevard
Central Milton Keynes, MK9 2BE
www.authorhouse.co.uk
Phone: 08001974150

This book is a work of fiction. People, places, events, and situations are the product of the author's imagination. Any resemblance to actual persons, living or dead, or historical events, is purely coincidental.

© 2006 LA'RON S. READUS. All rights reserved.

No part of this book may be reproduced, stored in a retrieval system, or transmitted by any means without the written permission of the author.

First published by AuthorHouse 6/12/2006

ISBN: 1-4259-3718-7 (sc)
ISBN: 1-4259-3719-5 (dj)

Library of Congress Control Number: 2006904426

Printed in the United States of America
Bloomington, Indiana

This book is printed on acid-free paper.

Table of Contents

Introduction 1

Prologue 35

Part One: The Beginning…

Chapter One 65

Chapter Two 105

Part Two: The Plot…

Chapter Three 139

Chapter Four 177

Part Three: The Climax…

Chapter Five 211

Chapter Six 241

Introduction

I

Darkness. Complete and utter darkness. Night when it is supposed to be day and extreme darkness at night. It has been like this all over the world for fifty years. No one knew how it happened, or who done this. Maybe it was the explosion of the sun. Maybe it was God punishing men for being disobedient to him. But I know what happened.

I know *exactly* what happened.

It started in the United States of America in the year 2250. The entire North American continent was suffering from a soon-to-be global plague. Greed. It is a plague in *all* of men's hearts. This viral disease could infect even strong-willed men. Soon the plague turned everyone against each other just for money, power, and fortunes of disbelief. But while America was spreading Greed around the world, they were blinded to what was coming.

In Kansas, a tornado formed. Everyone ran for shelter underground, and let the twister do its work.

It did not destroy a thing.

As the tornado was dying, a young boy went outside, ignoring his mothers' call to come back. The tornado as slowly fading away with every step the boy took. He reached out his hand, and touched the tornado, causing it to disappear completely. It seemed that this boy was not consumed by greed.

That is just what it wanted.

The tornado came back and engulfed the boy. Since his heart was clean from greed, it used him for its *real* purpose. The tornado turned into a black and purple vortex and started to grow as tall as the highest skyscraper. The only way people were hurt or killed were by the debris of fallen buildings.

In moments, the state of Kansas was destroyed.

It moved to other states in a circular movement, destroying them in the same way it did its origin state. It spread everywhere, but did not attack Canada or Mexico. After it hit every state on its way to New York, it settled in Manhattan. The vortex transformed into a purple crystal and fell in the remains of Times Square.

Unfortunately, the deed was not done. The jewel started to glow. It set off a sound explosion. It circled the globe, destroying buildings that were already destroyed in America. In other places of the world, it destroyed buildings, activated weapons of mass destruction, destroyed means of transportation, and erased computer information.

The entire world was damaged. All thanks to the Americans greedy spirits. To make sure it would not fall into the wrong hands, it sunk itself under the rubble, and then buried itself underground. However, after it buried itself, the young boy it used to destroy greed forever, reappeared in the rubble.

Fifteen years later, the boy discovered was Simon Sampson. The Sampson family was the richest family in the world, but was also consumed by greed. Five years after his resurrection, he suffered from a ten-year case of amnesia. Because he was inside the crystal when the sound explosion hit, he still has all the information he needed to survive.

If he could.

There were other survivors of the sound explosion and the vortex attacks, but Simon could not find any. It took him two and a half years to settle in what used to be Chicago. He decided he had to do something. He set off on a mission to find survivors from this pre-Armageddon. For twenty years, he searched all of America, except Hawaii. He checked Canada and Mexico.

No one.

He was in the ruins of Orlando when the thought of being the only person left in America entered his mind. He then took the murderous two and a half-year walk to Times Square, Manhattan, where he first opened his eyes to this New World. There was only one thought in his mind when he sat where he first woke up.

Simon Sampson was going to die.

He grew angry. His thoughts were crazed. What happened next left me speechless.

The purple jewel resurfaced!

It was not the crystals' will to come out but the washing from washing of rain on the land.

It was amazing to his eyes. The way it looked. The way it shined. However, when Simon looked at the jewel more closely, he saw an unbelievable sight.

The vortex.

That same vortex that kept him prisoner for at least seven hours that day was spiraling inside the purple jewel.

Simon was so angry at it. It took his life! It took his pleasure, his pain! It took human *comfort* away from him! He was about to snap this piece of crystal like a twig until he thought.

This was *his* fault.

Yes, yes, he was starting to remember. If he did not touch that tornado as a young boy, none of this would have happened. Everything would have been normal.

Simon then got angry with himself. *He* ruined his life. Then he heard something- human voices.

People were starting to resurface from the ground. Simon asked about his parents. Unfortunately, his parents were wounded badly. Because of the sound explosion, the doctors forgot what they knew about medicine and bondage.

His parents died.

Simon was then filled with guilt, anger, and sorrow. His life was overwhelmed by grief. Everything he treasured was gone. With the diamond choked in his hand, a teardrop fell from his eyes. It was the first emotion he uttered in front of people in forty years.

II

The jewel had amazing powers, and one of them was immortality. In Simon's hand, it kept him alive to see centuries. As long as Simon had the jewel, he could live forever.

Technology was replaced with magic. The continents took different shapes and remolded the inside of the earth. The seawater increased three hundred folds. Animals evolved, and some stayed the same. Oh, don't get me wrong, technology started to pop up places.

Hand-held weapons started to resurface.

Simon traveled back to Manhattan, which took him five years to reach. You see, that's where he buried his parents. He put a purple rose, a new species of roses, on each grave. He took the jewel out of his pocket, put it around his neck and tucked it under his shirt.

He started to cry.

Then Simon thought. Five hundred and forty years ago, he was just a toddler. He didn't know that so much could happen if he touched the tornado. This was all God's doing. God brought the tornado to earth. God needed a pure soul to touch it. God destroyed everything to rid the world of greed. There was only one explanation for all of this-

Man

What is your purpose, Simon? a voice said. *Are you just going to stand here while the people responsible for your suffering go unpunished? What is your purpose?!*

Simon tried to fight the voice that tempted his actions, but it was right. The race of man was responsible for everything he had lost, and everything he hoped for his future.

Then in what seemed like an endless headache to Simon's mind, a rush of clear thinking entered his sanity, until he himself became lost.

"Yes," he said. "My people are responsible for this doing." He started to frown. "I had no idea the hearts of men could be so easily corrupted," he said louder. Something happened to the jewel that it hoped it didn't.

Simon was slipping into darkness.

Simon's soul became evil. The aurora of his unleashed power stood over him in a purple light. This drew the nearest officers of

the law to his location. They were street enforcers; the only officers with hand-held firearm weapons, even though there was no crime in the year of 2790. They sensed he was dangerous and pulled out their guns.

"One more step, and we'll fire!"

<Go ahead, fire! > the voice of Simon's dark spirit spoke in the minds of the police.

Simon took another step.

"Fire!"

They fired, but Simon absorbed the bullets because of his immortal soul.

"It's *your* fault, humans!" he yelled. "It took me five hundred and forty years to figure it out." While he was absorbing the bullets, he lifted his left index finger. A narrow beam of purple light shot out of it.

Simon smiled.

"I am no longer called a '*man*'!" he said as he brought the beam down.

The officers of the law stopped shooting and ran. Simon's beam of light went through them like a hot knife through butter.

They were cut in two.

"My powers shall be used to destroy mankind!" He then yelled so loud, it started an earthquake that almost lasted for five hours. The fact that no one was killed made Simon even angrier.

"I am a *God* to mankind!" he yelled. "I am flesh that must punish all these corrupt souls with death! And none shall escape my fury!" He blew fire from his mouth and shot ice from his fingers. With the vortex crystal, he could not be stopped.

Your purpose is not to destroy mankind, the voice started again, *but to recreate it. With these powers, you can destroy God himself. Harness it, and you can be God!*

Simon smiled as he thought of what to do.

"But," he said in a more silent tone, "there might be a way to save your pathetic souls.

"If what's left of the world can create an army and *try* to beat me, I will spare your species," he said out loud. "Use weapons, technology, magic." Then Simon thought.

"But if you loose this *last* war," he said, "the remaining survivors from the war and the rest of the human race shall become my slaves.

I will only be known as **Yamalu**."

I received the news three hours later in the country of Mourtavia. I went to the ruler and told him.

"My lord," I said with a bow, "a man known as Yamalu has declared war to the entire world, against *him!*" He did not look surprised.

"I know Nostra. Get the troops ready. We must move out at once!"

Three months later, all of the armies on earth and every man that was willing to fight gathered in Canada. I had to stay and watch, thank heavens. The army was sectioned off in four ways. Arsenal, Self-Defense, Machines and Wizards. The army was lead by the world's greatest wizards-Sistro, master of light magic, and Endstra, master of dark magic.

This one war would go down in history.

When Simon, now called Yamalu, foresighted the army, it did not worry him. Knowing he did not need it, he put on battle armor that resembled his dark and tormented soul.

What is your purpose, Simon? the voice asked again.

"My name is no longer Simon," Yamalu said. "That is a name for mortals. I am a *god.*"

Then show the race of man your fury like a real god does! the voice antagonized.

Yamalu smiled. "Oh, I will," he agreed. *"Believe* me, I will."

The battleground was set. North America. The army was on one side and Yamalu was on the other. The American men grew arrogant, thinking this was a waste of precious time. British and Japanese troops grew brave. Vietnam, Israeli and Mexican troops started to worry. The Wizard troops expressed nothing. Then the words of a wizard soldier uttered,

"We will not win this war."

Endstra gave the signal to attack. The first wave started to run towards Yamalu. He just looked at them. When the first wave came within striking range, they exploded. Sistro was speechless.

"Impossible!" Endstra said.

"Attack!" yelled Sistro to every troop of men.

"Now things are going to get interesting," Yamalu whispered.

He raised his sword, and out of nowhere a demonic army of black shadows appeared. There were twice as many shadows than the soldiers running towards them. The shadow army hovered and met the army head on. They could not be killed because they were merely shadows. The humans lost fifteen hundred and seventy lives.

"Brother, if you please?" Endstra said to Sistro. He held out his staff of light and diminished the shadows. Yamalu applauded Sistro's magic.

"Well, I guess I have to fight sometime."

Yamalu floated over the men and wizards. He took all ten of his fingers and brought forth his purple beams of light. He fiddled his fingers over the army and sliced anyone who encountered the beams.

"Endstra! Bring out the heavy artillery!"

The bomb squad fired missiles and rockets at Yamalu. He smiled.

"Finally, some competition."

One raise of the hand stopped the missiles and detonated them. But one missile wasn't around his reach and hit him. When it collided with him it carried him all the way to the other side of the battlefield and exploded.

The army cheered in thinking that this war was finally over. Even Endstra was relieved. But Sistro heard something.

"Get down!" Sistro told everyone. The people who didn't listen to Sistro were hit with giant pieces of debris controlled by Yamalu, who was walking with an evil-like smile on his face.

"He's alive!" Endstra yelled to his brother.

"Yes, I know!" responded Sistro with a hint of irritancy.

"Till death!" Endstra yelled as he stood back up. The remains of the army barged toward Yamalu.

He stood there, waiting on them.

"Now, Wizards!" Endstra yelled. The wizards came on white horses and prepared to cast a spell. They raised their staffs toward Yamalu and fired their best attack spell, Minaforten O' Zulu.

Dragon of Light.

This attack caught Yamalu off guard. It blinded him; but since he had the jewel inside him (the jewel was originally created for good), the jewel absorbed the light and increased its power.

Yamalu smiled.

He took out his sword and walked toward the soldiers. When he swung his sword at the humans they were blasted away. He didn't touch the wizards.

He needed them after he won the war.

The wizards and humans continued this war until there were only five hundred survivors out of an army of five hundred thousand. There were three hundred wizards including the army's two wizard leaders and only two hundred humans.

The surviving soldiers charged towards Yamalu, knowing all hope was lost.

"Enough!" he yelled. He raised his hand and the army stopped unwillingly. He then lifted his index finger and made the army float in mid air.

"This war is over," yelled Yamalu. "You have lost. I have *won*."

The humans did not want to accept the truth. The wizards knew it was hopeless from the beginning.

"Tell all of your countrymen you have accepted defeat. From this day forth, I will rule this world by fear and evil. Those who oppose me shall die!"

"Curse you! You filthy demon!" one soldier yelled. Yamalu cut him in half with his finger energy beam.

"Just for that," yelled the new ruler of the Earth, "the entire world shall stay in eternal darkness!" He let the soldiers go and raised his left hand to the sky. A giant purple ball of energy appeared in his palm that looked like it was powered by the crystal itself. Yamalu shot it in the air and into the atmosphere. The ball exploded and the sky grew dark.

It started to spread everywhere after every inch of the sky had darkened in North America. In Mourtavia the people were scared, curious and amazed. The king came to me. I knew what was happening.

"Nostra! What sorcery is this?!" I started to get angry.

"Yamalu has cast the world in everlasting darkness."
I turned toward the king.
"The army has *failed*. Yamalu has won!"
The world was in darkness, Yamalu declared lordship over the world. The wizards were held captive. Science was non-existent to the people. Certain animals were captured for experiments. The human race was forced to reproduce and serve him as slaves.
Yamalu ruled the world.

III

Fifty years later, we are back where I started. Yamalu still had lordship over the world. The wizards unfortunately are still alive because the good Lord blesses you with immortality if you either practiced or were born with wizardry. I am a fortuneteller, so I am part wizard.

But out of this desolation came a sign of hope. Five years ago, Yamalu's magical servants Sistro and Endstra came to see what their "master" wanted.

"Yes, my lord?" they both said in unison. Yamalu, who now had the crystal attached to his chest, said, "I need a charge, dark wizard." Endstra frowned. He lifted his black staff and fed the crystal dark magic. He did this for seven years.

The jewel was pure *evil*, now.

"Sistro!" Yamalu yelled. He came back to the attention of his ruler.

"How goes the process of my new tower?" Sistro did not have a pleasant look on his face. He gave Yamalu the plans and a letter by the construction slave driver.

"Everything is in order," he said to Yamalu while he was reading the letter. "The tower will be ready in two days."

"Have all my things been transported?"

Sistro closed his eyes. "Yes, my lord."

"Where is the tower located, Endstra?"

"Manhattan, sir."

Yamalu smiled.

"Yes," he said. "The place where I awoke five hundred, ninety-two and a half years ago. Where I also found my source of power." Yamalu stood up from his chair and walked towards the exit.

"Where are you going?" Endstra asked. Yamalu stopped walking and turned around to face the wizards.

"*We* are going to Manhattan for the opening of my new home."

"B-But my lord!" Sistro interrupted. "We are in California! It would be a seven-year trip to New York!"

Yamalu took out his sword and put it an inch near his neck.

"Not unless I know two wizards who could get me there in two days!"

Sistro swallowed.

"Of course, my lord, how foolish of me."

Yamalu led Sistro and Endstra to an underground chamber. It held a giant bird of some kind. Only Sistro and Yamalu knew what this rare fowl was called.

"It's a Griffindale!" Sistro said in surprise.

A Griffindale was Experiment #35. Yamalu genetically combined a Griffin with one of the fastest extinct birds in the 21st Century. The Humming Bird. The turnouts were great. It had populated and adapted to the surroundings of the Dark World.

"We will get to Manhattan in *five* days on this bird," said Endstra. Yamalu turned to the wizards.

"Combine your powers to make this creature fly to Manhattan in two days, or I will take away your immortality and watch you turn to dust!" Yamalu was smiling during his entire statement. The wizards had no choice.

They were able to make the Griffindale fly to Manhattan in two days. Before they had reached New York, Sistro dropped a note on the new land that appeared in-between America after it split in two, called Atlantacore, home of the Water Lords.

The note glided toward the glowing blue city. One of the king's servants saw the note falling from the dark sky. The servant read the note and quickly informed the king. The city was a giant circular wall that was around the fortress where Neptoriana, king of Atlantacore resided.

The city and the fortress were illuminating a light-blue light. Atlantacore was a circular island that was created by a volcanic eruption ten years ago, that separated the country of the United States of America.

Neptoriana's servant finally reached the fortress. After he calmed down from running almost completely around the city, he found the king.

"My Lord! My Lord!" the servant said in Watersion. "This note fell from the sky from the great wizard Sistro!" King Neptoriana was a muscular man with a long white beard, long white hair and blue skin. He had a Mer-human tail. Because he was a Water Lord, he could float in both air and sea. He had large scales hanging from both sides of his neck to show seniority and greatness.

The servant gave the king the note. The note, by Sistro, was written in Watersion. It read "sacrifice Atlantacore's most sacred power to God in order to save the world from Yamalu."

"Get the Hydroscepter," Neptoriana told his servant. The Hydroscepter held Atlantacore's greatest power. The scepter held hydrokinesis, and the handle held infinite immortality. The servant ran with haste to get the weapon, but took his time coming back because of its extreme weight.

The king took the scepter from the servant with ease.

Neptoriana held the staff up with both hands and said a small chant in Watersion.

"I sacrifice this weapon to you oh, Lord, hoping in return to help save the world and the human race." Amazingly, the scepter disappeared into a glittery blue fog. It rose to the glass roof and went through it.

The servant was in shock. "Does that mean," the servant began to say, "that there really *is* a God?!" The king started to smile as he watched the blue vapor go into the dark sky.

"There was *always* a God," he said to his servant. "Let's just hope God uses our power to help the reconstruction of our lives."

The Griffindale slowly landed on one of Manhattan's new airstrips for Yamalu's carrier birds. The wizards left the bird first. They watched Yamalu walk off the bird in mid air. When he reached the ground, he continued walking with his arms behind his back. His captive wizards followed.

"My lord," Endstra began to say, "If it could be granted, my brother and I ask to retrieve the Informant Tractor for your tower you ordered from Dimbar."

"And the weapons of darkness you told Camenstra to construct," Sistro added.

Yamalu stopped walking.

"Dimbar and Camenstra are a ways from Manhattan," he said. He then turned around and faced the wizards.

"Travel on foot."

The wizard brothers' first stop was Dimbar, the only city created within the bowels of the earth. The entrance was where the city of Iraq once stood. It is now called the Hidden Death Ocean, a giant desert filled with endless waves of sand. Almost one hundred percent of the desert was filled with dry quicksand;

Whoever came to the Hidden Death Ocean never returned.

But the citizens of Dimbar used this to their advantage. Of all the quicksand traps, Dimbar was able to survive underground. Dimbar was a city of second chances. It was a city for a better life. Only three quicksand traps lead to the main entrance of the city.

Every other quicksand trap killed their victims instantly.

"How do we know which sand trap is the entrance?" Sistro asked.

"Have faith, brother," Endstra said. He took a stone out of his robes and threw it. It landed in the sand. There was a half-second delay before the sand around it swirled like a small tornado. The top of the tornado closed like a mouth and went back into the sand.

The stone was gone.

Sistro took a light stone out of his robes. It was the only source of light the desert had in fifty years. He threw it. The light illuminated more and more until it revealed the safe places to stand and where the real quicksand traps were. The wizards ran to the nearest safe spot before the stone landed. It turned out while they were running, they activated one of Dimbar's trap door entrances. Sistro and Endstra fell through the door. It automatically closed and refilled the hole with sand. Sistro and Endstra slid down the slim tunnel, and divided.

They landed next to each other, poured with the sand that was caught with them at the trap door. They brushed themselves off and exited the arrival area.

"Well, that was fun," Endstra said to his brother. They were walking out of the greeting area and saw the underground city of Dimbar.

The spectacular city was as big as the state of Nebraska used to be. People were able to replenish transportation needs from six hundred years ago when the vortex did its destruction. The city, on its own island, was surrounded by groundwater. Surrounding the water was the modern-day shelter. The buildings in both cities and the suburban homes were made of marble, granite, stone, and metal. Dimbar, a city, tried to resemble a civilization lost over six hundred years ago.

"Behold the city of Dimbar," said Endstra to his baffled brother. "Home of the Earth-Dwellers." They made their way through the suburbs, until they reached the city. There, they separated. Endstra went to transport the item Yamalu wanted. And Sistro went to talk to the king of Dimbar.

Kowatuu was the king of Dimbar. This tall, slim, muscular African American man was very proud of his city. Everyone who lived there loved this man. He was the perfect role model. He was looking over the city when Sistro walked in.

"Ah, Sistro!" Kowatuu said. "What did your dark master send you here for? More supplies?!" Sistro closed his eyes and smiled.

"You know my coming was not of Yamalu's will," he said with a sharp headshake.

Kowatuu continued to look out of the window.

"You also know," Sistro said as Kowatuu faced him, "why I *am* here."

Sistro looked at Kowatuu with confidence.

Kowatuu looked back.

He walked toward Sistro, and then stopped shoulder-to-shoulder. A giant diamond appeared in front of Sistro.

"This is Grodera," Kowatuu said, "the jewel of the earth." Sistro touched it, and it started to glow.

"This diamond holds two powers," said Kowatuu. "Biokinesis and infinite immortality."

Sistro smiled.

"Thank you very much, my friend," he said. Kowatuu put his hand on Sistro's shoulder.

"You are welcome, wizard. I just pray to God it would help terminate that demon for all eternity." Sistro took the diamond and started to head out the door.

"By the way," Sistro said, "are you familiar with the king of Yalutar?"

The noble king nodded his head.

"Can you tell him about my favor and see if you could get his most powerful weapon?

"I'll tell him you asked," Kowatuu said with a smile.

Out near the entrance to the desert, Endstra sacrificed the Grodera diamond to God just like Neptoriana. "So," Endstra asked his brother, "how do we get to Camenstra from here?" Sistro looked around and saw the other side of the HDO (Hidden Death Ocean)

"We go north," he said.

"North of *what?*"

"Past the ocean," he said as he pointed towards it. "We are not far."

The three-day journey to Camenstra was a long one. Sistro and Endstra made camp at the top of a mountain. They could see Camentsra's gates.

"When do you want to head down there?" asked Endstra.

"In a few hours. King Embora is not expecting us." Sistro looked up past the gates. The tallest tower beyond the height of the gates was where the king lived.

Sistro pointed at the tower.

"That's where King Embora dwells, he said. "It will be six o' clock in the morning in two hours. That will be the time we enter the city."

Endstra closed his eyes and smiled.

"Then what are we waiting for?" Endstra said. "Let's get some rest!"

Sistro smiled, lied down, closed his eyes and went to sleep.

IV

It started with Sistro riding a white horse. He rode to his village; a beautiful heavenly city with a white glow on every building. He was the King of all Wizards and his brother was second in command. For you see, this was his life <u>before</u> Simon Sampson became the man-demon, Yamalu.

"Summon the council of wizards immediately," he told one of his servants.

"May I ask what for, my lord?" he questioned.

"No, you may not. This is none of your concern."

The servant bowed, and went out the main door. Sistro grabbed his armrests and closed his eyes. When he opened them, the council of wizards was around a star-shaped table. Sistro was walking down a set of stairs leading to his seat at the table.

"Welcome, ladies and gentlemen."

"You are the one that should be welcome, Sistro," Lady Lunaris said to their master in command.

"Thank you, wizard of space," he said with a nod and a smile. "I have called you all here for one reason."

Sistro lowered his hand to signify the council to sit down.

"There is a rumor about a man by the name of Yamalu challenging every army in the world to have a war against himself."

The council was silent for at least five seconds, until Medosa asked a question.

"Who was this <u>'Yamalu'</u> according to history?"

"According to history," Sistro said, "this mortal should have <u>died</u> four hundred and ninety years ago."

"His name was Simon Sampson," continued Sistro. "He was the son of the richest family in the world back in the 23rd Century. Shall I continue?"

Everyone nodded.

"Simon Sampson was also the pure soul God needed for the vortex to rid the world of the greed plague.

Everyone knew what Sistro was talking about.

"So, the legend is true," whispered Lady Lunaris.

Sistro nodded.

"Unfortunately after it took crystal form, hid itself and revived Simon's soul, he found it and kept it for himself. Five hundred years later, he used its powers for evil purposes.

He became Yamalu."

Everyone was silent. Even though what they heard was true, they still could not believe it.

"So," said Sistro, "what shall we do, then?"

There was a moment of silence.

"There's nothing we can do," Medosa said. "Even if we join the mortals in battle, we all know in our hearts we will not be victorious."

Medosa stood up and looked at Sistro.

He stood, also.

"What are you, mad?!" he yelled at Medosa. "We won't be able to survive!"

"There is no other way, Sistro," said Medosa. "If we don't, we will spend an eternity in enslavement!"

"I refuse to abandon the Earth in its time of need!" He then paused.

"I _forbid_ it!!" he yelled.

Medosa sat down.

"I know we will not win this war, but if we don't participate, how can we help the future?"

Sistro sat down.

"After we lose the war, we will be enslaved. My brother and I will be his personal 'magic keepers'. But when we get the opportunity, we will send out messages to the four cities of power: Atlantacore, Camenstra, Dimbar and Yalutar. Some of these cities don't exist yet.

They will sacrifice a treasure or weapon to God, with some kind of kinetic power and infinite immortality.

"Years after our quest, God will bless four children each with kinetic and immortal power. They will grow up and rid us of Yamalu. Are there any questions?"

Lady Lunaris stood. "Is it possible we could do this, now?"

"No Lunaris, it is not."

She slowly sat down.

"Remember three of these cities don't exist yet, and doing this now would tamper with our future."

Medosa raised his hand. "Then I vote yes in your favor, Lord Sistro."

Lady Lunaris raised her hand. "Yes," she said with a nod. Soon the rest of the council raised their hands and accepted this prophecy.

Sistro stood up.

"Then it is agreed," he said. "The rule of Yamalu will be a short one."

The Council of Wizards took their leave; Sistro then turned around and suddenly was in the Last War. This was the war the armies of the Earth had against Yamalu. Sistro and his brother were on horses side by side watching Yamalu send human troops into the Earth's atmosphere.

"You know this war is impossible to win," Endstra told his brother.

"I know," Sistro said with a smile.

"Then why send these people to their deaths?" Endstra asked. "Why, brother?"

Sistro smiled.

"Because with their sacrifices," he said, "there will be hope of victory in the future."

Sistro looked at the humans fighting one man in hopes they can continue to live their lives in what they call "peace".

They were fighting for freedom.

Sistro understood why they were dying for their cause. He closed his eyes, and a tear ran down his left cheek.

When he opened them, he was standing in a dark wasteland.

Darkness filled the sky. Skeletons of men who died in this "ultimate" war were laid on the ground exactly where they lied during the Last War. Everything around Sistro was dark and gloomy. There was an eerie quiet until a Sakkaroid – a giant ten-legged animal with one eye – approached him.

Yamalu appeared on its head.

"You like what I've done to the place?" he said with a grin.

"What have you done with my brother?" Sistro demanded. He then noticed the vortex jewel molded on his chest. The energy inside started to turn black. Yamalu's evil laugh got Sistro's attention back on him.

"Oh, I'm sorry, wizard of light," he said. "But that's for me to know, and for you to find out."

Yamalu took out his sword. He held it over the ground and dropped it. It landed face up, the blade in the ground. It bled a dark purple liquid and trapped Sistro inside a giant circle. The liquid soaked into the ground; it transformed into a mini-army of one hundred demonic shadows with weapons and shields.

Sistro smiled.

"You don't really think an army of darkness can beat a magician of light, do you?"

Yamalu smiled.

"There's only one way to find out."

The demon shadow army ran towards him. Sistro put his staff in front of him and let the shadows cover him, but the shadows covering Sistro exploded out of existence. Sistro floated in the air with a sword of light replacing his staff, chest plate armor replacing robes and shortened hair instead of his long locks.

He was glowing white.

"Now," Yamalu whispered, "things are getting interesting."

Sistro was falling toward the remains of the dark army, he lifted his sword. As soon as he hit the ground, a light explosion knocked one-third of the army out of existence. The shadows kept coming, until Sistro knocked every one backed where they belonged.

"Well done, Sistro," Yamalu said with a clap. Sistro looked at him and in a burst of light, returned to his normal state.

"According to my knowledge," said Yamalu, "that was called a madrocellular transformation, was it not?"

Sistro smirked.

"A person with the power of the madrocellular," said Sistro, "can transform five times. Only one with a pure heart can obtain it."

Yamalu smiled.

"How about a pure energy source?"

Yamalu's hands swept pass his jewel. It turned purple again. He closed his eyes and started to concentrate. A giant purple ball covered him. The ball turned into a shell, cracked and exploded into thousands of pieces.

He was in his first madrocellular transformation!

"Inconceivable!" Sistro whispered to himself. Yamalu was muscular, with long black hair, a sword on each side of his waist. He had black pants made of leather with metal boots. There was a tattoo of a giant black head dragon on his chest and stomach.

"My soul may not be pure anymore, but I can create the illusion of a pure soul to transform!"

Sistro frowned at the fact that Yamalu had the power to create a pure heart in order to activate a madrocellular transformation. Yamalu jumped off the Sakkaroid and took his sword out of the ground.

"Tell me, Sistro," Yamalu said. "Are you up to the challenge of facing the world's first all-powerful dictator who just won a major war against the world about two hours ago?"

Sistro stood up tall with his staff in his left hand.

"If I win?"

Yamalu smiled.

"I surrender my dictatorship and release the human race from enslavement."

Sistro went back into his first transformation.

"Then it will give me great joy when I kill you!"

Yamalu and Sistro clashed their swords. Yamalu underestimated his opponent. They backed up and circled. Yamalu tightened his grip and charged toward Sistro. The charge, avoided by a flip Sistro performed over Yamalu's head.

The swords kept clashing until there was an equal amount of force between Yamalu and Sistro. They collided. The swords jumped out of the hands into the farthest places of the world.

"I guess we'll finish this battle with fists," said Yamalu. He then attempted to uppercut punch Sistro in the stomach. Sistro jumped out of the way. Yamalu then threw out a punch to the face. The wizard caught the punch with the strength of a heart-piercing bullet.

Yamalu frowned at Sistro, who was standing with his arms behind his back. Yamalu brought out two swords that were attached to each of his sides. Sistro took out a sword from a sword harness on his back. They were quite a distance away from each other. At the same time, they ran towards each other.

They started to fly.

When they collided, there was a mixture of purple and white light.

Sistro, on his feet, was holding a white katana with a scythe blade on the top. He was wearing a white silk shirt, a glamorous white metal covering his arms, and metal gloves. The aurora of white light around him meant one thing;

Sistro was in his second madrocellular transformation!

Sistro looked around. He saw Yamalu on the ground. In a quick shadowy flash of black light he returned to his original form. Sistro looked at the ground. He saw his swords lying side-by-side.

Unfortunately for Yamalu, his hands were still attached to the swords!

Yamalu got up and witnessed his missing hands. He also witnessed Sistro's new power.

"This isn't fair!" he said.

"You cannot rule the world, Yamalu," Sistro said with a smile. "No matter what power we possess it is not *us* who controls this place."

Yamalu frowned.

"That's what you think." He then thrust both arms in front of him. Tentacle-like tubes came out of the stubs of his arms and wrapped around Sistro.

Even with his newly discovered powers, Sistro could not break free. Every time he tried, they squeezed tighter. Eventually, he ran out of power and forced back to his regular form. Yamalu's remaining tentacles formed two new hands. He picked up his swords, took off his old hands and put them up.

"It seems that I am the victor!" Yamalu said to Sistro while walking towards him. "There is nothing you can to do to me that you have not already done," Sistro said in disgust.

"True..." Yamalu said. "So you shall become my slave." Yamalu walked away from him. He looked at Sistro and said,

"Like your brother."

He started walking towards the Sakkaroid, when five shadow demons with a barred carriage appeared.

"Put him inside," said the first dictator of the entire world. Sistro was tossed in the portable prison, with his brother.

"What happened to you?!" Sistro yelled.

"When Yamalu turned the skies dark, all of the wizards were teleported to the ruins of Denmark and were shackled. I escaped, but Yamalu found me while I was looking for you."

Sistro took his eyes off his brother and looked at the dark, desolate world before him. The buildings built after the Great Destruction of 2250 slowly started to become consumed by darkness. He looked at the sky. The sun, merely a star in the darkness.

A diamond in the rough.

The moon was not out yet. You could not tell the difference between the sun and the moon. What kind of a world is this when you cannot tell the difference between the sun and the moon?

What have we become?

Sistro closed his eyes. When he opened them, he was on the mountains near Camenstra's city gates.

He was back from his reminiscences. Or was he? After looking at the city of Camenstra, he could tell he wasn't. The city of Camenstra was on fire. He saw buildings collapsing. He saw people on fire and screaming in terror. Sistro noticed, before the fire, the buildings were aged more than ever.

This was a vision from the future.

Sistro felt a rumbling in the Earth. He turned around and saw a swarm of flying shadow demons. When they reached Sistro they went straight through him and destroyed the remains of the city. You see, they didn't see him, feel him or heard him.

Sistro looked shocked.

"Good Lord, what have I done?!"

Before they reached the city, a beam of light struck the swarm. It was Sistro's future self, helping a group of four people who went inside the burning city. The fires ceased and the buildings recovered. The future Sistro released the remains of the shadows. Sistro turned away from Camenstra and saw Yamalu's terrifying tower in Manhattan.

He looked up at its dark and gloomy sight. The tower itself had curves like an actual scorpion tail. The tower was unbelievingly bent like one. It even included what looked like a penthouse/throne room inside the scorpion stinger-shaped part of the tower at the very top. It was amazing how the tower had a bent curve and stingers part half the towers weight and had the balance of some of the best buildings. Sistro stepped on a human skull. He looked on the ground; skeletons were everywhere. They covered every inch of the ground, around the tower.

Behind him a mysterious voice said, "It will be like this for one thousand three hundred years." Sistro turned around and saw a person cloaked in brown wearing a hood.

"How do you know?" he asked.

"Darkness is everywhere. In everyone. In me, in him. Even in you, Sistro, master of light."

Sistro grew concerned.

"How do you know my name?" he asked. The hooded man showed no expression. The inside of his hood was too dark to see his face. He turned around.

"I know everything about you, Sistro. Even about the quest you are on now."

"This was all a dream, wasn't it?" Sistro questioned. The hooded man faced Sistro again.

"Yes," he said. He started to circle Sistro.

"I have blessed you with the visions of your past and premonitions of the future."

Sistro then asked everyone's favorite question.

"Why?"

The mysterious man continued to circle around him.

"I am here to tell you <u>about</u> your future." He stopped circling Sistro and faced him.

"After you visit Camenstra, you must not go back to Manhattan."

"What do you suggest I do?" Sistro asked.

"Continue your journey and find the secret to the vortex crystal. The whole truth will be revealed then."

Sistro grabbed his staff with both hands.

"And if I return?"

"Then Yamalu will remain our overlord. The world will continue to see complete darkness. The Chosen would not have a leader. You and your sibling are very valuable in the future."

The hooded man then came closer to Sistro.

"Once you see what I see, you will understand." He pointed to an area away from the tower. Sistro saw what he had not seen in fifty years.

He saw sunlight.

"It's beautiful!" Sistro said.

"Look." The hooded man pointed ahead. Endstra came flying across the field below them, landing back first.

"Endstra!" his brother said. The hooded man stopped him from going to him by blocking Sistro with his hand.

The great wizard of light was forced to watch.

While Endstra was on the ground, a man slowly walked towards him. He was wearing a tan silk shirt, tan dress pants and a pendant of Yamalu's sign around his neck. As he was walking towards Endstra, he had a smile on his face.

"If you kill me," Endstra said, "everything we worked so hard for will be destroyed by him! Please understand! You <u>have</u> to understand!"

The man took out a sword with a black blade from a harness on his left side.

Before Sistro knew what happened next, the vision faded away.

Sistro and the hooded man appeared in a black void.

"What happened?" Sistro said. He looked at the hooded man and grabbed him by the shoulders.

"What happened to my brother?!" he said as he shook the man.

"You will know in time."

Sistro looked angry and disgusted.

"In time?" he asked. "In time?! That's my brother you're talking about!"

The man pointed behind him. A small village in Turkey appeared.

The village was in darkness. The people showed no fear of Yamalu's power.

Sistro and the hooded man lead Sistro to a temple. This temple was different from other places of worship. Under the altar, there was a secret staircase.

They went down.

"Where are you taking me?!" Sistro asked. The hooded man was silent. The stairs led to an underground tunnel that was lightened by bright bulbs overhead.

"Keep up," he said. "Were almost there." At the end of the tunnel, there was a door that said "secret" in Turkish. From his sleeve, the hooded man pulled out his left hand. He put his index finger near the key lock. Sistro was amazed the hooded man's finger took the shape of a key!

The hooded man put the 'key' in the keyhole and unlocked the door. They both went inside. The door automatically closed and locked itself. Sistro went back to the door to see if it really was locked.

"We're trapped!" Sistro yelled. There was no light in the room, until the hooded man said these words:

"Munnatalu, munnatalu, munnatalu..."

As he kept repeating it, Sistro found out what language it was.

"Demarican tongue!"

More light was injected into the room. The hooded man stopped the chant and went to what looked like a box. At the wave of his hand, it opened. It showed four medallions. There was a circular red one, a diamond-shaped brown one, an N-shaped blue one and a rectangular yellow one with yellow spikes on the ends.

The hooded man put the pendants in a small bag and the room turned black. They were once again in the void.

"What was the reason for that?" Sistro demanded.

The hooded man stayed silent.

"Answer me," Sistro yelled, "you filthy Demaric!"

Oh, that really caught his attention.

"Yes, I know all about the Earth Demons! How they can manipulate dreams to make them <u>seem</u> important."

The Demarican turned his head toward him.

"Unlike my brothers and sisters, I speak the truth."

Sistro put his sword to what he thought was his neck.

"Who are you? Tell me." said Sistro.

The Demarican kept silent.

Sistro put the sword closer to his throat.

"Tell me now!" Sistro demanded.

He looked at Sistro. "I am Marblus," he said, "fortuneteller of the Demarican Race."

Sistro removed his sword from Marblus' neck.

"You must believe me when I say do not go back to Yamalu after your quest. The vision of the Chosen will perish! The vision of your brother? He will die!"

Marblus gave Sistro the small bag.

"Take these medallions," he said. "Give them to the Chosen once they're ready. The world is depending on them."

Sistro looked inside the bag.

"Only through your guidance, will the Chosen succeed."

Sistro closed the bag.

"I do not blame your doubt of me," Marblus said. "My kind is a despicable race."

Sistro shook his head. "No, he said. I should have listened to you in the first place."

"To find the secret of the vortex diamond, you must find the source of light," Marblus said. "Being a wizard master of light, this should be no problem for you." Sistro smiled. He put his right hand on Marblus' left shoulder.

"Thank you, my friend."

Then he heard a familiar voice.

"Sistro! Sistro!"

"Sistro!" his brother Endstra called out. Sistro awakened and was relieved to see his brother.

"What time is it, Endstra?" Sistro asked.

"It's almost six o' clock," Endstra replied. "Almost time for us to enter Camenstra."

Sistro couldn't believe it. The dream was over. It also didn't seem he was asleep for only two hours!

Sistro got up. "Very well then, Endstra," Sistro said. "Let's be off."

The brothers then gathered their staffs. Endstra was almost at the city gates.

"Come on!" he yelled to his brother.

"On my way," Sistro replied. He felt his pocket with the bag of medallions inside. He then looked at the dark sky and smiled.

"Thank you, indeed."

V

It took the brothers two hours to head down the mountain to the city gates. Eight o'clock in the morning and no sunlight.

Just utter darkness.

"Will I really witness by brother's death in the future if I return?" he thought. When they reached the gates, the gatekeeper stood present.

As they walked towards him, he looked despised.

"You cannot enter," he said to the wizards.

"We are here for business," Sistro said to the gatekeeper.

"For what?!" he said disgustingly. "To take something to that *demon* you call a man?"

Endstra approached the guard.

"We are not here for *his* pleasure," he yelled, "but for our *own* business!"

The guard took his attention off the dark wizard and looked at Sistro.

As he put his hand on his shoulder, he said, "Yamalu's reign will soon end, my friend. Believe me."

The gatekeeper stood aside and opened the gate.

The city was beautiful! It took up more land that it looked and were more buildings than expected. The city was glowing in a fluorescent red like its blue counterpart, Atlantacore was. Like Atlantacore, Camenstra's buildings were surrounding the tallest tower in the world so far, which happened to be the home Embora, King of Camenstra dwelled in.

When Sistro and Endstra entered the city, Endstra's mood changed.

"Camenstra," Sistro said with a smile. "Home of the fire masters. We finally made it." They started to walk towards the inside of the city. The red light from the city was the only source of light the city had. It illuminated from buildings, sidewalks, and streets. But there were places in this giant city that were kept in the dark.

Sistro and Endstra were inside one of those areas.

"Where are we?" Sistro asked his brother.

"The dark of the city," he said. "I need your light, brother."

Sistro bounced his staff on the ground. The tip of it illuminated a white light. The light came on, he saw someone standing across from him and his brother. The light was not strong enough to fully see him, but it revealed the lower half of him.

"Excuse me," Endstra said to the person loudly. "Do you know the way to the Camenstrian Tower?"

The person started to run away.

"Come on," Sistro told his brother. They started to pursue him, in the darkness.

Sistro's light was able to pick up his footsteps. They actually saw him running when they reached the lightened area. By the way he was running, they could tell it was a male.

They continued to run after him down the road.

"We just want directions!" Endstra yelled to him. Then the most amazing thing happened. In the blink of an eye, the person disappeared! Before Sistro and Endstra could stop themselves, they both tripped and rolled down a hill that signaled the end of the road. When the brothers reached the bottom of the hill, they realized the hill inside the city was a giant ditch holding King Embora's Tower!

"Well, that was ironic," Endstra said as he rose from the ground. Sistro and Endstra walked to the door and were greeted by one of the king's servants.

"Hello, masters," he addressed them. "Are you here to see the king?"

"Just for old time's sake," the master of light magic said with a nod. The servant led them into the first floor palace and headed up stairs to Embora's throne room.

"The king was not expecting this visit," the servant said to start a conversation.

"This will be brief," said Endstra. "We do not want to keep up his tome." They continued walking until they reached the top floor, which was King Embora's throne room. Embora was dressed in black and red. His robe was a fiery red with a few stripes of black. His shirt was a black Alligator zip shirt, and black leather pants. His red gloves and boots were suede. As he looked at the fire in the bright red room, he noticed Endstra and Sistro near the door.

"Leave," he said, pointing to the servant. He left and closed the door.

"What are you two doing here?" he said with a strict tone of voice. Endstra stood forward. With just that done, Embora figured out why they were there. Embora rose from his throne.

"You are not here under the will of Yamalu, are you not?"

Endstra shook his head. "He thinks we're delivering certain parts for his master tower."

Sistro stepped in front of Endstra to where Embora stood.

"My friend, your city has been chosen – hand-picked by God – to partake in a prophecy that will rid the world of this fowl demon forever."

Embora smirked with a little blow of breath. "You are wasting your time, wizard of light," he told Sistro. "It is hopeless to fight this man that possesses the world," he said as he turned around. "If man and wizard could not destroy this beast forty-five years ago in the Last War," he said as he took his seat, "what could you two wizards do now?"

Sistro angrily frowned.

"We could do a lot more than what you're doing now!" he yelled. "And all *you're* doing is sitting in your chair you call a throne feeling sorry for yourself and calling yourself a king!"

Embora rose from his chair. "Are you trying to say that I have not the courage to lead my people?!"

"No, Embora," sighed Sistro. "No. I'm not."

"Then what *are* you trying to say?!"

"That you have the chance to change the world we know it!" Sistro yelled. "You may not live to see it, but Yamalu *will* fall!"

Embora looked at the ground, then at Sistro.

"What must I do?"

Sistro turned around and nodded at Endstra. He left and went to see about Yamalu's delivery. Sistro then took Embora to the viewing patio. They both looked at the spectacular view of the city of Camenstra.

"How far would you go to save this city from destruction?" Sistro asked Embora.

"To the ends of the Earth," Embora replied. "When I saw my brother killed by Yamalu instantly after we lost the Last War, then punished the entire Earth to everlasting darkness after his remark to him, my world crashed. I then devoted my life to destroy that beast of a man. I just can't find a way."

Sistro smiled, and then put his left hand on Embora's right shoulder.

"There is, my friend," Sistro said.

"How?"

They returned to the throne room. "I need a weapon of great importance. Four cities that have a very valuable weapon or item that contains a powerful kinetic ability and infinite immortality. The four cities with these items are Atlantacore, Dimbar, Yalutar and of course Camenstra. The weapons from Atlantacore and Dimbar have already been retrieved and sacrificed to God.

"How are these weapons going to save mankind?"

Sistro sat down in a chair. "It's not the weapons," he said, "but the powers inside them."

"What happens to them?"

"After God retrieves the powers, he will pick the Chosen. The Chosen are four people who will be born with the powers of the weapons given to God. They and they only, will have the power to destroy Yamalu and bring peace to the world."

"And you are sure of this?" Embora asked.

"Very."

Embora nodded his head. "Then I shall do my part." He took out a sword from his belt harness. Its handle was pitch-black with a red swirl around it. The three blades were shaped like a wild flame, with the two outer blades colored red and the middle blade colored black.

"This is Hikulo," said Embora. "The Camenstrian people call it the Fire of Death, but its pronounced Black Fire in the forgotten language."

Sistro already knew that the forgotten language was Japanese that was lost after the Last War.

"Its kinetic power is pyrokinesis; the ability to create, control and manipulate all forms of fire." Embora handed Hikulo to Sistro.

"The immortality is in the handle," he told Sistro.

"This is beautiful," said Sistro.

"Do you know what's funny?"

Sistro looked at Embora and started to listen.

"The first time I tried to use the sword," he began, "it almost killed me."

Sistro looked frightened as he held the sword in his hand.

"Is that why the citizens call this the Fire of Death?" Sistro asked. Embora nodded with his eyes closed.

"Well," he said, "there's only one more thing to do." Sistro walked to the middle of the room and held the sword by the handle over his head with his right hand.

"I sacrifice this item to thee, oh Lord, in hopes of destroying Yamalu and to rebuild the foundation of man!"

The sword transformed into a red glittery vapor. It floated through the ceiling and into the dark sky.

"I guess you weren't kidding about God's plan," Embora said.

Sistro smiled.

"When it comes to God, I never kid." Endstra then came through the main door.

"Did I come at a bad time?" he said. Sistro turned and saw his brother at the door.

"No, Endstra," he said. "We are finished." Sistro faced Embora again. "You did the right thing, King of Camenstra." Embora smiled.

"If you need anything," he said, "just let me know."

Sistro then thought.

"There is."

Back in Dimbar, Kowatuu and Sonita, King of Yalutar were almost done discussing the wizard of light's concerns.

"So you see," Kowatuu said to Sonita, "this is the only way to save the Earth." Sonita was old and wise. He knew he was telling the truth.

"So be it," Sonita said Kowatuu. He snapped his fingers on his right hand to summon two servants each carrying a side of a giant golden shield.

"This is Natunga O Lioben; the Lord of all Shields. It holds Electrokenisis and infinite immortality." Kowatuu was given the shield by the two servants.

"If this shield would rid the Earth of that foul creature, Yamalu," Sonita said, "then I will not stand in its destined path." Both Kowatuu and Sonita stood up and shook hands.

"Thank you, King of Yalutar," Kowatuu said.

"You are most welcome, King of Dimbar." With that said, Sonita and his servants left the throne room.

Kowatuu noticed his communicator was online.

In the undergrounds of Camenstra, where the Camenstrian Army of machines and all other sources of technology were being held after the Last War, Sistro was standing in front of a holo-projector, waiting for Embora to receive a returning signal from Dimbar after they sent one out about three minutes ago.

Then Embora received a signal.

"Going online..." he said, "now!" He pressed a button and a holographic projection of Kowatuu appeared.

"Hello, Sistro," Kowatuu greeted. "I would like you to know that Sonita made his judgment and decided to give you the weapon." Sistro smiled.

"What is the weapon?"

Kowatuu chuckled. "It's a giant gold shield with immortality and Electrokenisis."

"Perfect," Sistro said. "Do you have it?"

Kowatuu smirked. "Yes," he said. "It's ready for teleportation now. Are you ready?"

Sistro nodded at the holographic Kowatuu. His hand pressed a button, and within seconds, the shield appeared inside the giant metal box. Before Sistro picked up the shield, he concluded his conversation with Kowatuu.

"Thank you, my friend," Sistro said. "Our adventure is finally over. Sistro, going offline," he said.

"Ditto," said Kowatuu. They both turned off their holographic projectors and Embora turned off the communicator.

"A scepter, a diamond, a sword and shield," Sistro said. He looked at Embora.

"It must be done."

Sistro, Endstra and Embora went outside to get ready for the sacrifice. Sistro had the shield in one hand and his staff in the other. He looked at Embora and the shield.

"Would you like to do the honors?" he asked him. Embora smirked and nodded. He lifted the shield with both hands over his head.

"Lord," he yelled, "I give this shield to you in which you use this power to rid the world of Yamalu!"

The shield turned into a burst of yellow glittering light and floated into the dark sky.

"He accepted it!" Embora whispered to himself. "I don't believe it!"

"God accepts everyone," Sistro said. "He just wants you to accept him."

Embora's eyes started to water. They shook hands.

"Thank you for giving me faith, Sistro."

"I never gave it to you," said Sistro. "Faith is in everyone."

Embora nodded as a tear ran down his cheek.

"Over there are stairs that lead back to the city," he said. "Keep straight to go to the city gates."

After one final farewell, Sistro and Endstra left the city of Camenstra.

It was ten thirty in the morning, but of course you could not tell. Sistro and Endstra were walking to the coast of the mountains.

"We better head back to Yamalu," Endstra said.

"No," Sistro said. "We cannot go back."

"Why?"

Sistro looked at his brother.

"Because we have a job to do."

Endstra was almost sure of his decision.

"In my dream," Sistro began again, "I saw the fall of the Chosen. I saw the destruction of Earth."

"So this will happen," Endstra began, "if we return to Yamalu.

Sistro shook his head. "It will only happen if *I* return."

There was a silence for five seconds.

"I must find the secrets of the vortex crystal. That is, after you and I train the Chosen."

Endstra smiled. "If we are not to return," he said, "we should stay in an uncharted city."

Sistro looked at the ocean and saw a giant island he had never seen before.

"We shall *build* a city on *that* uncharted island." Sistro turned to his brother.

"Are you ready?"

Endstra smiled. "As I'll ever be."
They then left to the island with no name.

And so it is written that this would be the beginning of the greatest journeys in the history of the world. I, Nostra, the great ancestor of the late Nostredamus, prophesize that one thousand years from now, the Chosen – four human beings gifted with a great kinetic power and immortality given by the four cities of the 29th century which are Atlantacore, Camenstra, Dimbar and Yalutar – will stop the demon who rules the Earth and his evil forces and will purify and protect the vortex crystal so it will never again fall into the wrong hands.

But the question remained:

Will the Chosen's special abilities be enough to stop Yamalu?

Prologue

On the uncharted island of Kiputrina, where the wizards Sistro-master of light magic-and Endstra-master of dark magic- reside, the clocks stroke twelve.

It was January 1st, 3840.

Endstra awoke from his sleep. "It's here!" he said in a whisper. He went out of his room to alert his brother and *king*, Sistro, who was in the most beautiful part of this island city, the Kiputrinan Tower. Its reflecting white walls were the source of light for the entire island. Everything illuminated from the walls, giving the entire island the imitation of light.

Sistro was standing in the balcony, looking at the spectacular view of the island. Endstra stood next to the king of Kiputrina. He could tell by the way Sistro was looking that he knew the New Year was here.

"It is time," he said to Endstra.

"We still don't know exactly when they will be born," Endstra said. Sistro smiled.

"We don't," he said, "but *he* does."

Sistro pointed to a man whom Endstra had never seen before.

"May I present to you, Nostra," Sistro said, "the great ancestor of the late Nostredamus. He knows exactly when and where they will be born."

"It is an honor," Nostra said with a bow.

"So," Sistro began, "what are the children's names?"

Nostra closed his eyes and silently chanted a verse. When he opened his eyes, he was in a trance.

"The names are Mercutio, Goddum, Eviana and Ginzolo."

"Tell me about Mercutio," replied Sistro.

Nostra nodded. "Mercutio is the immortal bearing the power of the Hikulo sword, Pyrokinesis."

"What about his parents?"

"Father is unknown. Mother is Brittany Wulbarow."

Sistro suddenly was paralyzed. He even started to breathe heavily. His staff slipped out of his hand. He bent down to pick it up when his pulse started to quicken.

Then he stared at Endstra with a suspecting glance.

"You okay?" his brother asked.

Sistro came out of his feared state. "I'm fine," he said with a fake smirk.

"No you are not."

Everyone in the room heard the mysterious voice that came from nowhere.

"Who are you?" Endstra asked.

"You should ask your brother," it said.

Sistro suddenly knew who it was.

"You may show yourself," he said, "Nostra and I already know who you are." In a small cyclone that suddenly appeared in the middle of the throne room stepped a hooded man. His dark brown robe symbolized he was a Demarican. His hood was too dark inside to see his *true* face, even in the enlightened room. His sleeve covered his hands, signaling he was of great importance.

"Marblus, old friend," Sistro said, "welcome. Great to see you." Marblus nodded once. "It's been a long time, Sistro," he said.

"A thousand years to be exact," replied Sistro. Marblus walked to where Endstra was.

"The parents of the Chosen must be aware of their abilities."

"You can do that, Marblus," Sistro said. "Go to each parent and let them know about their child. Demonstrate if you have to. Visit them in the order they are born."

Even though you could not tell, Marblus was smiling.

"Meaning," he said, "visit first the babe *Mercutio*."

Sistro suddenly stopped walking.

"Yes, he said, "visit Mercutio first." He faced Marblus and Nostra. "Why do you trouble me about the Pyrokinetic?"

"Because I know a secret," said Marblus, "But I promise you, after you find the source of light, the secret *shall* be revealed."

Sistro started to frown. "How long have you known?" he said as he gleamed at Endstra.

"Since I first met you," replied Marblus.

"Have you told anyone else?"

"None," said Marblus. "None so far." Marblus was silent for two seconds.

"During their trial on their 16th year of life," he said, "I will check on them to see how they would handle their situation."

"Have the medallions been set?" asked Endstra.

"The water, earth and thunder medallions have been entered in their episodes of life," Sistro said. "I will deliver the fire medallion to Mercutio *personally*."

Marblus nodded.

"When will the Pyrokinetic be born?" Sistro asked Nostra.

"Five months from now. It will be on the 28th day at 4:14 a.m."

"Then it is decided," said Sistro. "Marblus will inform the Chosen's parents and watch them at the age of 16. Nostra will let us know when they will be born and if they passed their trials. And *I* will deliver the pyrokinetic's medallion when he is ready."

Endstra nodded. "Very well," he said as he headed to the door, "I'll see you in sixteen years."

He left Sistro's throne room.

Nostra followed.

In a gust of wind, Marblus disappeared, leaving Sistro alone. He sat on his throne and said to himself,

"We must be patient."

When his new magic servant, Mascool, walked inside, Yamalu was asleep in his new home. He awakened automatically as the hallway light pierced his eyes.

"What is it, Mascool?" he eerily spoke.

Mascool was Sistro and Endstra's replacement after they "mysteriously disappeared" according to Yamalu. Unlike Sistro and Endstra, Mascool loved his position. He saw it as being the "right hand of God."

Maybe loved it a little *too* much.

"My lord," he began, "the year of the prophecy is here. According to rumor, four immortal babes will be born this year with supernatural powers. Possibly greater than *yours,* my lord."

Yamalu rose out of bed.

"Who made this 'so-called' prophecy?"

"The Lord of Prophets, my liege."

Yamalu's eyes widened. "*Nostra?!* But we don't even know where he *is!*"

Yamalu put his left hand on his head.

"When the four grow to be adults, they shall journey on a quest to fulfill their *real* purpose."

"And what is *that?*"

"To destroy *you,* my lord. Also to purify the Vortex Crystal, and keep it safe."

Yamalu got out of bed.

"May I make a suggestion, my lord?" Mascool asked.

"Speak," he said. He snapped his fingers, and was dressed instantly.

"Let's track these children down and make sure we get a DNA sample of each."

That brightened Yamalu's mood. "Yes," he said. "If we were to get a sample from each of the babies and put them in one of our experimental embryos, I could not be stopped!"

Yamalu began to calm down. "Have you located any of them yet?" he asked.

"The Rodriguez woman started to glow yellow after she found out she was pregnant."

"Keep an eye on them," Yamalu said. "Once the babe is born, capture it and kill the parents."

"As you wish, my lord." With that said, he left from Yamalu's sight. Yamalu rose from his throne and went to his viewing mirror.

"Sistro, Sistro, Sistro," he said. "You count on your God to help you with my destruction. If God wants me dead, why not he do it himself?"

It started to rain.

"The world is mine, God," he said. "And soon, the entire galaxy will be." He then looked up in the dark sky he created.

"Not even *you* can stop me."

As prophesized, Mercutio Wulbarow was born on May 28th, 3840 at 4:14 a.m. As a young boy, he and his mother, Brittany lived in Yamalu's slave region. They were able to escape to New Dimbar when he had just learned to walk. When Mercutio was 16, fifteen years after the prophecy was made, he was a junior at Kowatuu High School. Dimbar didn't really change in the past one thousand years. Talutarr, who was in Kowatuu's bloodline, was the king. Mercutio and his best friend, Theodore turned out to be the weirdest ones in their class. Theo was weird because of his passion for music, and Mercutio because of his obsession with fire.

The main reason is that it couldn't burn him.

Of course, in every high school was the class bully. His name was Castro Brown. Very tall and had a mixture of muscle and fat. Everyone feared him except for Theodore and Mercutio.

That's why Castro hated those two.

Mercutio and Theodore were talking at their shared locker when Castro paid them a visit.

"Hey, Murky," he called him. "What're *you* doing on *my* side of the hallway?!"

Mercutio continued his conversation with Theodore.

Castro grabbed Mercutio's shirt collar, picked him up and slammed him on the wall.

"Don't you ever in your life ignore me, you freak!"

That caught everyone's attention.

"What did you call me?"

"You heard me!" Castro yelled. "I know all about you, Murky. According to the laws of nature, you've died *twice!*"

"What are you talking about?" Mercutio said with a sigh.

Castro threw him on the ground.

"You were tossed in front of a transport vehicle as a baby," he said, "then you got butchered alive by stalagmites here in Dimbar. You don't even get burned by *fire!*" Everyone was speechless. Mercutio's secret of immortality was revealed!

"You're lying," he said. "I never died before."

"Oh yeah?" Castro said. He suddenly entered a boxing stance. "C'mon," he said. Mercutio sighed, looked at his watch and shrugged his shoulders.

"I'm passing that class anyway," he said.

The fight started with Castro giving out continuous punches with both hands at Mercutio's face. Mercutio dodged every one of them, caught the last one with his right hand and kicked him in the groin with his right leg. It allowed him to do a back flip, and

land on his feet.

As Castro recuperated, he began to charge. Mercutio quickly moved out of the way, and tripped him. Castro slid on the concrete floor face first.

The left side of Castro's face was bleeding.

"You're dead when I get over there!" he yelled.

"I thought you said I couldn't *die?*" Mercutio replied. Castro was blazing with anger. This 16-year-old ignored him, didn't fear him and now was being a *smart aleck!* Consumed by anger, Castro ran to Mercutio and kicked him in the ribs.

Everyone heard his ribs crack as Mercutio slid backwards on his back towards Theodore's feet.

"You all right?" he asked. As he helped Mercutio up, he heard and *saw* Mercutio's ribs mending together again!

"G-g-go get 'em!"

Mercutio was back on his feet and perfectly calm.

Castro punched him in the gut four times and knee-kicked him in the forehead. He roundhouse kicked him on the left side of the head, causing Mercutio to fall on his side. Castro suddenly started to stomp his face, his legs, his chest and stomach. Bruises were all over his body. His blood was everywhere. As Castro started to walk away, Mercutio stood up.

"I'm not done yet!" he yelled. Castro and the other students looked at him; they were amazed.

Mercutio looked normal!

"What?!" Castro whispered to himself.

"Stop whining and fight me!" Mercutio yelled.

Castro was starting to get irritated.

"I'm about to hurt you so bad," he said, "you'd wish you'd stayed on the ground!"

He took out a pocketknife.

The fight was getting intense now. People started to gather to see the action. Castro swung the knife, cutting Mercutio's shirt in the process. He swung it frontward, horizontal, vertical, until he slit Mercutio's throat.

Mercutio was left for dead when he fell on the ground, but his throat mysteriously started to mend! People were amazed as they saw Mercutio, murdered by Castro, stand up with no scratches!

"Are you *serious?!*" he yelled. He walked up to him and slit his throat again. He watched the wound heal and watch him come back to life!

Again!

"I guess you found out my secret," said Mercutio. "I am immortal and I'm not even a *wizard!*"

Castro frowned.

"Now that you know my first secret," said Mercutio, "I might as well show you my other one."

Castro started running towards Mercutio, but before he reached him, Mercutio ran his left index finger over the floor. A line of fire formed on the floor. Castro tried to stop running, but tripped and landed face first in the line of fire. The burn on the right side of his face resembled the scraping on his left. Mercutio waved over the fire.

The flames retreated from the ground to the air in a whip-like manner and through the fingertips.

"No way!" Castro whispered. One of Castro's followers came in the circle and tried to punch Mercutio in the face, but Mercutio ejected a burst of fire from his left palm, blinding him in the process. Castro was full of fear as Mercutio came closer. He tripped over his own feet. Suddenly Mercutio saw a hooded man in the audience. HE nodded his head at him.

Mercutio nodded back.

He then disappeared.

Mercutio put his attention back on Castro.

"P-pl-please," Castro cried. "Please don't kill me!" Mercutio looked down at the once feared bully of Kowatuu High School.

"Why?" he asked. "Why should I spare your life after you put so much fear in others?" He bent his knees and looked in Castro's eyes.

"You deserve to die."

Mercutio blew fire on his hands and threw it on Castro's lower torso. When Castro and his followers were able to put it out, Mercutio's waist down to his toes were useless.

He was paralyzed.

"Next time," Mercutio said, "I will not miss."

Mercutio left school that day with no disciplinary action whatsoever. The students who reported about the "fire boy" were immediately rejected.

No faculty member believed them.

Once out of the school, Mercutio was at a crossroad, when he saw a man dressed in white. He had a long white beard and hair.

But it *definitely* wasn't *Santa Claus.*

Mercutio was eager to introduce himself.

"Hi," he said as he held out his hand. "I'm Mercutio."

The man shook his hand.

"I am Sistro."

"Nice to meet you, Sistro."

As he looked in his hand, Mercutio saw a red, circular medallion. He figured Sistro gave it to him by accident. But as he was about to give it back to him, Sistro was gone. He decided to wear it around his neck and went on home. That felt good to a teen that had died at least four times that day.

Eviana Johnson was born July 5th, 3840. Her father, Joshua, took her from her mother before she sold her like her other three babies, and took her to Tritunia, the city of dreams. When she learned to walk, she was one month old. Joshua was very proud of his daughter. He loved her so much, he ran for kingship over Tritunia and won. He said Eviana, his daughter, inspired him.

At thirteen months, she almost spoke proper English. She even started to read a little.

No, *a lot!*

She read and understood a Shakespearian play at one-year-old. She learned how to add, subtract, multiply, divide, round, square root and Sine, Cosine, and Tangent figures. At the rate she was learning, she could be in the Tritunia Senate at the age of 10! As Joshua watched his daughter do all of these things at a year and one-month-old, he started to wonder.

Should *he* be the one taking care of her?

Or is he just watching her until she is able to go on her own and do what *God* wants her to do?

At age sixteen, Eviana was in her senior year of college. She was promoted to the 9th Grade and received a perfect score on the Tritunia College Aptitude Test. She went to Tritunia University, the only college in the city, which was founded by her father. Even though she was sixteen, there were others who shared Eviana's intellect and were given the same treatment. There was Alicia; her best friend and the only one besides her father who knew she was immortal, and David, her boyfriend ever since kindergarten.

In her dorm room with her roommate Alicia, Eviana was getting ready to go to the school aquarium for the fifth time this week. Alicia came through the front door. She was African American, which is an endangered species in the Dark World. She was a very beautiful girl for the age of sixteen. Her good looks and black hair with blonde highlights brought any strong male senior students to their knees.

"Are you going to that aquarium again?" Alicia asked. Eviana smiled while putting on her make-up.

"Girl," Alicia said with a tone, "one of these days you're going to *turn* into a fish!"

Eviana giggled at Alicia's comparison. Even *Alicia* knew she could breathe underwater!

"Do you know where else I can go at 8:00 in the evening on a Friday night?"

Alicia put her hand on her lip. "You could try going out with David!" she said. "He told me to ask you if you wanted to go to your daddy's party tonight."

Eviana and Alicia were best friends ever since preschool and were both geniuses. Along with her underwater breathing, Eviana could tell when someone was lying. So could Alicia, which is why they never lied to each other.

"B-b-but that's an hour from now!" she said excitedly. "Where is he going to meet me?! What am I going to *wear?!*"

Alicia went to Eviana and said, "Now hold on girl, slow down! He said he'd meet you at Joshua Hall in thirty minutes and to wear something blue."

Eviana pulled her locks of hair behind her and took a deep breath.

"Now," Alicia said, "go have fun, and tell me all about it when you get back."

In thirty minutes, she was dressed in a glittery powder blue dress, complete with matching shoes and scarf and waited in the lounge of Joshua Hall. In seconds, David Peterson, her boyfriend ever since kindergarten, walked through the doors. Officially, they didn't start dating until the 6th Grade, but they admired on another from afar. She was also the reason why his grades were outstanding. He wanted to be around her so much, that he got all A's in his classes, a perfect score on his Aptitnde Test the first time and got promoted to college.

His suit was blue, but a different shade than what Eviana was wearing. His suit and white shirt was collarless. He had a sapphire button piece on his shirt, which matched his eyes. His hair was gelled and combed back. There were no blemishes on his face or hands. When he spotted Eviana, he showed off his blindingly perfect white teeth with a smile. Eviana walked towards him.

She suddenly was in his arms.

"Hey, baby," he said before they kissed. They left the dorm house to his car and drove off.

At the Mansion of Champions, Tritunia's 1st Annual Aqua Ball was in session. Eviana and David arrived. The valet parked his car. They were greeted by her father, King Joshua.

"Hi, daddy," she said as she hugged and kissed him on the cheek. He then noticed her date and smiled.

"David!" he said as he shook his hand. "Long time no see!"

David smiled. "Ditto, you're Majesty," he said. "I heard you have something to present that might change the outcome of the human race. That sounds interesting." Eviana could always accept the fact that David enjoyed her fathers company.

Even if *was* about money.

"Well," said Joshua, "in a few minutes I'm going to make my presentation. Just follow the waiter to your table and I'll catch up shortly." The couple then entered the giant blue room with tables, a dance floor, a stage, and everyone was wearing a shade of blue.

Go figure.

As soon as they took their seats, Joshua walked up to the stage.

"Ladies and gentlemen," he said as the audience quieted down. "I give you, the sun!"

He pulled out a small yellow ball.

Eviana closed her eyes in embarrassment.

"This little ball once squeezed can release at least eight times more light than this city alone," he said. "Enough light to light the world from Yamalu's spell. If you would please put on your sunglasses provided by your waiters."

Everyone put on their blue sunglasses, including Joshua.

"Now," he said, "let there be light!"

When he squeezed it, the entire room was covered in white light. There were people who were blinded even with the sunglasses *on!* Joshua squeezed it again and the light went off.

Everyone applauded.

After the presentation, the band started to play. David whispered something in Eviana's ear. They both went to the pool and fountain area.

"I heard you loved water," David said, "so I rented this out for the two of us."

They sat on a bench next to the seven-foot deep pool.

"This is very beautiful, David," she said. "Thank you." But as she leaned toward David for a kiss, her hand slipped off the bench. She lost her balance and fell in the pool.

She resurfaced and started laughing, but started to get a headache.

"You okay, Eva?" David asked. Her headache overtook her. All the water in the pool was entering into his body-through her eyes, fingernails, toenails, nostrils, and mouth. When it was finished, she and her dress were bone dry. Not a single drop of water was left in the pool.

David climbed into the pool to check on Eviana.

"Eviana, what just happened?" he asked his girlfriend.

"I don't know," she said, "but I'm going to find out." She walked out of the empty pool towards a giant fountain. David wasn't far behind. When he reached her, she put her hand above the water, closed her eyes,-inhaled and exhaled.

The water then started to float out of the fountain.

David was astonished. As he saw Eviana's hand move from side to side-to-side and the water following it, he was amazed. As she opened her eyes to the somewhat miraculous sight, she smiled. She waved her other hand and the water froze in an instant. When David touched it, his fingers were burnt from the extreme cold of the ice block. She realized her very powerful talent.

Eviana could control water.

"Ever since I was a little girl, I was different," she said to David as they walked to his car. "I knew high school math at the age of seven, and even more things at nine. I was three when I found out I was immortal."

"Wow," he said, sounding disappointed. "Immortal. Looks like you have it made." Eviana looked at David who looked depressed. They stopped and looked at each other.

"You know," he said, "I think we shouldn't see each other anymore."

Eviana looked confused.

"After what I saw, I believe anything you say. If you are immortal, that means you would survive after my passing. I don't want you to grieve over me forever."

Eviana was smiling because he cared so much for her.

Yeah, right.

"I understand." They went to his car and drove off.

When they reached her dorm hall, Eviana came out of his car.

"Before you go," David said, "I have something for you." He reached into his pocket and pulled out a medium-sized box and gave it to her.

"Don't forget me, Eva."

She started to cry.

"Never," she said. They then kissed one last time. David drove into the everlasting darkness.

Eviana wiped the tears from her eyes and smiled. She opened the box and saw a blue N-shaped medallion. She smiled as she put it on. She headed up the stairs to her dorm hall; she turned and saw a hooded man in the street looking at her. He soon disappeared, in the darkness.

Eviana went down the hall, and into her dorm room.

In the year 3840, Goddum was born. It was a cold autumn night on November 30th at 9:00 p.m. He tipped the scale of weighing 20 lbs, 13 oz. He was the son of Shateria and Kowatuu V, who, like his great-great-great-grandfather, the late Kowatuu, was the king of Dimbar. They were surprised at their son's unnatural weight. Like his father, he was an African-American, and the first race of humans to be put on the endangered species list.

At the age of 16, Shateria and Kowatuu V's reign as king and queen of Dimbar was over. Goddum couldn't be heir, because he was a minor. But another from Kowatuu V's bloodline took the throne. His name was Talutarr. He was the cousin. He was Kowatuu's great-great-great-grandson. Now, don't get me wrong. Just because he was not king anymore, didn't mean his family was poor. The city of Dimbar paid all of their bills, because of how well he ruled for the last 30 years. Money was no problem. His five bank accounts totaled 150,000,027,370.00* with interest added every Tuesday.

He was filthy rich.

Goddum was just now waking up. As he got out of his king-size bed, he went and bench-pressed 1200 lbs! Yes, yes, the unbelievable had happened. Even though he weighed 277 lbs, he had developed super-strength! He scratched his back after bench-pressing 1200 lbs fifteen times. He headed to his bathroom, closed the door and washed up. When he exited, he had on no shirt, but had on his pajama bottoms.

Goddum's body was weirdly shaped. His belly was round, and his chest and arms were like that of a body builder. You barely saw his double chin. His *belly* was forming a *six pack*. As he was putting on his clothes, he heard his mother's voice.

"Goddum," she said, "breakfast is ready."

Goddum sighed.

"On my way," he hollered, as he headed towards the dining room, fastening his belt.

You see, after Kowatuu V found out about his son's immortality, he made special preparations for him. He stayed home for school, and exceeded higher than anyone in Dimbar. He was officially an adult in the laws of Dimbar. For many years, Goddum took an interest in the environment. He worked for Dimbar's Environmental Science Plant, which paid him very well.

Goddum walked toward the table, and looked at his mother and father.

"I start my next project today," he said grabbing a powdered doughnut, "so I can't stay long." Kowatuu V smiled, knowing his son was finally independent.

"Okay, son," he said. "See you when you get back." He put one powdered doughnut in his mouth and grabbed another and headed out the door.

"He's growing up so fast," Shateria told her husband. Kowatuu V watched Goddum leave the house and looked at his wife.

"That's what I'm *worried* about."

Their mansion was on the wall-side cliffs with a driveway and staircase leading to the suburban streets and sidewalks. It was a very safe place to live. Goddum loved the view of the entire city, including the surrounding houses. During his father's last year as king, Dimbar was changed to New Dimbar. The city of New Dimbar was supposed to become more useful of their natural resources, which gave Goddum the opportunity to become what he always wanted to be, an environmental scientist.

As Goddum headed towards the extremely long stairway to the suburban sidewalks, a sniper was watching him in one of the wall dunes. The sniper had a view shot of his neck and took it. Goddum's neck was immediately broken. He stumbled down the steps, then fell over, falling and collapsing a roof of an abandoned suburban corner store, breaking every bone in the process. The wood and debris from the collapsed roof piled on top of Goddum's crippled body. As the last of the debris fell, Goddum's bones snapped back together! The hole in his neck from the bullet started to reform. As Goddum opened his eyes, he got up from the heavy load of debris.

"Ow!" he said as he rubbed his neck. He cracked his back and neck and started to walk towards the door. He felt a sharp pain shoot into the back of him. As Goddum turned, he saw what looked like a tranquilizing dart in his back near the waist. Goddum took it out to examine it. He felt dizzy. His vision blurred. Every time he took a step, he felt unbalanced. He tried to reach for the door. He tripped over his own feet. He touched the doorknob, and passed out.

"Clear!" someone from outside yelled. An entire team of some organization entered the room with Goddum's sleeping body in it. A man with long white hair in his 30's and wearing a dictator-like black trench coat, red boots, black gloves, black leather pants, and a white shirt entered. By the looks of his black military hat, he was a General.

"Everything's in order, General Solara," a soldier said. Solara went to Goddum. He bent his knees, and grabbed his head with his right arm and said, "We have something very special planned for you." He raised his other hand that signaled the soldiers to take him away. As the soldiers carefully loaded Goddum into a van, Solara walked out of the building and into his ride. His driver soon took off after the van.

When Goddum awoke, very thick chains bound him around the wrists and ankles. He looked around. He was in a black room full of laboratory equipment and giant tubes with a special liquid that looked like it had child embryos inside each one. He then looked at the door in front of him. It mechanically opened, when General Solara came through.

"We finally have you," he said. He nodded at the scientist, who put certain stickers on his forehead and arms.

"What do you want with me?"

"In a few minutes," said Solara, "you will have the privilege of becoming a very beautiful asset to Lord Yamalu."

Goddum shook his head.

"Don't give me that crap," he said. "I figured it out already."

Solara's eyes widened.

"You're going to transfer my powers into those embryos."

Solara clapped very slowly.

"Good job," he said as he walked to the door. "Then you should know that we're going to *kill* you after the process."

The door opened; Goddum saw a hooded man looking at him. He was not visible to Solara's eyes.

"Begin!" he yelled.

Goddum's body was then being electrocuted.

It's been five seconds and one embryo was complete. With the remaining strength he had, he pulled the chains from the wall that held his arms and legs. He peeled the stickers before the second embryo became complete and destroyed the computer with one punch. He kicked the wall open, and punched the completed embryo through its tube into the outside sand.

It was dead.

Goddum then ran through the mechanical door. When he was outside, an entire fleet of Yamalu's soldiers were waiting to charge under Solara's command.

"Attack!" he yelled. They were roaming toward him. As he waved his hand, Goddum smiled. The soldiers, stunned, ran into a ground-made wall.

"Biokinesis!" Solara whispered to himself. Goddum then punched the wall, which busted into flying rocks and boulders. Half of the army was immobile. With both hands, Goddum punched the ground twice, and made it come up in the form of a wave. The soldiers were lifted and fell on their backs. Goddum released boulders, dirt, and rock from the palm of his hands over the soldiers, suffocating them and made it extremely challenging for them to get up.

He saw Solara, driving off in his jeep.

Solara was near the exit to New Dimbar. Goddum ran in front of it and kicked the car back a block. His palm faced the ground. The ground immediately came to his hands. He shook it, like one would shake a sheet. The ground formed another wave. Solara saw the wave coming his way. He took off the seat belt; the wave hit the car. It lifted the car and the General into the air. Solara landed on the ground first, and moved out of the way as the car crashed to the ground.

Solara got up just in time to feel one of Goddum's flying power punches. His left arm was broken.

"My people have been living in fear long enough!" Goddum yelled.

"Yamalu shall forever *rule* this world!" Solara said. He took out his gun. "And there's nothing you can do to change it!"

Solara shot Goddum in the head, killing him instantly. But when he put up his gun, Goddum stood up, untouched, with the bullet in his hand.

As Solara ran towards him, Goddum put his right hand behind his back in the horizontal area and a giant boulder appeared. Solara stopped running as soon as Goddum had smashed him.

"Watch me!" he said.

Goddum left the boulder on the remains of Solara. All of the soldier's were dead. He looked on the ground. He saw a diamond-shaped medallion and decided to keep it for good luck.

Goddum looked at his watch. He had one hour before his first day of work started.

"I better get out of here," he said. He headed out of the military camp. He saw the hooded man standing a few feet in front of him. Goddum put the medallion on a string, and put it around his neck. The hooded man faded away.

Goddum went to work.

Ginzolo Rodriguez was born December 27th, 3840 on the island of Mexico. At a year old, his parents were sentenced to death just for *conceiving* him. They were butchered alive right in front of him. Yamalu kept Ginzolo alive because he knew what was inside. They kept him inside a dark cube for three months, even though he was a baby.

Now, his story began.

Inside Yamalu's new home in the remains of Manhattan, he sat on his eerie throne, thinking.

"Mascool!" he yelled. Mascool came into the throne room.

"You called, my lord?" he asked as he bowed in courtesy. Yamalu pointed to the cube containing Ginzolo.

"The DNA you got from the babe," he whispered to Mascool. "What were the results?" Mascool sighed. "There were no traces of any kinetic power whatsoever.

He's no threat to you."

Yamalu looked at his new wizard. "Good," he said.

"My lord, what should I do with the child?" Mascool asked. Yamalu looked at the cube containing the boy.

"Take him to a child center."

"In his homeland?"

"Yes."

"As you wish, my lord." Mascool said a few words in Demarican tongue and transported the child to an orphanage on the island of Mexico.

"That will be all Mascool," he said. The wizard then walked out of the throne room.

Five seconds later, Ginzolo appeared on the porch of a Mexican orphanage. One of the older boys went to the door and brought him inside.

"Mrs. Santana!" the boy said in Spanish. Mrs. Santana, the main worker of the orphanage came to the boys' attention and saw the baby he was holding.

"Where did you find him?" she also said in Spanish.

"On the porch," he said. "His dog tag says his names Ginzolo."

"Does it show a birth date?"

"Yes, Mrs. Santana?"

"What is it?"

"12-27-3840."

Mrs. Santana's eyes widened. "Oh, my goodness," she said. She took Ginzolo from the boy and put him in her arms.

"He's only a year old," she said. "You can get back to the play area. I'll get him registered."

The boy nodded his head. "Yes, Mrs. Santana," he said as he ran off.

Mrs. Santana got a baby bottle with a special baby formula and fed it to Ginzolo. It was the first nourishment he had for three weeks. This was unknown to Mrs. Satara.

"Now, now, Ginzolo," she said to the babe. "You'll be safe with us. You'll make friends, learn to talk, read and write, and best of all, you'll never be abused again."

Suddenly, Ginzolo sent an electric charge through the baby formula that accidentally went through Mrs. Santana. After the slight shock she looked on the ground.

"Oh," she said with a laugh. "Forgot I was on the carpet." She got on the hardwood floor and continued to hold Ginzolo in her arms.

Back in Yamalu's lair on November 30th, 3856, Mascool was inside the bioengineering lab. He noticed a yellow glow from one of the DNA samples on the reject shelf. Suddenly, he received a call from an exhausted soldier.

"Mascool, sir!" he said gasping for air. "I have important news! Please come to New Dimbar at once!"

Mascool hung up the private line and left for New Dimbar.

That same day, Ginzolo was sixteen and wouldn't dare leave the orphanage unless he wasn't forced. During his middle-school years, he learned and mastered a second language, English. He took up self-defense, and later discovered that he was able to move at the speed of light. And the sound of color! But the rules of the orphanage said that once you're sixteen, you must move out and into the world.

Now Ginzolo wasn't the only one moving out. His best friend Antonio was, too. The orphanage was giving the two a big farewell party. Mrs. Santana burst in tears as she saw two great children she raised go out into the Dark World. As they headed out the door, Ginzolo embraced Mrs. Santana one more time.

"I promise I'll visit you as soon as possible," he said. Mrs. Santana wiped her tears.

"Don't worry about me," she said, "I'll be fine. Now go before I kidnap you!" That made Ginzolo smile. He kissed her on the cheek, waved good-bye to the children, and left the orphanage. When they left, Antonio and Ginzolo loaded a bus to the Boat port. They moved to the American Republic, formerly known as the United States of America.

When they arrived in New Los Angeles, the two friends said goodbye.

"Well, it's time for me to go," said Antonio. "A bus to my new house is loading over there." Ginzolo nodded his head, showing that he understood. After a handshake and a hug, Antonio went to his bus, leaving Ginzolo alone.

From this point on, Ginzolo's language was English. He mastered it in the orphanage. It would be easy to translate. He asked for directions to his new home.

His own home Mrs. Santana paid for him.

It was modern. Elegant, but modern. It was the size of a miniature mansion. As Ginzolo entered his house, and found a note on the front door in Spanish.

"Dear Ginzolo," it began. "I would like you to know that you do not have to worry about any payments on this house. I have paid off the mortgage, the light and gas are free, and you never have to worry about water. Have a good life Ginzolo. Your nanny, Mrs. Santana."

Ginzolo couldn't believe it. A tear streamed down his right cheek as he opened the door.

The inside was huge! The living room was very exquisite. He checked the kitchen and found out how organized it was. He checked the entire house and counted seven guest bedrooms and two master bedrooms. Ginzolo still couldn't believe the mortgage was paid for this big and beautiful house. He dived into the bed in the master bedroom that he selected.

"Thank you, Mrs. Santana," he said to himself in Spanish. He got up after he heard the phone ring. Since no one in Mexico knew the number, he figured it was an American solicitor.

He answered it, anyway.

Before he greeted, the voice on the phone said, "We have your friend, Antonio." Ginzolo didn't know what to say, but when he heard his voice crying out in Spanish, he knew this was real.

"Where?" he asked.

"Macula Plaza," the voice said. "7:00 p.m. Don't be late."

Ginzolo hung up the phone and checked his watch. It showed 6:58. He ran out of the house, faster than the speed of sound, literally.

At 6:59 p.m., Mascool showed came from New Dimbar and brought two dozen of Yamalu's soldiers. They were hiding on the first floor of the plaza, with Antonio gagged and tied in a chair. At 7:00 p.m., Ginzolo opened the main door and saw his friend shaking his head. Ginzolo removed the gag, Antonio yelled in Spanish, "It's a trap!"

A dozen soldiers cane out and overcame Ginzolo with gunfire.

Even though Ginzolo was dead, he still was standing. Mascool watched from a distance. It was amazing to everyone, including Antonio, to see every single bullet that entered Ginzolo's body pop right out and see the wounds and insides heal. Ginzolo's heart started to beat. He opened his eyes. They turned yellow as he frowned. Mascool signaled the other troop. Ginzolo raised his hands.

"Feel my wrath!" he said in Spanish.

Electricity came from his fingertips. It shocked and killed every one of the shoulders. He then calmed down. He pointed his index fingers at Antonio's ropes. A small lightning bolt burnt through the ropes that came from Ginzolo's finger. Antonio got out of the ropes and stood.

"Let's get out of here," Antonio said. Ginzolo heard a very slow clap come from the back. The person who had clapped had walked into the middle of the room.

Mascool smiled. His clap stopped.

"I know you..." Ginzolo said in English.

"Of course you do," said Mascool. "I was the one who found you and sent you to Yamalu."

Mascool circled him, and tossed the soldiers bodies into a pile with his telekinetic ability.

Ginzolo pointed at him.

"You're Mascool," he said.

"You remember!" said Mascool. "How cute. Do you *also* remember being locked up in a cradle-sized cube with no light? No food? No water?" He then stopped walking.

"It was then when I knew you were one of *them*. One of the *chosen* that gypsy Nostra was talking about."

Mascool smiled. "But when I got a DNA sample of you, there was no trace of immortality *or* kinetic power in you, until we sent you to that orphanage. As soon as we sent you, you accessed your powers for the first time."

Ginzolo couldn't remember.

"I was in my lab when your DNA I placed on the reject shelf started to glow yellow." Ginzolo took a deep breath.

"I have come here to do what I should have done fifteen years ago."

Mascool pulled out a sword with a purple blade. "This is called a Hito blade," Mascool introduced. "This blade," he continued, "can *kill* an immortal."

Ginzolo smiled.

"Bring it on, *wizard*."

Mascool swung, swung again and swung again very professionally, but missed Ginzolo every time. Mascool then aimed for his head. Ginzolo caught it with both hands, but his hands soon bled. When he let go, Mascool prepared his blade to swing at him. But Ginzolo shocked Mascool's sword out of his hand and out of the plaza. Ginzolo kicked Mascool in the gut again, and again, and again, and again, then punched him in the face, knocking him to the ground.

"Give up, Mascool," Ginzolo told him. "It's over."

Mascool then smiled. "This is only the beginning."

Mascool extended his right hand. It turned into a metallic blade and went through Antonio's heart, ripping it out in the process. His heart fell off the blade as it turned back into his hand. In an instant, Mascool disappeared. Ginzolo ran to his dying friend.

"H-he-here," Antonio said. He then gave Ginzolo a rectangle spiked medallion that was yellow. The most unbelievable happened.

He spoke English!

"Tr-treasure it," he said, "as I treasured you."

Then he died, right in his arms. Ginzolo said a prayer to the mother of the Savior, Mary, and laid him down in peace. He put the pendant around his neck and walked outside.

Ginzolo made a promise to himself. He would avenge Antonio's death, even if he had to bring down Yamalu in the process. It was now his life to find and kill the immortal, Mascool. On the way to his home, by the bus station he saw a hooded man looking at him. He nodded at Ginzolo, and Ginzolo nodded back.

He disappeared.

Ginzolo's eyes widened.

"Weird," he said in English.

He proceeded to his house.

After his check-up visit with Ginzolo, he returned to Sistro's living quarters on the island of Kiputrina. Marblus walked through the walls to his sleeping chambers. Sistro was at his desk, writing a letter to someone, unaware of Marblus' attendance. Marblus silently transformed into a shadow, sliding on the floor. He closely watched as Sistro fell asleep. Then, without any feeling from Sistro, Marblus quickly slid up his back and into his ear, so he could talk to Sistro inside of a dream.

In Sistro's dream, they were inside a black void.

"How was your trip to visit Ginzolo?" Sistro asked.

"That is what I am here to talk about," Marblus said. "Goddum and Ginzolo's trial included Yamalu. When Ginzolo was born, Yamalu found out about the prophecy for some reason. He killed his parents and took a DNA sample of him. And when Goddum turned sixteen, they captured him and took some of the strength he was blessed with, which had some of his biokinetic ability."

Sistro grew concerned. "Have Mercutio and Eviana been discovered?"

Marblus shook his head.

"Make sure they don't," Sistro demanded. He was about to leave the dream until Marblus called out his name.

"Sistro!" he yelled. Sistro turned around.

"I think he's using the powers to create something to face us in the future."

"I think so, too," Sistro replied. "We cannot allow my brother to know this information."

"Agreed."

Sistro once again headed to the exit.

"Oh, Sistro, one more thing," Marblus said. Sistro turned around again.

"He doesn't know."

Sistro awoke, still on his desk. Marblus' shadowy form exited Sistro's head and quickly slithered out of his room. Sistro smiled and continued to write his letter.

"*What?!*" Yamalu yelled at Mascool. "You had a sword with a Hito blade, and you *still* lost?! How!!" Mascool stayed in his disciplinary position.

Standing still.

"Speed," he said. "Endurance. Ginzolo is faster than the sound of color. Even with a speed spell, you couldn't catch him."

Yamalu sighed and grabbed the sword.

"Fast or not," he said, "this sword was created to kill immortals. And all you were able to do was scratch him on the *palms?!*"

He dropped the sword.

"I thought this was going to make up for the incident at New Dimbar that killed my best General and killed the embryo infused with Goddum's *strength!*"

"That day was not a *total* loss," Mascool said smiling.

"How?"

"After Goddum left the base," he said, "I transported there and found the baby. It was alive. It's here inside the lab."

Yamalu started to calm down.

"And what about Ginzolo's-"

"I already inserted his DNA in the same embryo. We have just created our first genetic baby."

Yamalu started to smile. "Perfect," he said. "We hold a creation with immortality and a genetic fusion of Electrokinesis and Biokinesis."

"Don't forget super speed and super strength," Mascool added. "It's like you said before; no one will stand in your way, my lord."

Yamalu left Mascool and went into the lab. There he saw an African-based baby floating inside a tube filled with a neon-green liquid. The yellow and brown lightning shocking it told Yamalu one thing.

This is the creation to defeat those four.

Yamalu's right hand reached out and touched the tube. He saw it suddenly grow about one foot. He smiled. He could tell it was a male. He put *both* hands on the tube.

"Do not worry, my sweet," he softly cooed to the baby. "Once you are ready, you will crush those four meddlesome little pests and rule by my side."

Yamalu took his hands off the tube.

"Everything is going according to plan."

Nine years later on the island of Kiputrina, the citizens of the island gathered by Sistro's balcony to hear his speech. Sistro was getting ready when Nostra walked into the throne room.

"Nostra!" he said. "Thank *goodness* you're here." Nostra smiled.

"Sistro," he said, "I need to talk to you."

They went to the table and sat down.

"The Chosen are ready," he said. "All four of them have now reached their twenty-fifth year of life. Once an immortal is twenty-five, they will look that age forever."

"Only human immortals," Sistro said. "Wizards stop aging when they desire it."

Sistro stood up.

"Anything *else,* Nostra?"

"Twenty-five years ago," Nostra said, "Marblus set out to let their parents know they were the Chosen. Now *they* must know that they are the Chosen."

Sistro touched Nostra's forehead and it started to glow white.

"You now have the power to sight them."

"But what should I do?" he asked.

"Find them and bring them to the location I gave you just now."

Sistro put his right hand on Nostra's left shoulders.

"I want you to get them for me," he said. "Just you. I'm sending you, because only you can get them."

"There is one more thing, Sistro," Nostra said. "As you know, Yamalu is growing a creation as we speak."

Sistro's eyes closed.

"Do not worry about him," he said. "It will not be long until this creation is destroyed."

Nostra nodded.

"Everything's happening so fast," he said. "Are you sure *we're* ready?"

"We wouldn't be if we weren't, Nostra."

Sistro then headed for the balcony.

"It is time," was Sistro's last words to Nostra before he left.

Sistro headed toward the balcony. He saw thousands and millions of people all over the ground. Some cheered and clapped at the very sight of him. Others watched.

"People of Kiputrina!" Sistro yelled. "The Chosen are ready!!"

The crowd cheered even louder. Sistro smiled as they chanted his name. And finally, Sistro whispered,

"So it begins…"

That same day, Yamalu had summoned Mascool inside the throne room.

"Did you find the other two?" he asked the wizard.

"I am sorry, my lord, but-"

Before he was able to finish, Yamalu shot electricity through his fingers and electrocuted Mascool. Yamalu stopped, and looked at the fingers on his right hand.

"I feel better," he said. "Now why couldn't you find them?"

Mascool took a deep breath.

"The remaining two have slipped through our fingers. They must have found out about our plan."

Yamalu smiled at the fact Mascool kept using the word *"our"*. As if Mascool was his partner. He rose from his throne.

"I have some things to do." Yamalu walked out the door. Mascool stood there with his head sown in grief.

Yamalu entered the lab, where his *real* treasure was.

His creation.

You see, Yamalu secretly chipped off a piece of the Vortex Crystal and put it inside of the creation's concoction. Already the human looked twenty-three. Yamalu once again put his hands on the glass tube.

"Soon, you shall be awakened," he cooed. "And only you shall rule by my side, *Napoleon*."

The creation's eyes suddenly opened. They circled the tube, but the first thing he saw was Yamalu. It felt the glass. He wanted out. It pushed until it cracked the eight-inch glass tube. The liquid sprayed out of the tube. Soon, the entire tube was destroyed by the creation, making it fall on the ground. His naked body dripped from the substance.

"Father," he said to Yamalu.

Mascool was watching from outside.

Yamalu smiled at his creation.

"So it begins…"

Part One
The Beginning

Chapter One

Twinkle, twinkle little star. For that what was in the sky that night. As Mercutio looked at the sky over his mother's grave, he noticed one solitary star. Mercutio is an African-American and Twenty-five years old. He held a dark secret.

He was immortal.

But he could not save her.

At the age of twenty-one, Mercutio's mother was shot by one of Yamalu's soldiers. Yamalu was and still *is* the ruler of the world.

Yes, the world!

He ruled under evil and fear. Those who resisted were killed. Like Mercutio, he was immortal. But Yamalu was all-powerful in everyway.

Yamalu could kill with the snap of a finger.

Mercutio discovered his mother's assassination attempt when he saw her lying on the sidewalks of New Dimbar, their home. Dimbar is an underground city, right under the Hidden Death Ocean. He ran to his mothers bleeding body.

"Mom?" he said to get her attention. She smiled at her son, knowing he cared so much about her.

But she knew her time was up.

"C'mon," he said, "I have to get you to a hospital." But his mother shook her head as he tried to pick her up.

"It's too late for me, baby," she softly said. A tear started to form in Mercutio's right eye.

"I'm not gonna just watch you *die,* Mom!" he said loudly. "I love you too much."

"Then let me go!" she said. "Release my burden from your shoulders!"

Mercutio was speechless. His mother *wanted* to die.

"*Yamalu* did this, didn't he?" he asked his mother with a frown.

She nodded. "Ever since you were born," she said, "you were especially unique.

Mercutio nodded, agreeing with his mother.

"You are immortal," she continued, "you are blessed with the power of fire, and most importantly, you are *my child*." She smiled.

"I cannot hold you back any longer."

"What are you talking about?"

"You are chosen to be part of a team of individuals like yourself to get rid of Yamalu."

Mercutio heard of this as being the prophecy he was born in.

He knew his mother spoke the truth.

She smiled as she put her right hand on Mercutio's left cheek.

"I wish I could see it," she said.

Mercutio started to cry.

"I love you, baby," she said. "Let *God* take me now."

"I love you too, Mom."

She smiled as she uttered the small speech she said when she brought him in this Dark World as her last words.

"My boy," she whispered. "My beautiful little boy." And like that, the same God she wanted to go to released her invisible soul out of her earthly shell to live forever in the light. No longer having to serve the demonic dictator again.

But leaving her son alone in the darkness.

Mercutio stopped focusing on the memory of his mother's last moments and focused once again on the star. He pulled out his pendant a man mysteriously gave him in New Dimbar at the age of sixteen. A tear rolled down his face as he looked at the star.

"I miss you, Mom," he whispered.

"Your mother's death was not in vain," a voice behind him said.

Mercutio turned around and saw a short man. He was about three feet, nine inches tall. He was bald, bony, had an extremely big nose and his robes was dirty.

"How do you know my mother?" asked Mercutio.

"I don't," the man said as he shook his head, "but I knew when, where, and *how* she died."

Mercutio smirked. "You're the prophet?" he said sarcastically. "You're *Nostra?*"

"Yes, I am."

Nostra is the prophet that predicted the coming of the Chosen. He is also the last surviving member from the bloodline of the late Nostredamus.

"Why trouble me?" said Mercutio. "What do you want to tell me?"

"That it is time for you to take hold of your destiny."

Mercutio walked towards Nostra. "If there were anything in this world that would give me enough pleasure beyond my imagination," whispered Mercutio, "it would be that I had the opportunity to kill my mother's murderer."

Nostra smiled.

"But I will kill Yamalu alone."

Nostra frowned.

"You can't do this alone, Mercutio!" he yelled.

"Why? Why can't I?"

"Because there is still a secret you must know." Mercutio sucked his teeth and turned the other way.

"Who is your *father,* Mercutio?" Mercutio stopped walking. He has been on a search to find his father ever since his mother died. He looked at Nostra.

"You know my father?"

"I have seen him in a vision," said Nostra with a smile.

Mercutio walked towards Nostra again.

"You're not gonna make this easy for me, are you?"

"Not a single step."

Mercutio looked at the ground. He looked at the star in the sky and felt a kind of comfort in his heart that he never felt before.

"Where are the others?"

Nostra smiled. "Follow me."

As they were walking, Nostra snapped his fingers and a spiraling white hole appeared. The two walked through the spiraling white abyss; then it disappeared.

The other end of the spiraling white hole opened at the city of Cotendra, the only place where the earth was not affected by Yamalu's spell of darkness. Mercutio stepped through the white hole to a balcony of a building. As he stepped, the white hole disappeared behind him.

Nostra wasn't there.

He noticed two giant doors with a strange symbol on them. It was based on a red upside-down V. There was an aqua blue line through the middle, a yellow line from the blue forming another V. And a brown line under the somewhat star formed symbol.

In curiosity, Mercutio opened the doors.

Mercutio entered the room, and the doors closed with haste. Mercutio ran to the doors and they were locked. Not to mention there was no light, leaving him in the dark.

Like the world wasn't!

Suddenly he heard other human voices. One a female, one a very low voice and the other had a Mexican accent. He ran around tripping over things in the dark at least three times, until he decided to use one of his super-enlightened senses.

He used his hearing.

Mercutio closed his eyes so he could concentrate. According to his ears, the voices were coming from the far left. With his eyes still closed, he started to walk towards the sound of their voices. The floor felt different. He opened his eyes. He was inside a hallway lightened by torches of fire. Mercutio lifted his hands. The flames grew bigger, creating more light.

Mercutio smiled as he walked down the winding hallway. As he walked, he noticed a closed door with the same symbol that was on the two front doors of this crazy place. Three voices came from the other side of the door. Mercutio's curiosity grew. He decided to see if the door was open.

Of course it was.

Mercutio went through it.

The other side of the door led to outside. It also led to the ledge of the wall of the building he was in. Even though he was immortal, he didn't want to fall from such a monstrous height. He noticed another building. It was made mostly of glass from the outside. He saw the same symbol on the top of that building and heard the same three voices.

He saw a bridge leading from the ledge around the building he was on to the building he wanted to go to. It looked well supported under it. He decided to go for it. Besides, the door behind him magically disappeared into the wall, so he had nowhere else to go. As he slowly scaled around the building, not looking down at the ground, he noticed the bridge was made out of the ground. It had no handrails, and looked like it was made of rock.

He reached the bridge, and slowly walked over it. He felt it shake a little, alerting him that the bridge was not that sturdy. He turned his head back and saw the bridge start to fall apart. He looked down and saw one of the support row beams come apart and fall to the ground. The bridge started to fall like a line of dominoes, gradually reaching Mercutio.

"Great."

Mercutio ran towards the other side of the bridge where the glass building was. The bridge of rock and soil was falling and hoping to take Mercutio with it. Mercutio saw the other side of the bridge. He felt a sign of relief, until a great portion of the bridge fell from the end, creating an impossible jumping distance from the bridge to the glass building. It was collapsing behind Mercutio!

He was trapped. He continued running, and realized he had to jump. So when he reached the point, he jumped amazingly high. It exceeded the impossible jumping point. The bridge behind him was completely destroyed and fell thousands of feet to the ground. Mercutio stood up. He was on the surface of a canyon with the entrance to this spectacle glass tower only two feet away from him.

He took two steps, turned his head and saw the bridge was back in place!

"Nah," he said to himself, and entered the tower.

Mercutio walked through this glass tower. It was supported by concrete from the inside. The stairs were painted red, blue, brown and yellow. He heard the three voices coming closer from there. The tower it was dark. With the snap of his fingers from his left hand, a fireball the size of a tennis ball appeared in his palm.

He went downstairs.

The dark hall the stairs led to resembled the one he was in before. Mercutio decided not to open any doors. He headed down the long, dark hallway. He came to a holt. His left hand grabbed the fireball. It disappeared. He was at the end of the hallway, but a giant room separated him from a door that was hopefully the exit. He heard the three voices that lured him there in the first place. The ground was at least twelve feet below him, but it was filled with water.

"Great."

Mercutio tried swimming once. He was seven years old, and had discovered his power of fire. His mother pushed him inside a pool, and the water nearly took his life.

Literally!

Water beats Fire!

Mercutio paced back and fourth. He realized something. Mercutio stood tall and placed his hands over the water. He closed his eyes and pushed. He pushed until molten lava oozed out of his palms and into the water. Mercutio made sure to keep away from the steam. When it cleared, a path from the hallway to the door was built by the cooling of molten lava from the water.

As Mercutio walked across the cooled lava, and hoped this was over. When he reached the door, he turned the knob and pulled it.

It was locked!

He turned and saw that the cooled lava was starting to crack!

"Perfect," he said to himself. He looked up and saw an opening to what looked like another hallway entrance over the door. He jumped to grab the ledge of the entrance; the path of lava broke and sunk to the bottom of the room.

Luckily, Mercutio had a hold on the entrance floor.

As Mercutio climbed the narrow hall, sat down and leaned against the wall. He was breathing heavily. He looked below and saw his bridge at the bottom of the room underwater. Mercutio rolled the other way, and got ready to stand up, and saw that it wasn't a hallway, but a slide! Mercutio slid on a silver metallic lining that seemed to never end, but it did.

Right inside a black room.

When the slide ended it sent Mercutio flying in the air. He started falling. Endlessly falling inside this black room.

But as he was falling, he fell inside a clear tube feet first, and slid out of the room.

He slid through a frozen room of ice.

He slid through a room filled with fire.

He slid through a room filled with electricity.

He slid through a room buried in the ground.

The tube slide ended, and Mercutio was dropped inside a clear box and into another giant black room.

"What's going on here?!" he yelled as he stood up.

"*You* are," someone responded in an eerie whisper. Mercutio then saw what he wanted to see for the first time in four years. It was so amazing; a tear ran down his left cheek.

Mercutio saw his mother and smiled.

What he was seeing was the beginning of his life. The clear box disappeared under his feet, but he started floated instead of falling. After he saw his mother give birth to him, he witnessed the hooded man he had seen when he fought Castro Brown in high school, throw him in front of a monorail as a baby. He saw himself come back to life *after* the incident.

Mercutio's life was being presented to him.

"How can this be?" he whispered to himself. Unfortunately, it was not done. He witnessed his *second* death as a toddler in Dimbar.

He witnessed the high school fight he had with Castro Brown.

He saw the stranger he met called "Sistro" give him the very medallion he was wearing around his neck, tucked under his shirt collar this very moment.

After that, the visions grew faster and faster. He witnessed the death of his mother all over again. He witnessed her dying, her last words were amplified.

"My boy," she said. "My beautiful little boy."

Mercutio soon grew angry as the visions showed his darker side. He witnessed himself set buildings on fire and lava flows around innocent people.

Even his failed suicide attempts.

"No," he whispered. He yelled the same word.

"No!!"

As he tried to grab the vision, it disappeared. He started to fall feet first.

As he was endlessly falling down the black void, Mercutio saw a small white speck below him. It grew into a spectacle of light. It grew, and grew, until it absorbed his entire body. Not only was Mercutio falling, he was blinded. He yelled a painful yell, and continued until he could no longer take it.

"Let me out!" he yelled.

Mercutio burst through the two doors he had originally entered and landed on his back. He responded to the pain in his back, neck and the back of his head, he heard the three voices again. He opened his eyes, and saw three unfamiliar faces around him.

He saw a white woman, another black man and a Hispanic man.

"Well," Mercutio said with a chuckle, "that explains the voices."

The other black man helped him up.

Mercutio looked at the double doors with the symbol that apparently were the entrance *and* the exit.

"Did all of you go through that door, too?"

The three nodded.

"How did you cross the bridge?" the Hispanic asked.

"I ran."

The other black man spoke.

"I think it would be appropriate to introduce ourselves." He smiled and held out his left hand.

"I am Goddum."

He shook his big hand.

"Mercutio," he replied. The white woman smiled.

"I'm Eviana," she greeted.

"Ginzolo," the Hispanic said with a small soldier's salute.

Goddum folded his arms. "So, Mercutio," he said. "How many times have you *died?*"

What kind of a question is *that*?

Did they know he was immortal?

He tried to look confused. "What?!" he said jokingly.

"You can cut the act," Ginzolo said with a smirk. "Every one of us survived that crazy building. According to history, if you come out *sane,* you're immortal."

Mercutio looked at the star-like symbol again.

"Now," Ginzolo continued, "how many times have *you* died?"

Mercutio looked at the three immortals.

"You first."

Eviana raised her hand. "Eight times," she said.

"Six," Ginzolo said with a nod.

"Twelve," said Goddum.

Mercutio went to the handrails of the balcony and sighed.

"Twenty-two times," he said. Eviana looked shocked. Goddum nodded and Ginzolo looked at him. "Twelve of them were suicide attempts," he finished.

That caught Goddum's attention.

"*Suicide?*" he questioned.

"Yeah," Mercutio desperately said. "You see my mother was killed by one of Yamalu's soldiers when I was twenty-one. After that, I didn't want to live anymore."

"I had an experience like that, too," said Ginzolo. "One of my best friends was murdered by one of his wizards. In order to take *him* down, I have to take down Yamalu in the process."

Mercutio nodded. "Well, I guess that's another thing we all have in common," he said. "We all have something against Yamalu."

Mercutio walked around the balcony.

"What are we waiting for, anyway?" he asked.

"I don't know," said Ginzolo as he shrugged his shoulders. "I don't even know why I left with that little prophet."

That caught Mercutio's attention.

"Nostra came to you, too?"

"He came to *all* of us," Eviana said. "We were all convinced by something to come with him to this place. He said I would find my true love."

"He said I would find my true place in life," said Goddum.

"He said you guys would help me find my friends' killer," said Ginzolo.

Mercutio thought, and then remembered what Nostra told him.

"He said I would find my father."

"Wow," Goddum said. "That's deep."

Mercutio nodded. "I know," he said, and again looked at the symbol on the doors.

"You know what?" Mercutio said to everyone. "The symbols on these doors are the same colors of the medallions I see on *you*."

Eviana stood next to Mercutio and pulled out her N-shaped medallion. She compared the color to the aqua blue line.

It was an exact match.

"Hey," she said to Mercutio, "you're tight!" Goddum and Ginzolo noticed the same thing with their medallions and looked at Mercutio.

"What about *your* medallion, Mercutio?" Goddum asked. Mercutio took out his red circular medallion, and held it up. Not only did its color match the red upside-down V, but his medallion glowed.

So did the upside-down V.

"I think we're *all* supposed to go inside this door," said Mercutio. He then turned towards the others and said,

"Together."

Ginzolo nodded, agreeing with Mercutio. All four of them opened the two doors, the room changed. Instead of complete darkness, it was a beach with a sunset.

The four went through the door, and were amazed. The doors closed and disappeared. They were in Cotendra, just the outskirts.

Near the shoreline, Mercutio's enhanced sense of sight saw what he thought was Nostra, and two cloaked men in hoods.

One was in white and the other in black.

The three came in visual distance. They wondered who the two men were.

The short one was indeed Nostra.

That the four figured out.

These two men were a mystery. As the three came in front of the four, the two removed their hoods.

Mercutio knew the man in white.

"I know you," he said to the old man in white. "You're Sistro. You're the man who gave me this medallion."

"The *wizard*, who gave you that medallion," Sistro said with a smile. He put his attention on the other three.

"The rest of you," he said, "I have not had the pleasure of meeting.

"I am Sistro, Master Wizard of Light." He pointed to the one cloaked in black, who lifted his hood. "That is Endstra," Sistro introduced, "Master Wizard of Darkness, *and* my brother."

Sistro put his attention on Mercutio. "And you," he said with confidence, "are all related."

Ginzolo chuckled. "That's funny, wizard," he said.

Sistro with a concerned look on his face, said,

"Oh, but it's true, Ginzolo, Possessor of Electrokinesis."

Ginzolo stopped laughing.

He knew his name and special power.

"For *all* immortals are related in spirit," continued Sistro.

He started to pace in the sand.

"Wizards are related by technique," Sistro continued. "You four are related in three different ways."

"And what are those?" asked Goddum.

"One," Sistro began, "you all are immortals. Two, you all have an elemental kinetic power. And three…"

He stopped pacing.

"You were all born in the same year. 3840."

Mercutio nodded. "May twenty-eighth," he said.

"July fifth," said Eviana.

"November thirtieth," said Goddum.

"December twenty-seventh," Ginzolo said.

Sistro smiled.

"Well according to the prophecy," he said, "human immortals who are born with elemental kinetic powers born in the year 3840, are the *Chosen.*"

"The Chosen?" Ginzolo said with a confused look.

"Yeah," said Mercutio. "The Chosen are four human immortals born with special powers, whose destiny is to rid the world of Yamalu, the ruler."

Mercutio looked at Sistro with a slight squint.

"Also to protect the Vortex Crystal and the earth for all eternity."

Sistro nodded. "Yes," he said. "That is the prophecy told by Nostra one thousand twenty-five years ago." Sistro looked at Nostra with gladness, and looked at the four individuals.

"You four are the Chosen, the ones who will destroy Yamalu and save the world."

Ginzolo wasn't impressed. "What are the four powers we're supposed to have?" he asked.

Endstra stepped up.

"Pyrokinesis," he stated, "Hydrokinesis, Biokinesis, and Electrokenisis. Each of you has those powers." Endstra looked at Ginzolo. "*Now* do you believe or do I have to draw a *picture?*"

Ginzolo frowned.

"Like it or not," Sistro said, "you are the Chosen."

He pointed to a building near the beach.

"That is where you will be spending the next two weeks for your training."

He faced the Chosen.

"You begin at dawn." Sistro pointed his staff at Mercutio. "I must talk to you," he said.

"*Alone.*"

After the other three went inside the tower, Sistro and Mercutio walked the shoreline.

"You are very clever, Mercutio, possessor of pyrokinesis," Sistro said looking forward. "Not only did you take, survive *and* accomplish the hardest test back there, but you also figured out one of the secrets behind the unified symbol."

"And what's that?" Mercutio asked.

They stopped walking.
Sistro faced Mercutio and said,
"Unity can overcome *anything*."
"What *was* that place?" he asked Sistro.
"It is called the Tower of Crystal Dreams," stated Sistro. "Whoever enters is tested by their greatest fears, strengths and weaknesses ever imagined." Sistro stopped talking about the tower. Mercutio had a depressed look on his face.
"The prophecy tells of this," he began again. "According to Nostra, *you* are the leader of the Chosen."
Mercutio stopped walking.
"Now wait a minute," he said. "I can't lead a team! I'm barely a *follower*!"
Sistro went back to Mercutio and they continued to the tower.
"When the time comes," Sistro said, "you will be ready."

The Scorpion Tail Tower.
One of the most disturbing buildings in the rubbles of Manhattan.
Everything around it was covered in chaos.
The humans living there were unwillingly pulling up a statue that resembled the cruel, evil, and sinister dictator, known as Yamalu.
This African-based man was definitely evil itself. If this immortal were to die and sent straight to Hell, he would be the darkest soul down there.
Even darker than Satan.
He was on the top floor of the tower, which was the actual tip. He looked through a giant window, frowning.
"Mascool!" he yelled. A wizard dressed in a white and black robe with a rectangular shaped hat immediately came into the throne room.
"Yes, my lord," he said as he bowed. Yamalu turned around and faced Mascool. With his left hand, he snapped his fingers and a thunderstorm appeared.

It made it even harder for the slaves to pull up the statue.

"If they mess up my statue, have them exterminated," he told his wizard servant with no remorse whatsoever.

Mascool started to write it down as a memo.

"Have they been successful?" Yamalu said as he sat on his throne. "Experiments fifty-one thru fifty-three, I mean." Mascool stood in front of him and gave the report.

"Numbers fifty-one and two are doing well together," said Mascool. "Number fifty-three is breeding with the dogs we've captured."

That raised Yamalu's left eyebrow. *"Really!"* he said with a smile.

He stood up. "Let's go see." Yamalu walked to the transportation device with Mascool following. They were then transported to the underground part of the tower;

The Scorpion's Lair.

This is where all of the experiments took place, to the keeping of the Sakkaroids to the mating of Gastrulas. As Yamalu and Mascool moved to the more dangerous experiments, covered in darkness he saw a two-legged monster, bonded in chains, forcefully mating with what looked like a dog.

When it was done, it picked up their scent. It then attempted to attack the two.

"Light!" Yamalu yelled. A light appeared on the monster's body. It looked like a werewolf, but it looked a lot stronger. It was a dog that was designed to walk on its hind legs and its front legs as hands. Its hind paws were feet. Its front paws were hand-like claws. This dog's new body was muscular and strong.

Thus, it was bonded in chains.

The mutant dog barked and sometimes attempted to bite the immortals. His head was two times the size of any human.

So was its body.

Yamalu smirked. He blew in the mutant dog's face, and it stopped barking. It wiggled its nose and sneezed. Yamalu smiled and said,

"Hello, experiment number fifty-three."

The mutant dog frowned.

"Who are you?" it said.

Mascool applauded. "Brilliant, my lord!" he said. Yamalu nodded once.

"Thank you, Mascool."

He put his attention back on the dog.

"I am Yamalu, your ruler."

The dog automatically got on one knee and bowed his head.

It *knew* its place.

"It would be an honor to serve you, my lord." Yamalu grinned and grabbed Mascool's collar.

"Check on fifty-one and fifty-two," he told him. When he let go, Mascool immediately left.

"Rise," he told the dog. It stood straight. It was a foot taller than Yamalu.

"I see you are enjoying your task," Yamalu noticed. The mutant looked at the next dog he had to impregnate. He looked at Yamalu with an evil grin and nodded his head.

"Good," said Yamalu, "because I want you to impregnate different animals."

The dog looked cautious. "What kind?" it asked.

"Gorillas, Lions, Tigers, Cheetahs, Bears, Panthers, Alligators, Bulls. Basically any animal that walks on land and is ferocious."

As Mascool headed back to Yamalu, he heard the dog say, "I would like that very much, my lord."

Yamalu nodded. "Good," he said. "Continue with your pleasure." As Yamalu and Mascool left that part of the Scorpion's Lair, they heard number fifty-three grunting. He was mating with its next victim.

"I noticed there are *male* dogs in the line. Why?"

"Fifty-three's genes are unstable," Mascool said. "He can impregnate both male *and* female animals." Yamalu frowned.

"That's disgusting!" he said, with a smirk. "I like it!" he said.

"Have all the animals in Sector 17 lined for impregnation by number fifty-three."

"Yes, my lord," Mascool responded.

The four headed to their rooms. Sistro relaxed. A small wind cyclone appeared in front of him. It then stopped and Marblus appeared. Marblus was a Demarican; one of many earth demons who could sneak into dreams and manipulate them to be good or evil. Sistro once despised them, but found friendship in Marblus.

"What news do you give me from amongst the cites, Marblus?" Sistro questioned.

"Much," Marblus replied. He took a seat.

"The Chosen are here, are they not?" he asked.

"They're here," Sistro answered. "They are headed to their rooms, getting ready for bed."

Marblus nodded. "I have looked into the mind of Yamalu, and I have this to say"

Sistro leaned forward.

"You are already aware of the 'creation' be ready, am I right?"

"Yes, of course," Sistro replied with a nod.

"There is something else."

"What?"

"Yamalu is breeding a new type of animal called Trimals," said Marblus. "These animals are some of the most ferocious from this century and centuries past. They are being transformed into humanoid warriors via trimacular diffusion of cells. Thus, the name Trimal."

Sistro felt his heart drop. "How fast are they reproducing?" he asked.

"One of the first one's genes were so unstable, it could mate with any species and any sex. They *instantly* become impregnated. He has at least five thousand, now."

Sistro took a deep breath.

"Sistro," Marblus called,

"He's creating an army of humanoid animals."

Sistro looked at Marblus, frowning.

"This cannot interfere with the plan," he said. "By the time I have the Chosen ready, they will make sure *none* of them will have the ability to *walk!*"

"By the time you have the Chosen ready," said Marblus, "there will be *eighty* thousand of the monsters! We don't have enough time!"

"Like *Hell* we don't!" Sistro yelled. "You said that the Chosen would *fall* without my guidance. If I guide them, they can *definitely* destroy eighty thousand Trimals!"

Marblus nodded. "Well said, my friend." That instantly told Sistro that this was a test to see if he were *really* ready for the trials to come.

"I was serious about the Trimals," Marblus said, "but you have to work faster." With that, Marblus disappeared inside another cyclone, leaving Sistro alone.

"Harder..." he whispered to himself.

Cotendra was the only place in the world a sunrise could be seen. The Chosen were outside on the balcony near the entrance of the Tower of Crystal Dreams before the sun came up. Sistro was on his way up the stairs to the balcony.

When he reached the balcony, the sunrise was in effect

"Today," Sistro said, "you will learn how to fly."

Goddum's jaw dropped with a smile on his face. "Fly?" He said.

Sistro nodded. "Yes, Goddum, possessor of Biokinesis, fly. From the simple flotation to flying as fast as Griffindales."

"But I warn you," Nostra said, "that if you attempt to fly from here to Yamalu's lair whereabouts, you will not obtain victory."

Ginzolo didn't understand.

"Basically," Mercutio said, "each obstacle we face makes us stronger. If we go through each obstacle we face, we'll beat Yamalu."

Nostra nodded. "Exactly," he said.

"Well," said Sistro with a smile on his face, "let's begin."

The four were lined side-by-side. Goddum was in-between Mercutio and Eviana. Sistro put down his staff and stood in front of the Chosen.

"To learn how to take the sky," he began, "you must first find the energy within you."

Sistro put his left index finger in the air near his face.

"What I am doing," he said, "is channeling my inner energy outward by focusing on flight." Sistro then closed his eyes.

"You will be able to do this faster with more practice."

Sistro's body was covered in a white glow. Once it disappeared, his body started to float in the air. He flew higher and continued to float.

"Once you four get up here with me," Sistro yelled to the four on the balcony, "I shall continue to train you in flight."

"Showoff," Ginzolo whispered to himself.

"All we have to do is focus on flying," Eviana said.

"So," said Mercutio, "are you three ready?" The three nodded.

"Okay," he said. "Let's do it."

The Chosen took the same pose as they saw Sistro in. They closed their eyes and started to focus on flight. Mercutio's red aurora covered his body as soon as he closed his eyes. When the other three's aurora disappeared, they started flight. Mercutio's aurora turned to fire. Sistro saw Mercutio, who was shivering in his own flames. As the aurora completely turned to flames, his eyes suddenly opened. The retina of his eyes turned an orange-like yellow. He was shivering in flames, still in the energy gathering position. The only part of his body he could move was his mouth.

Goddum looked at Mercutio.

"I'll put him out," Eviana said. As two water balls appeared in Eviana's hands, Sistro put his hand on her right shoulder.

"No!" he yelled. "Eviana, possessor of hydrokinesis, you cannot interfere!" Sistro looked at him. He said, "Besides, his elemental weakness would *kill* him!"

As the flames grew bigger, Mercutio's shivering body rejected something. Sistro sensed what was inside of him. And for the first time in his immortal life, he was afraid.

"My *God!*" he whispered. "The legend!"

Mercutio let out a cry. The other three and Sistro heard it. It was like a dog whistle ringing in their ear. Once Mercutio stopped the yell, his fiery body was telekinetically blasted off the balcony and was heading straight to the giant pond, fed by a waterfall underneath the balcony.

"No!" Sistro yelled. He went flying down to the pool to save him. But halfway to the pool, the flames on Mercutio were sucked into his body. Sistro hoped to catch him, but missed.

"Mercutio!" Sistro hollered. Mercutio regained control of his body and flew away from the pond just in time. Sistro smiled as he watched him fly from the pond to the others.

"Well done," he whispered.

But as he reached the other three, he slowed down. Eviana saw something was wrong with him as he reached them. His eyes were still orange-like yellow, but he looked as if he were in a trance.

"Mercutio, what's wrong?" Eviana asked. Mercutio stayed silent. Sistro watched beneath the balcony. Once Eviana touched Mercutio's right cheek, hoping to get a response, Mercutio fell out. His body weight forced him to fall backwards. As Sistro watched Mercutio crash land on the balcony, He was concerned. He flew towards Mercutio's body.

So did the others.

According to the other three, this was his twenty-third death.

Mercutio's bones mended and his wounds rapidly heal. His eyes opened once. They were the same color as they were before, but his eyelids were heavy.

He went to sleep.

"What happened to him?" Goddum asked. Sistro and Ginzolo got him up and started to float.

"Something that could either help us," said Sistro, "or *destroy* us."

Back inside their Cotendran living quarters, Eviana and Ginzolo were looking after Mercutio, who was asleep. Sistro, Endstra, Goddum and Nostra were in the lounge area discussing what had happened.

"As Mercutio came up to us," Goddum explained, "he had orange-like yellow eyes and looked like he was in a trance."

Nostra nodded as if he had witnessed the phenomenon.

"What happened after that?" Endstra asked.

"Mercutio blacked out and fell back to the balcony," he said to his brother.

"Something is happening to Mercutio. I think it's the GF."

Nostra and Endstra suddenly looked terrified. Goddum thought now was the best time to put his curious mind to work.

"What's the GF?" he asked.

Nostra sat on the front edge of his chair.

"The GF stands for many things," he said. "Great Future, Gigantic Foretelling, and Genuine Flame-"

"A long time ago," Sistro interrupted, "one thousand years before all of you were born after my brother and I settled on the island of Kiputrina. The volcano used to form Atlantacore exploded a second time. The city was destroyed."

"When Atlantacore was destroyed," Endstra started, "a Phoenix engulfed in flames emerged from the rubble. It was called the Fox Phoenix; the very last, and also the strongest."

"According to legend," continued Nostra, "the Phoenix was wild and eagerly wanted to become part of the prophecy."

"About *us*, right?" asked Goddum.

"The same one," answered Nostra.

"Did it succeed?"

"Unfortunately," said Sistro, "*yes*. It found the pyrokinetic power inside the weapon that held Mercutio's power, the Hikulo sword. Even though his future power was in heaven, the Phoenix was able to unite with the power of fire."

"So you're saying," Goddum said, "that this 'Fox Phoenix' is inside of Mercutio? Wouldn't it just increase his power?"

"Maybe," Nostra said as he scratched his chin, "but the Phoenix has a mind of its own. Until Mercutio can control it, he will have worse episodes than the one he had briefly."

"But it also represents another thing," said Sistro. He looked at Mercutio, who was on a couch asleep and guarded by Eviana and Ginzolo.

He then looked back at the three he was sitting with.

"Mercutio is the *leader* of the Chosen," he said loudly.

Eviana and Ginzolo heard.

"How?" Ginzolo said. "How is this person the leader of us and he can't even control his *own* power?"

Sistro grew angry.

He stood and looked at Ginzolo. "Because, Ginzolo," he yelled, "Unlike *you*, with your smart lyrics of foolishness and sarcasm, *he* can perform a madrocellular transformation!"

Ginzolo became quiet.

Goddum chuckled beneath his breath.

Sistro sat down.

"According to Nostra's prophecy," Sistro said, "the one who can perform a madrocellular transformation first shall lead the Chosen to victory. I knew *he* would be the one to do it, but I never figured he would with the GF."

"You *still* didn't answer my question," said Goddum.

"The GF is Mercutio's new source of power," said Sistro. "With the power of the Fox Phoenix and another spirit that is almost equal to *its* power level, Mercutio can merge with any fire animal and spirit on this earth and madrocellularly transform into his *ultimate* form."

Sistro looked at Mercutio again and said,

"The Genesis Fire."

One week later, Mercutio woke from his coma. The Cotendran sun woke him at sunrise. His eyes were back to normal. He was in his room. As he got out of bed, across from him was Marblus, sitting in a chair. Mercutio had seen him once before, during his fight with Castro Brown back in high school, but never met him.

"Who are you?" he asked. "How did you get in here?"

Marblus was silent for two seconds.

"Your father asked me the same question."

Mercutio was stunned. "Y...y...you know my father?"

Marblus nodded and introduced himself.

"I am Marblus," he said. "Fortuneteller of the Demarican race. I am here to tell you of your power. It is starting to grow out of your control."

"What are you talking about?" Mercutio said with a frowned face. "I am in *complete* control of my fire capabilities!"

"Is this why you collapsed on the Tower of Crystal Dreams last week?" Marblus sarcastically asked. "Oh yes!" he added. "That's right! You were in a trance last week, so of *course* you can't remember."

Mercutio grew angry. His eyes turned red.

"That's it," Marblus whispered.

Mercutio charged toward him, and missed Marblus because he teleported. Mercutio went through the main door of his room to the hallway. The others heard the noise and immediately went to see what was happening. When they reached the hallway, they saw Mercutio and his glowing red eyes.

"Get away from me!" he yelled. His voice was mixed with his and the darker force within him.

Ginzolo didn't respond the same way that everyone else did. He walked towards Mercutio.

"I'm not going anywhere!" he told him. Mercutio saw Ginzolo come towards him. He signified him to stop by holding out his hand.

"I'm warning you Ginzolo," Mercutio's demented voice said.

Ginzolo pushed him.

"Who are *you* to warn *me?!*" he yelled.

He pushed Mercutio again.

Mercutio fell to the ground.

Mercutio stood. Ginzolo grabbed him up by the collar.

"If you really *are* the leader of us," Ginzolo provoked, "transform! Perform a madrocellular transformation!"

Mercutio stopped frowning and smiled as his demented side took over.

"As you wish," the darker force said.

Mercutio grabbed Ginzolo and threw him all the way down the hallway and then through the wall. Before he plummeted to the ground, he was able to use his flight.

Mercutio grinned and started to float. Eviana put her hands in front of her.

"I'm sorry, Mercutio,"

She shot a water ball at Mercutio.

Even though it was a direct hit, it showed no effect! He turned his head and gazed his blood red eyes into Eviana's.

He smiled at her evilly. He flew down the hallway and headed towards Ginzolo.

"What do we do *now*?" Goddum asked. Eviana looked at her hands and the hallway opening that lead outside to Mercutio and Ginzolo.

"Watch," she said.

Mercutio flew outside. He saw Ginzolo dusting himself.

"*Come on!*" he yelled. "*Transform!*"

"Don't do it!" yelled Eviana as she flew from outside. "You don't have to prove *anything* to Ginzolo."

She put her hand on his left shoulder. Mercutio regained control. His eyes started to turn back to normal. He turned his head and looked at his friend.

"Eviana," he whispered. But, something happened. Marblus was inside his mind. Mercutio saw *him* instead of Eviana.

"*I know a secret,*" whispered over and over within his mind. He saw fire all around him. He felt cold and started to shiver once again. He no longer could see or feel Eviana. He lost his touch of reality. Then he saw the Fox Phoenix stare at him from the fiery sky, piercing through his soul with its glowing red eyes that rendered him helpless.

It had taken over.

Back in reality, Eviana tried to get Mercutio to fight it, but he blasted her away with a burst of energy.

His eyes turned blood red.

He smiled deviously at Ginzolo, who was awaiting a fight. But this time Mercutio's dark side decided it was time for something different. The three Chosen watched in amazement and in horror, as Mercutio changed.

It started with his hands. They morphed into red claws with long black fingernails. His feet started to transform into human-sized bird talons. A red ball was formed by his own energy. He was trapped inside. Sistro sensed the energy and quickly ran towards the wall opening down the hallway. He flew and joined Goddum and Eviana.

"What's going on here?!" Sistro yelled. "I don't know!" Goddum yelled back. "I think the Fox Phoenix is transforming Mercutio!"

Sistro looked at the red ball of energy Mercutio was trapped inside.

"It's his first transformation!" he said to himself.

Soon the ball of energy exploded and showed a floating cocoon. As it opened, Mercutio's morphed hands and feet came out. The rest of him was a somewhat-spectacular sight. His body was muscular and with red feathers covered it with white feathers on his breastplate. He had the head of a hawk with a yellow beak, black feathers around his original blood red eyes with red feathers around the rest of his head. On the lower torso was a belt holding the bottom half of a brown toga and a red fox tail waving side-by-side behind him. Once the cocoon shattered, it fell to the ground. A giant pair of fire wings appeared and started to take their spectacular form.

"The Fire Griffin!" Sistro said to himself.

For once, Ginzolo was speechless. He had just seen a man transform into a man-bird! Mercutio deviously smiled.

"ARE YOU READY TO PLAY?" Mercutio's demented voice asked. Ginzolo frowned.

"I will not," he began, "become second best!" With that, Ginzolo threw a lightning bolt in Mercutio's direction. He avoided it by flapping his wings once. This allowed him to fly faster than ever before. The air rushed from his wings and made the lightning bolt bend downwards. It hit one of the supporters of the building.

Mercutio let out a bird screech and nose-dived towards Ginzolo. Ginzolo repeatedly shot thunderbolts from his hands. Mercutio dodged them during his nosedive. Mercutio threw a fireball at him. He dodged it with his super speed. It turned and hit him in the back, leaving four-degree burns.

"Those things are navigational!" he yelled.

Mercutio's nosedive crashed into Ginzolo's chest, knocking the wind from him and made him fall back a little. Mercutio repeatedly sent out *more* navigational fireballs. Even with Ginzolo's super speed, every single one hit him. Ginzolo once again tried to hit him with another thunderbolt while he was distracted. It hit him, but it bounced right off his chest!

Mercutio smiled.

Ginzolo was becoming weak and he didn't like it. With both hands at the same time, he conducted a thunder blast. Mercutio blocked it with a fire blast, which was at least twice the size. Spinning around spontaneously, Ginzolo tried to keep up his strength to feed his electric power. You could tell by Mercutio's face, he was tired. His body caught on fire. He blasted another fire blast through his mouth, feeding his original blast.

It was now *six* times the size.

Ginzolo couldn't keep up the energy. The blast stopped.

His entire body was drenched in stampeding flames.

When Mercutio stopped, Ginzolo's skeleton had floated in the air. It turned into his human form and was revived.

Clothes and all.

Mercutio floated towards Ginzolo's floating body. He lifted his right hand. The nail of his index finger grew sword length. It turned from black to purple.

Sistro knew it was a Hito blade.

So did Ginzolo, who remembered his battle with Mascool.

Mascool pulled out a sword with a purple blade. "This is called a Hito blade," Mascool introduced. "This blade," he continued, "can kill an immortal."

Ginzolo smiled.

"Bring it on, wizard."

Sistro saw Mercutio was about to ram it into Ginzolo's heart, he decided to interfere.

"No!" he yelled at Mercutio. He looked at Sistro and smiled. He headed towards Sistro with his Hito nail blade. Before he stabbed Sistro, he forced his staff in front of him and a blinding white light came from the staff that covered the battlefield.

"Hell shall *not* consume you, Mercutio!" he yelled. Mercutio let out another bird screech and flew backwards.

"Be purified by the light!"

With that said, all of the darkness from the GF blasted from his chest. Mercutio let out one of the loudest bird screeches that even *Yamalu* heard it! Once the light disappeared, Mercutio fell out and his wings were put out.

Ginzolo got up from his flashback. The two spectators came to Sistro. They all saw Mercutio back to normal in a burst of red light.

"*Now* do you see why *he* is your leader, Ginzolo?" Sistro asked.

"Could he do it again?" asked Ginzolo.

"The Fox Phoenix and the GF are *still* in his body," Goddum said. "His transformation will be the same as this one, but because Sistro purified it, the Fox Phoenix and the GF are now pure. It's on *our* side, now."

Mercutio awoke. He had no idea what had happened. He looked around and saw all the destruction his transformation had done.

"What happened?" he asked. "All I remember is seeing Eviana, and then I was trapped in this room of fire with this fiery Phoenix inside of it."

Sistro put his right hand on Mercutio's left shoulder.

"Everything is fine now, Mercutio," he said.

The Chosen and Sistro floated inside their living quarters.

"Mascool!" Yamalu yelled. Mascool busted through the throne room doors.

"I heard it too, my lord!" he said. He was trying to get the ringing out of his ears.

"What was it?" Yamalu asked.

"It sounded like a Griffin," answered Mascool.

Yamalu frowned.

"That was more than a mere Griffin." He turned and faced Mascool.

"One of the Chosen has made their first madrocellular transformation," he said. "I think it was their leader."

"Mercutio, my lord?"

"How do you know that?"

"I can see into the present far beyond this tower," Mascool answered. Yamalu got even angrier.

"Then how come you didn't tell me where Sistro and Endstra were?! No! How come you never told me where the Chosen are *now?!*" In two seconds, Mascool answered with this.

"You never *asked,* my lord."

Yamalu punched Mascool all the way to the other wall, breaking his neck. Yamalu cracked his neck.

"I feel better," he said.

Mascool's neck mended itself. When he was revived, he stood and bowed in respect.

"I did not mean to upset you."

"Just tell me where they are, Mascool."

"Cotendra, Land of Light."

"The Japanese Ruins?"

"The same."

Yamalu thought. "Have a group of the Wolf Trimals handle them. See if they survive."

Mascool bowed. "I'll send them immediately." Yamalu looked at Mascool in disgust.

"Then why are you still here?!"

The Chosen's training session drew to a close. Mercutio, Eviana, Goddum and Ginzolo were lined side-by-side. Sistro looked at them.

"Show your medallions," he said. They each either got them out of their pockets and put them around their necks, or took them out from the inside of their shirts. After Sistro noticed each had their destined pendant, he pulled out four belts with buckles the same shape as their medallions.

The belts and buckles were white.

"What do our medallions have to do with any of this?" asked Eviana.

"The medallions were *put* into your lives," said Sistro. "You should never have gotten them originally 'till now, but Nostra told me it would be wise to give them to you at a young age."

Mercutio looked around.

"Then how come you gave me mine *personally?*" he asked.

He must never know, thought Sistro as he thought of Endstra at the same time.

"Because," he said, "you would've overcome anything that crossed ways with it." He passed out the belts, according to the shape of their medallions.

"When you put these belts on," he said, "you will be cloaked in your armor, and given the weapon your-"

Sistro looked at Mercutio.

"*Original,* powers came from."

They waited for Mercutio to put his on first. Mercutio put on his belt. An aurora of red glowed over him. When it disappeared, he was in his armor and held the Hikulo.

His armor consisted of a red collarless silk long-sleeved shirt, a red version of the belt he put on, red dress pants with a sword harness attached and black shoes from the twenty-first century.

"Some armor," Ginzolo said.

"You're already immortals," said Sistro. "You don't need *that* much. Now, the rest of you."

The others put theirs on. All three were the same as Mercutio's armor, except for the colors. Goddum's was brown, Ginzolo's was bright yellow, and Eviana's was sky blue. Each had the weapon of their original powers.

"Mercutio," Sistro began, "you have the three-bladed Hikulo sword. In the ancient language of this city, it means Black Fire. Ginzolo, you have the Natunga O' Lioben. It means the Lord of all Shields in Lingu. Eviana, you possess the Hydroscepter from the now destroyed city of Atlantacore. And Goddum, you own Grodera; the jewel of the earth." He looked at the four warriors and smiled.

"You are ready," he said.

Soon after that, Mercutio heard footsteps, snarls and barks from the Far West. He turned and saw nothing. He used his enhanced vision. He saw a small army of Wolf Trimals, running towards them.

"We have company coming, guys!" he yelled. The others turned around and saw the army as they came within normal visual range.

"This is an unexpected obstacle," Sistro said. The Chosen got ready to fight.

"*We're* an unexpected obstacle," said Ginzolo. As they got their elemental powers ready, Goddum asked Mercutio, "Do you need to transform?"

"I can handle this without it," he said. "Besides, it might take me over again."

Sistro smirked. "I think I will help you with this," he said as he stood next to Mercutio.

Sistro closed his eyes. In a burst of light, he transformed to level one, then two. Covered in white light, he made his third madrocellular transformation! He had the same kind of armor as the Chosen, only white. The difference was his hair was short, his beard and mustache was cut off and his belt was black.

"You're a *Chosen?*" Ginzolo asked. Sistro shook his head.

"I am a *wizard*," he said. "Let's get ready." The mutant wolves came close enough for the Chosen to attack, but they struck first. Ginzolo ran inside the swarm at the speed of light bombarding them with his shield and punching. Eviana started to drown a third of the army by forming a pool of water over their heads. She froze the survivors in blocks of ice.

Goddum formed two giant boulders and crushed any Wolf Trimal he saw walking. Mercutio used a combination of martial arts and pyrokinesis to trap the beasts. Sistro with his newly found power used his new ability:

Telekinesis.

With one wave of the hand, Sistro knocked several Trimals out of the earth's atmosphere, like Yamalu did his troops during the Last War.

The Chosen were on a roll; until an even bigger troop of Wolf Trimals started to aid the survivors. They moved in fast and hard. Ginzolo was knocked off his running course by a very powerful punch. Eviana's freezing method was useless. They broke free from her blocks of ice. They broke Goddum's powerful boulders and out trapped Mercutio's fire traps. Sistro was challenged.

"Mercutio!" yelled Ginzolo. "You have to transform!" Mercutio used self-defense and failed. He frowned.

"I can beat them without it!" he yelled back.

"Mercutio!" Eviana yelled. "Mercutio, *please!*"

"No!" he yelled as he started to shoot firebombs.

Sistro got irritated.

"You must perform your madrocellular transformation, now!" he yelled. "I mean it! Stop this foolishness *immediately!*"

The way Sistro said those words made Mercutio stop fighting and was hit with a giant sledgehammer while in thought.

He went hurtling in the air.

He flew over the army was fought his friends. Mercutio closed his eyes and focused all of his power on transforming. That's where the GF came into effect. The Fox Phoenix came out him and circled his body. It spun faster, faster and faster until the Fox Phoenix covered his body. The Phoenix re-entered his body. A ball of fire formed around him.

The Trimal army and the Chosen watched in amazement. Sistro smiled and floated to the sky level of Mercutio.

Mercutio's ball of fire exploded.

Parts of it hit certain Trimals. Mercutio was in level one madrocellular transformation, the Fire Griffin. But, this Griffin was different.

Mercutio opened his eyes. The Chosen found out they weren't red. He looked at his transformed hands.

"I'm in control," he amazingly said to himself. He looked at Sistro.

"If that's only your *first* transformation," Sistro said, "imagine what your *second* shall be." Mercutio smiled and flapped his wings of fire twice.

"Shall we?" he said.

"With pleasure," Sistro answered.

"Chosen," yelled Mercutio, "stand down."

The three did not hesitate to get off the battlefield.

Sistro and Mercutio nose-dived towards the army. Mercutio let loose several navigated fireballs. Sistro threw out white energy blasts. The mutant Wolf army fled from the sources of energy. They declared retreat. Sistro and Mercutio combined powers. They floated side-by-side, both of their hands next to each other and released blasts. Mercutio released a fire blast and Sistro an energy blast. With both blasts combined, the retreating army of Wolf Trimals was annihilated.

Mercutio and Sistro flew towards the other three. When they landed, Sistro transformed his normal form. Mercutio folded his wings.

"That was just a taste of Yamalu's power," Sistro said.

"How can *we* transform?" asked Goddum.

"Once you begin your quest," Sistro said, "you shall learn."

"We need to move out as soon as possible," said Mercutio. "Yamalu might send more troops."

"Not without *me* you're not!" said Endstra, who had walked towards them with his staff in his right hand.

"We shall *both* go," Sistro said. "My brother is everything that I am and more."

Mercutio nodded.

"Good," he said. "We need all the help we can get."

"Remember," said Sistro. "United we are invincible, but divided we fall."

Mercutio nodded again. "I fully agree," he said. Mercutio put out his left claw-like hand.

"Remember this always," he said. "We are not a fellowship. We are family."

Goddum placed his hand on top of Mercutio's.

"Family," he said.

"Family," said Eviana as she put her hand on Goddum's.

Everyone looked at Ginzolo. He looked at the unified three and decided to join. He put his hand on top of Eviana's.

"Family," he said.

The Chosen let go of each other and waited for Mercutio to make a decision. Mercutio looked the way the Trimal armies came. With his enhanced sense of sight, the land zoomed in front of him past deserts, past oceans, until he saw the Scorpion Tail Tower, where Mercutio concluded that was Yamalu's lair. Mercutio blinked and his vision became normal.

Mercutio transformed to his normal form.

"We go west," he said. "If we do, we'll head straight to Yamalu's lair.

Sistro nodded.

"Then that's where we go," he said.

And soon the Chosen and the wizard brothers journeyed off on one of the greatest adventures of all time.

"The wolves were no match for Sistro and Mercutio put together," said Yamalu. "We need something more," Mascool suggested. "Something more powerful than a wolf or a dog." "I do not want to send in any troops besides dogs," Yamalu said. "I want to save the troops of the different species when we need them."

Yamalu knew no matter what he threw at them, the Chosen would destroy it. Except…

He turned to Mascool. "Experiment #50," he said. "Experiment #50!"

Mascool frowned.

"You mean the *creation?*"

The same," answered Yamalu. "Bring him to the roof of the tower."

Mascool bowed. "As you wish, my lord." He then walked out of the room. Yamalu then walked through his giant glass window without breaking it, and flew upwards to the top of the tower. He saw Mascool bring the creation Yamalu bred in chains so he wouldn't escape. Once the creation saw Yamalu, he immediately bowed.

"Father," he said in a raspy voice. Because Yamalu was the first living thing he saw when he awoke, like an animal it would call it their parent. Yamalu smiled. He could easily control him.

Or so he *thought*.

"Rise," Yamalu demanded. The creation's skin was that of the endangeved Africans and his eyes were blue. His hair was black and spiked wildly. He had a muscular physique and showed a sign of intelligence.

The creation rose broke from the chains and sent them flying. They flew so fast they spun around the world in five seconds. The creation caught them as they came behind him.

"Impressive," said Yamalu. "I see a lot of me in you."

The creation sighed an exhausted sigh.

"Now listen," Yamalu said. "Your name is *Napoleon*. Your mission is to find and *destroy* the Chosen."

Mascool couldn't believe it.

He gave him a *name!*

"They are people like you," continued Yamalu, "and like you they have extraordinary powers. You won't fail me, *will* you my son?"

Napoleon shook his head. "Never, father."

Yamalu waved his hand and Napoleon was clothed in the same armor as the Chosen, only tan. He carried a black sword with a Hito blade attached to it.

It is the only blade that can kill an immortal.

"You do not know the meaning of *pain*," he told his son. "Now go! Spread your wrath through the world and do not return until they are *dead!*"

Napoleon floated in the air and flew north. Yamalu looked at Mascool.

"Place Experiments 21 through 24 in the Toxic Sewerway."

As the six left Cotendra into the Dark World once again, they started to worry.

"We'll camp here," said Mercutio. The others quickly sat down, exhausted from their four-hour walk. It was 9:00 in the evening. Two of the Chosen fell asleep.

Mercutio and Goddum decided to eat.

"Your leadership skills have improved," said Goddum.

"Thanks," Mercutio replied.

As Mercutio bit into a sandwich, he thought. "So what's your story?" he asked. Goddum shrugged his shoulders.

"I was born in a wealthy family back when my father, Kowatuu V was king of New Dimbar," he said. "I was captured at sixteen by some of Yamalu's soldiers. They transferred my powers to three embryos. One was complete I escaped before the other two became complete."

"What happened to the other one?" asked Mercutio.

"I made sure it was destroyed," he said. Mercutio pointed his index finger to the ground. A fire started.

Goddum chuckled.

"Now *that's* cool."

Mercutio chuckled, too. The friendly conversation ended when Mercutio heard someone walking there way. He took out his sword and stood up.

"What's wrong?" asked Goddum.

"Wake the others," Mercutio demanded. He woke Ginzolo and Eviana; Sistro and Endstra joined Mercutio.

"You heard it, too?" Mercutio asked Sistro.

"Indeed," he replied. The three joined the others who were standing, waiting to see whom it was. The footsteps got closer. The person was in the light. Sistro was surprised when he saw him.

"Run," Sistro said to his brother. "Go hide," he whispered. Endstra slowly backed up, then ran and hid.

"I am Napoleon," the stranger said. He pulled out a black sword with a purple blade. "I was ordered by my father, Yamalu, to kill you *all!*"

Mercutio blasted the purple bladed part of Napoleon's sword away with a fireball.

"You may try," Mercutio said, "but it will take you longer than you expected."

Napoleon frowned. He put up his sword and ran towards Mercutio. When he got close enough, Mercutio chopped off his head with the Hikulo. But what he did not expect was for a new body to grow from Napoleon's decapitated head!

Napoleon smiled as he landed.

"He's *immortal!*" yelled Ginzolo.

"I can *see* that!" Mercutio yelled.

Napoleon walked stalking-like towards Mercutio and took out his sword. Even though the purple part of the blade was gone, the black part of it was still very lethal. It contained a mysterious poison with strange effects on immortals.

It could help, or *cripple* them.

Mercutio grasped his sword and blocked Napoleon's attacked. Napoleon kicked him with his left foot in the stomach, all the way to the borderline of Cotendra!

"*Sheesh!*" he said to himself. He flew where Napoleon was fighting the others and landed next to Goddum.

"He has your strength!" Mercutio yelled.

Goddum thought.

"No!" he said. "It c*an't* be!" He grabbed Grodera.

"Sistro!" he yelled. Sistro looked at him.

"The creation!" Goddum yelled. "Napoleon is the *creation!*"

Sistro frowned, knowing this was true.

"I thought you *killed* it?" said Mercutio.

"I did, too," answered Goddum. "Yamalu must have found and restored it."

Goddum put his left palm on one side of Grodera. It glowed red. A chain and handle appeared on it.

"Shall we?" Goddum asked.

"Let's," answered Mercutio. Together, they ran towards Napoleon with weapons in hand. At the same time, Goddum and Mercutio thrust their weapons on both of Napoleon's sides, tossing him and spiraling upward in the air. He fell back on the ground and stood back up. The deep cut from the Hikulo healed rapidly. Along with his clothing, and the big chunk from his other side along with his clothing re-healed and re-mended from the Grodera.

"Well," Goddum said to Mercutio, "it was worth a try." Napoleon once again pulled out his sword and attacked Mercutio. Goddum tried to help. He was tossed away by telekinesis.

Sistro noticed that.

Eviana forced a water blast from both her hands. With a wave of Napoleon's hand, the water turned to light blue goop, which turned and engulfed her. Napoleon and Ginzolo struck lightning bolts. Napoleon's was more powerful.

Remember that he was still fighting Mercutio.

"A genetic human cannot do all of this!" Sistro said to himself. Mercutio and Napoleon clashed swords, until Mercutio broke his black blade in three parts. As they fell, Napoleon caught each, flipped Mercutio over and threw each part at the Chosen. One blade went in Goddum's arm, one in Eviana's leg and the other in Ginzolo's stomach.

"No!" yelled Mercutio. Napoleon elbowed Mercutio in the stomach, turned and punched him in the face with Goddum's strength, causing him to slide on the ground after falling.

Napoleon walked towards Mercutio, who was on the ground, trying to recuperate from that serious blow. Napoleon stood over, bent down and looked at him. He shook his head.

"Pathetic," he said and repeatedly punched him in the stomach with Goddum's strength. Mercutio was being pounded into the ground with every single punch. When he was punched in the ribs and heard every rib on his right side crack, he actually felt pain.

This gave Napoleon great joy. He laughed at Mercutio's pain. He stopped suddenly and put purple knuckles on his right hand made from a Hito blade. As he was getting ready to punch Mercutio in the face to finish off the Chosen's leader, a lightning bolt destroyed the knuckles. Napoleon turned, and a giant yellow thunder blast hit him head on, knocked him from Mercutio and further into the darkness.

As Mercutio got up, he could not believe what he was seeing. A male lion's head attached to a male's human body-covered in fur. The muscular body wore a gold sleeveless leather turtleneck, cream dress pants on, and no shoes. Its four-toed feet were too big for shoes. Its right hand held a sword shaped like a thunderbolt. His left hand held the Natunga O' Lioben; the Lord of all Shields.

"Ginzolo?" Mercutio said in awe.

"You were expecting the Easter Bunny?" Ginzolo said sarcastically.

"It must have been the black part of Napoleon's blade," Mercutio said. "It must have unlocked your potential to form a madrocellular transformation."

Ginzolo smirked.

"Why don't we work together?" said Mercutio. "You saw how strong Sistro and I were when we combined powers."

Ginzolo shrugged his shoulders.

"I guess it wouldn't hurt," he said. Mercutio nodded.

"Good," he said. "Because I hear Napoleon running this way, with your speed."

Ginzolo didn't understand. How did Napoleon get his speed? Or his *power* even?

He flashbacked to the battle with Mascool.

"But when I got a DNA sample of you, there was no trace of immortality <u>or</u> kinetic power in you, until we sent you to that orphanage. As soon as we sent you, you accessed your powers for the first time."

Ginzolo couldn't remember.

"I was in my lab when your DNA I placed on the reject shelf started to glow yellow." Ginzolo took a deep breath.

"I have come here to do what I should have done fifteen years ago."

In a burst of red light, Mercutio transformed and took out Hikulo.

"He's almost here," he said. "You take his left and I his right." Mercutio looked at the newly transformed Ginzolo. He put his shield behind him and pulled out his sword.

"Understand?" asked Mercutio. Ginzolo nodded.

"Fine by me," he said. By the time Napoleon reached the two, Mercutio flew to his right and Ginzolo ran to his left.

The battle was on.

Mercutio blasted navigational firebombs to Napoleon's right side. The bombs were faster than Napoleon's speed and hit him every time. Ginzolo's eyes zapped pure electricity at Napoleon. He was getting badly beaten. Mercutio and Ginzolo flew up and got ready to proceed with a fire and electric blast. But Eviana had freed herself from her goopish prison and Goddum, who broke his telekinetic boundary, joined their transformed members in blast combinations with a hydro and rock blast.

Before they attacked, Sistro and Endstra flew behind them and got ready for their blast. Napoleon noticed everyone was there. It would make it easier to kill them all. He flew towards them, yelling.

"Fire!" Mercutio yelled. A giant ray of fire, water, rock, electricity, light and darkness quickly hit Napoleon, and forced him on the ground and buried him hundreds of thousands of feet beneath the earth's crust.

Goddum shot rock, stone and dirt inside the hole and mixed it with Eviana's water. It dried quickly with Mercutio's flamethrower. They successfully made a concrete prison with no possible way of escape. Mercutio and Ginzolo transformed to their normal form and went to the others.

"That was no regular genetic human," Sistro said to the Chosen.

"Tell me about it," said Goddum.

Sistro shook his head. "No," he said, "not like that.

"None of you had the other abilities that Napoleon character showed today. Telekinetic abilities, transformation of elements." He then looked at Mercutio. "Only the person you are destined to destroy have these powers and many more."

"Yamalu..." Mercutio whispered while nodding his head.

"He must have control of him, somehow," said Eviana.

"I don't think its control," said Sistro. "If I am correct, I think he gave Napoleon a piece of the Vortex Crystal, which is why he said Yamalu was his father. He is *connected* to him."

"We must avoid him at all cost," said Mercutio. He looked and stepped on the concrete. "This prison will not hold him forever." He looked at Sistro.

"We need to leave with haste," he said, "before he escapes."

Everyone agreed and continued west.

About four hours later, the surface of the concrete trap cracked. The ground started to shake. Napoleon burst through the concrete and floated into the air, frowning and breathing hard.

"I need reinforcements, father," he said out loud. Yamalu's voice then telepathically said something in his mind.

<I'll send a fleet of Trimals to you, > he said. <They should be on their way in five seconds. >

Napoleon turned and saw a small group of at least twenty Gorilla Trimals come towards him. Napoleon smiled menacingly.

"Time to have fun," he whispered.

As the Chosen and the wizard brothers were walking, not aware Napoleon and an even powerful Trimal fleet were picking up their trail, they saw an enormous hole. There was a gigantic metal pipe with bright, dull green algae growing inside. Mercutio went to the beginning of the pipe and swiped his finger through it.

"This is pleasant," he sarcastically said.

"The only way to Yamalu," Sistro said, "is to go down there."

"No way," said Ginzolo. "We all know what this is. Who knows what's down there, anyway?"

"The land curves left," Goddum said, "back to Cotendra. If we follow the land, we'll *never* get to Yamalu's lair."

Mercutio looked inside. With his enhanced sense of vision, he saw a liquid illuminate from the walls.

"There's water down there," said Mercutio. "Water's *toxic* to me."

Sistro was getting very irritated.

"Look," he said. "No matter what's down there, we have to go through." Mercutio nodded.

Ginzolo nodded.

Goddum and Eviana were near the entrance.

Mercutio and Ginzolo headed inside, followed by Sistro and Endstra. Yamalu sensed they were entering his trap in the Posa Seagta.

The Toxic Sewerway.

Chapter Two

"How I wonder where you are, Sistro," Yamalu said to himself. He was sitting on his throne with his eyes closed, but not asleep. He opened them to see Mascool's face. He sighed and rolled his eyes.

"You're going to be the death of me," he said.

"You can't die, my lord."

"I can if I choose to."

Yamalu closed his eyes again. "Have you transported the Gorilla Trimals to my son?" he asked. Mascool felt insulted. It was *his* idea to create a human containing the powers of the Chosen, but it was Yamalu's idea to gather samples. But it didn't add up to the generosity that he showed that creature whom called him "father" nor the kindness that he never received. Mascool felt like he wanted Napoleon more than he wanted *him*. But with all this jealousy within him, he said,

"Yes, my lord," with a bow.

Yamalu sensed Mascool's jealousy and smiled.

"Why are you so worked up over something so meaningless?" he asked Mascool. "He's just an artifact I brought to life. A monster to my Frankenstein."

He opened his eyes with a smirk on his face.

"He is merely my pawn."

Mascool showed no emotion.

"Feel better?" Yamalu asked as he raised an eyebrow.

"I think not, my lord."

"Good," Yamalu said as he closed his eyes again. "Now go," he shooed, "before you feel even worse."

Mascool frowned and left the throne room.

"Now back to Sistro," Yamalu said. Mascool was watching without Yamalu's awareness, even though he already *knew* he was being watched.

"Ah, good," Yamalu said. "You and the Chosen are headed down the Toxic Sewerway with my son and his army closing in on you. You'll be trapped *or* eaten alive by the surprise I have in store for you."

As the Chosen and the wizard brothers moved into the darkness of the sewerway, Mercutio accessed a match light flame by flicking his thumb and index finger of his right hand.

"It's not enough light, Mercutio," said Ginzolo. The small flame turned into a fireball and enlightened the entire area. On what looked like the ceiling, were kerosene lamps. Mercutio pointed to each lamp with the other hand and fire from his finger lit each lamp. Mercutio grabbed his fireball and it disappeared. He looked at the floor.

The remains of the metal pipe were filled with water.

"Great timing," Mercutio said. Eviana touched the surface of the water and waved over it.

"This water is absolutely pure," she said. "No toxins, whatsoever."

"Water beats fire," Mercutio said. "If I go in, I'm a dead man."

"When I put my hands in water," Ginzolo said, "I electrically charge it."

"Plainly," Goddum said with a chuckle, "I can't swim. I'd sink to the bottom like a rock."

"How ironic," Ginzolo said sarcastically.

Eviana shook her head and put her right hand in the water.

"The temperature's right for swimming," she said. Eviana put her long blond locks in a bun behind her head.

"I'm going in," she said.

"You don't know how deep it is," Mercutio quickly responded. "You can't hold your breath that long."

Eviana looked at Mercutio. "Air is not the *only* element I breathe."

She smirked and dove in.

Four minutes later, Eviana resurfaced. She walked on the surface of the water until she reached the others.

"The water is twenty-five miles deep," she said. "But while I was swimming, I saw a giant air bubble alongside a wall in-between seventeen and nineteen feet. There's a door inside that leads somewhere. If we keep going down, we would be heading straight to the earth's core."

"So how do we get to the door without getting in the water?" Goddum asked.

"Fly over the water," she told Goddum.

Goddum trusted her judgment, so he flew.

Controlling the water, Eviana made it slowly float towards Goddum's feet. The water formed a ball around him until it covered him completely.

"We'll travel in bubbles," Eviana said.

"Well, that's something you don't see everyday," replied Ginzolo. Goddum touched the water wall with amazement. Eviana lowered her hand. The bubble containing Goddum descended into the water. Eviana put her head in to see if he was okay. Goddum was inside the bubble and looked at her.

"Can you breathe okay?" she asked.

Goddum nodded. "Just fine," he said.

Eviana removed her head from the water.

"Okay," she said. "Who's next?"

Ginzolo raised his hand. "I'll go next," he said and flew over the water. Eviana did the same as she had done with Goddum, then lowered him in the water.

"No need for us," Endstra said. The wizard brothers put away their staffs and transformed into fish. Sistro was an albino clown fish and Endstra a black puffer. Eviana tossed them into the water.

"Do you want me to come with you?" Eviana asked Mercutio.

"Wha-wha-wha-what?" he hesitated.

"Do," she said slower, "you, want, me, to, come, with you?"

"Uh…" Mercutio thought out loud.

"Well," he said, "sure. I guess it wouldn't hurt." With that, they flew over the water. Eviana summoned the water to cover them.

Mercutio started to worry.

"It's okay," Eviana said as she gently touched the left side of his chest. "I'm here."

The bubble formed and they submerged.

The others waited for Mercutio's commands. With his enhanced sense of vision, he saw the air bubble held the entryway to the door.

"Let's move!" he yelled.

Goddum and Ginzolo walked downward towards the bubble. Sistro and Endstra swam behind them.

Eviana and Mercutio walked slowly.

"Why are you afraid of me?" she asked.

"Afraid?!" Mercutio replied with a chuckle. "You think *I'm* afraid of you?"

"Yes."

"And why is that?"

"Because every time I try to act friendly towards you, you push me away," she said. "*And* the fact that I can easily kill you." Mercutio smirked.

"Now I don't know about that," he said. "Maybe *weaken* me, but not kill me." Eviana looked at her leader.

"You don't think I can kill you?"

"No," he said as he shook his head, "not really."

Eviana formed an icicle and pointed it at Mercutio's throat.

"This is made of absolute *pure* water," she said. "If you melt it, the first drop can *destroy* you!"

Mercutio swallowed hard.

"Okay," he said. "I'm convinced."

Eviana put the icicle on the bubble and watched it melt.

"You never told me your story before, Eviana."

"You don't want to hear my story."

"Yes, I do."

"You sure?"

"Yes, I am."

Eviana thought. "I found out who and what I was at sixteen," she began. "I told my boyfriend I was immortal. He wanted to break up so I wouldn't bear the pain of his passing when he did."

Mercutio nodded. "Sounds reasonable," he said.

"My father," she continued, "resigned from the throne of Tritunia."

"You're a princess?"

"I *was*," she said. "He resigned when I was eighteen. I decided it was time to go on my own and moved to Camenstra."

"That's where I got my powers from."

"I know!" she said. "Isn't that ironic?"

"Yeah!"

As they continued walking inside their bubble, Mercutio and Eviana found they had a lot in common.

"Wow," Mercutio said, "you're right. I *didn't* want to know your story."

Eviana laughed. "Told you so."

As they talked, Mercutio noticed the giant air bubble on the opposite side of them. Mercutio pointed to it.

"Is that it?"

"That's it."

He saw Goddum, Ginzolo and the transformed wizard brothers near it.

"All right," Mercutio said out loud, "go in." Ginzolo entered first. When his bubble attached to it, he easily walked into the bigger bubble.

The same with Goddum.

Eviana and Mercutio entered after them. The wizards in their fish forms jumped with the rest of them. After squirming and flipping on the floor a couple of times, they transformed to their normal form.

This door was cut out of the pipe. It had a metal floor inside and outside. It was rust covered with algae and dark inside. Ginzolo shot a lightning bolt inside it. The bolt reflected off the walls long enough to see inside. Turned out it was nothing but a very long hallway.

"Do we follow it?" asked Goddum.

"Of course," Mercutio answered with a nod. He created a fireball in both hands and went in first.

"It's clear," he said. The others followed except for Endstra.

"I'll wait here for your return," he said cowardly.

Sistro pulled him inside.

The hallway was damp and smelled sickening. The taste of raw sewage was in their mouth. And, even though they couldn't see without Mercutio's fireballs, they felt calm. Unaware of the dangers Yamalu had in store for them.

"We need more light," Endstra said. Mercutio got a little irritated since Ginzolo *already* complained. His arms caught fire, illuminating the entire hallway.

"Better?" asked Mercutio.

"Yeah," Endstra said. "Perfect. But where *are* we?" Mercutio looked around and saw what looked like the end of the hallway. They headed inside the other room and took out their weapons, just in case. Like the door that led to this place, it was rusting and filled with algae. A giant circle of rust on the floor was waiting to collapse any second.

The room was a metal deathtrap.

"Be on your guard," Mercutio said. "We don't know what's in here." With that said, a black shadow swiftly passed through the walls.

"Marblus," said Sistro loudly, "is that you?"

No one answered.

The shadow quickly moved through the floor, making Goddum trip and fall through the rusting floor. He was able to fly back to the surface before he fell forever.

"Show yourself!" Mercutio yelled. The shadow slid towards Sistro. It rose from the ground and had taken human form.

It transformed into Mascool.

"You!" hollered Ginzolo. Sistro and Endstra held him back as he tried to attack him.

"That's the guy who killed my best friend!"

Mascool smirked.

Then he looked at Sistro.

"Sistro..." he said softly.

"Mascool," Sistro replied. "I see you are swimming in the very soul of evil."

Mascool put his arms behind his back.

"My deeds may be wrong," he said, "but unlike *you*, I *enjoy* my job."

"You are a *disgrace* to the race of wizards."

"That's because Im not a wizard."

"You're a *Warlock?*"

"I am a *Sorcerer*," he yelled. "And a powerful one at that. All I have to do is destroy you and your brother and take your powers to be declared the most powerful Magic-like being on earth next to the all-mighty dictator!"

Mercutio stood in front of Sistro.

"That's not going to happen with *us* around," he said.

"Will you bet your *life* on it?"

With that said, Mascool grabbed Mercutio's sides and threw him into the ceiling. He went straight through.

Mascool followed him.

Mercutio landed in a room with algae and purple mold. Mascool flew and took out a sword with a Hito blade attached.

"So you're the leader of the Chosen," Mascool snarled. He pointed the sword at his throat. "You look like a coward in *red* to me." Mercutio pushed the sword away.

"Only cowards' use *weapons*," he said. Mascool smirked. He threw the sword away and punched him in the gut. Mercutio kicked him with a backward flip, sending him to the wall.

Mascool floated towards Mercutio and stopped when he reached the middle of the room.

He put his right hand in the air. It turned into a metal scythe.

"How dare you hit me?!"

Mercutio pulled out Hikulo. "You *started* it," he said. "I guess I have to *finish* it."

Mascool smiled.

"Give me your best shot," he said. Mascool's scythe hand stretched towards Mercutio's head. Mercutio flipped frontward over the scythe before it could reach him. It stuck in the wall. While he was still in the air, he cut off Mascool's scythe hand with a trail of fire from the sword.

The scythe melted. Mascool's overly outstretched hand shrunk back and formed a new hand.

"You will regret that," he said.

"You will regret *living* in a minute," Mercutio replied.

Both of Mascool's hands turned into metal double-edged swords.

"Impressive," Mercutio said.

"*Very*," replied Mascool. He attacked Mercutio with both blades. He swung his left sword at Mercutio's head and the right under his feet at the same time. Mercutio blocked the attempt to his head with his sword and a back flip before Mascool chopped off his legs.

Mascool repeatedly swung left and right at least four times, with Mercutio blocking each blow. Mascool stabbed Mercutio in the heart, twisted around to show off his black and white robe and cut off the tips of his three fingers. He then took his right sword and thrust it in Mercutio's throat.

"What?" said Mascool, "no pain? You must really *be* immortal!"

Mercutio took his right hand and pulled Mascool's sword-like hand out of his throat as his fingertips grew back. Like a twig, Mercutio snapped the sword.

"And *you*," Mercutio said as his throat started to mend, "are *done for!*"

As the swordfight continued, Mascool fought with one hand while the damaged one transformed back into his hand. Mascool quickly attacked and Mercutio quickly defended. Mascool had his sword hand in the air getting ready to slice his head open, Mercutio did a back flip, kicked Mascool's sword hand off of his arm. It stuck to the wall, blade first. Mascool's hand regenerated. A silver liquid metallic substance came from his arm. Mascool frowned at Mercutio. His right hand morphed again. This time, the liquid substance transformed his hand into a twentieth century weapon.

A buzz saw!

Mercutio tilted his head.

"Perfect."

Mascool stretched his hand abnormally to where Mercutio was standing.

"Well," said Mercutio, "here we go!" When Mascool's buzz saw reached him, he ran around the room near the walls with the saw right behind him.

Mercutio ran on the walls.

He estimated the right time and Mercutio flipped off the wall and punched Mascool in the face head-on. Mascool went circling in the air and fell to the ground. When he got on his knees to get up, Mercutio kicked him in the chin with such a force, Mascool flipped over and landed on his head.

Mercutio put up his sword.

"Get up," he yelled. Mascool slowly got up and coughed black blood. He realized that no weapon he could create could stop this man.

"Now we end this."

Mascool let loose a punch towards Mercutio's face. He dodged it, grabbed his hand, twisted Mascool's hand and himself and kicked him in the chin. He crashed through the ceiling.

Soon after, the others made their way up. Sistro came in first, followed by Eviana, Endstra, and Ginzolo contained by Goddum. With Goddum's extreme weight and strength, Ginzolo wasn't going anywhere.

"Are you okay?" Eviana said as she touched Mercutio's heart wound. Mercutio put his hand over hers.

"I'll regenerate," he said. "You and Goddum need to take care of those poisonous wounds."

"Mine healed," Goddum said. "You don't have to worry about me."

"Mine, too," said Eviana.

Sistro smirked at the sight of Mercutio and Eviana.

"You did a better job with Mascool than Ginzolo would have."

Ginzolo broke through Goddum's grip, flew around the room and grabbed Sistro by the collar.

"Mascool and I have a score to settle!" he yelled. "He killed Antonio in cold blood!"

"Get a hold of yourself!" Endstra yelled. "Mascool's an immortal just like everyone in this room. He cannot die easily."

"And Hito blades only work on *human* immortals," Sistro added.

"So how do you kill a wizard?" asked Mercutio?

Ginzolo let go of Sistro.

"I do not know," he said.

"Maybe I do," Eviana interrupted. "There are two materials that make a Hito blade and another material that may kill a wizard."

Endstra nodded. "I know where to find such a material."

Sistro grasped his staff tighter. "So do I," he said. He remembered a very important dream.

"To find the secret of the vortex diamond, you must find the source of light. Being a wizard of light magic, this should not be a problem for you."

This area was where Marblus told Sistro was where the secret of the vortex crystal was.

"Cavirielta O' Zulu; the Cave of Light."

"How far is it?" Sistro's brother asked.

"It should be on the way to Yamalu's lair." Sistro looked at the hole in the ceiling.

"Even if we don't know what's up there," said Mercutio, "we must go."

"I agree," Sistro said. As the Chosen flew up to the top of the hole, they were surprised who was up there.

Mercutio shook his head in disbelief. He saw Napoleon and a group of what looked like Gorilla Trimals across from him and the others.

"So we meet again, Chosen," he said. "I hope you don't mind the company. You see, they've been dying to meet you."

The humanoid Gorillas were armored with shoulder pads, helmets, metal knee pads and elbow pads and metal groin covers on the front and back. Their carnivore teeth were grossly enlarged. They started to grunt, drool and beat their chest.

"That's nice," Mercutio said. "Are they relatives of yours? Because I see a great resemblance." Napoleon frowned at Mercutio's smart remark.

"Take 'em," he said.

The Gorilla Trimals rushed to the Chosen.

These Trimals were a lot stronger than the wolf army they faced in Cotendra was. The three Ginzolo faced could tear him to shreds. He punched, kicked, flipped all three and couldn't bring them down. He punched the one in the middle in the face and split kicked the other two. Before he landed, the one in the middle returned the punch Ginzolo gave him. This time it was in the gut, which tossed him to another one across the room, who took his legs and threw him on the floor continuously like the tossing of an old rag. It then spun him around and threw him in the wall.

Goddum almost met his match. One Trimal matched his strength almost *exactly*. The two he faced seemed vulnerable. As he continuously punched one in the stomach, he picked it up and threw it at the other one. Unfortunately, two behind him head butted him back into the hole of the first floor.

Eviana was floating in the air spinning around and around shooting water blasts and ice balls that almost froze them completely. But just like some of the Wolf Trimals she froze in Cotendra, they broke through with a greater force. It seemed like the water blasts worked, so she increased the force with both hands. But one of the Trimals grabbed her legs and tossed her in a wall.

Mercutio saw what had happened to her. "Hey!" he yelled. The one who tossed Eviana looked at him.

"That's no way to treat a lady," he said. He flipped a fire blast from his mouth and set the mutant monkey on fire. The gorilla ran around, setting other gorillas on fire, until it died, followed by the others set on fire. So far only five out of twenty were dead, and the Chosen were drastically losing power.

Napoleon felt happy at this scenario.

Sistro once again made his third madrocellular transformation. Even his power couldn't match these gorilla mutants. As he was fighting one with his new telekinetic ability, one behind him punched him in the head and the gorilla's giant hand and Sistro's head crashed on the floor. Sistro automatically transformed to himself and was knocked out cold. Endstra tried to help him, but that same Trimal smacked him, and tossed him to the wall, knocking *him* unconscious.

Only Mercutio stood. He was about to face fifteen Gorilla Trimals. Mercutio took out the Hikulo and tightened his grip. He saw Napoleon float in the air, smiling sinisterly.

"Finish it," he signaled.

As the Trimals moved in to destroy Mercutio, small sharp stones flew out of the hole of the floor and hit the gorillas in their hearts. Then out of the hole flew Goddum in his first madrocellular transformation!

Goddum's muscle toned body was covered in black fur and a head of a black bull. His hands were normal but his feet were hooves. His pants and belt were black. He had an earring on his left horn and a gold nose ring. He took out the Grodera, grabbed the chain attached to it and started to swing it around.

"Now you didn't think you were gonna have all the fun, did you?" he asked.

Mercutio smiled.

Napoleon frowned.

Mercutio flew up beside his friend, and transformed. Mercutio's Hikulo ignited a fire on the three blades.

"Let's party," he whispered. They circled the room shooting navigational fireballs and rock darts. Ginzolo awoke and saw the two fighting.

"Now why didn't I think of that?"

He madrocellularly transformed and joined in.

Mercutio and Napoleon noticed Ginzolo's awakening and transformation. Mercutio was glad to get extra help.

Napoleon showed no emotions.

He watched.

By the time the Trimal army was down to five, Eviana and the wizard brothers came to and watched the three men finish them off with their weapons.

"Is that *Goddum?*" asked Eviana.

Sistro nodded with a smile. "Yes," he said, "I believe it is."

Soon the room had piles of rock and dirt, small flames and thunder markings on the floor.

Napoleon slowly clapped, making sure everyone heard him. Mercutio's fiery wings folded back.

"Are you ready to face us *now,* son of Yamalu?"

Napoleon looked at the three like a selfish rich man would look at beggars in the street. Then he smirked with the same looked on his face.

"A Griffin, a Lion and a Bull," he said. Napoleon looked at Sistro.

His eyes glowed purple.

"Are you creating warriors, Sistro, or a *zoo?*"

Napoleon's voice was mixed with Yamalu when he said that.

"Yamalu..." Sistro whispered.

Sistro flew to Napoleon's flight level.

"These are their first transformations, Yamalu," said Sistro. Goddum and Ginzolo were wondering why he called Napoleon Yamalu.

"Yamalu is connected to Napoleon because he has the Vortex Crystal in his blood," said Mercutio. "He can possess Napoleon whenever he wants."

Sistro pulled out his staff.

"Once they are complete, you shall fall," said Sistro. "And the Vortex Crystal shall once again be safe.

Napoleon laughed, then folded his arms.

"Do you think these three and *she* together can defeat me?" he asked. "The only thing they could do to my son is bury him. Even *that* couldn't sustain Napoleon."

"You shall see, Yamalu," said Sistro. "The day you realize you are no match for the Chosen will be the day Napoleon will fall. Your creation will die *six* different ways by Mercutio's hand."

Napoleon's face showed no emotion.

Mercutio was dumbfounded.

"You get to have all the fun," Goddum teased.

Napoleon didn't move for at least seven seconds after what Sistro said. Yamalu left Napoleon's body when Napoleon's eyes returned to normal. He looked at Eviana, who was on the ground, on the other side of the room. With a smirk, Napoleon flew towards her. She repeatedly threw water balls and ice balls but Napoleon easily whisked them away like annoying insects. He took out his sword. He was about to slice her, Mercutio's shoulder tackled him to the floor.

Napoleon got up. His focus was once again on Mercutio. Napoleon ran towards him-stopped suddenly on his right foot-spun around in the air-landed-flipped over Mercutio and his wings-kicked him in the back, causing him to land on his back. Because Mercutio was transformed, Napoleon's strength wasn't damaging.

Mercutio flew into the air and set his sword blades on fire again. Napoleon flew up in more of a charge. Mercutio did a back flip and started another nosedive toward Napoleon, who was still flying toward Mercutio. They met and both clashed their swords. They spiraled in the air with their swords still attached to one another. Once they let go, Mercutio was at the high top of the room and Napoleon at the bottom. They let out blasts of enormous power. Of course, Mercutio's was a fire blast but Napoleon's was a darkness blast. Mercutio seemed to become stronger, somehow. His fire blast quickly consumed Napoleon's dark blast.

Then, it happened.

With a loud yell, Mercutio's fire blast tripled in size and overtook Napoleon. Once the blast stopped and Napoleon's skeleton fell to the ground, another red ball of light engulfed Mercutio.

It exploded. Mercutio's second madrocellular transformation was formed!

He had a long red robe with gold trimmings. His feet were covered with red boots and his gloves were sunlight yellow. His hair was lengthened and permed. More facial hair had grown. His new mustache was attached to a new regular-sized beard. His shirt was an orange silk with the symbol of fire in Demarican text. His pants were black but his original red belt and medallion remained the same. His sword was in a harness attached to his belt, and he carried a smooth, slender red staff with a circular red crystal on top.

"What *is* he?" asked Ginzolo.

"Pioferia E' Magiciono," said Sistro. "The great Wizard of Fire."

Napoleon sucked his teeth when he regenerated himself and looked at Mercutio's second madrocellular transformation.

"It makes no difference," said Napoleon.

He started to fly towards him. Mercutio put his right hand in front of him. When Napoleon was about to shoulder tackle him but was blasted by Mercutio's new telekinetic ability. Napoleon took out two daggers, each with a Hito blade. He threw them at Mercutio; his eyes shot lines of fire and destroyed them. With his left hand, Mercutio grabbed the end of his staff. Napoleon flew towards him again but Mercutio front flipped over him. While still in his flip, he shot rays of fire from his eyes on Napoleon's back.

Napoleon turned and faced Mercutio. He scowled at him, then smirked. Napoleon tried to punch him.

Mercutio dodged and slapped him in the face with the end of his staff.

Napoleon attempted a kick his stomach.

Mercutio jumped back then flipped forward for a kick to the top of the head.

Napoleon grew angry. The maged Mercutio was calm as he took out Hikulo.

"I sense it is *you* I am fighting," Mercutio's new deep voice said. "Yamalu is not controlling you."

Napoleon smiled.

"You have not yet witnessed *my* true power," he said. He threw out a punch that knocked Mercutio straight into the wall. Napoleon's hand turned into a giant horrendous looking morphed hand with long nails and bubbly skin. Napoleon grinned and started to laugh. The laugh grew deeper, deeper and deeper. His entire body changed but not before he sent Mercutio plummeting to the ground with *his* telekinetic ability. Fortunately, he wasn't hurt enough to unwillingly transform back to normal.

Napoleon's muscles bulged insanely out of proportion. His clothes were torn off. Spikes grew out of his back, arms and legs. Once his head transformed, he plummeted. The room soon started to fall apart and land directly on Napoleon. As the dust settled and debris cleared, they saw no sign of movement from where Napoleon landed.

Eviana walked forward. Mercutio stopped her with his staff.

"No," he said. "We do not know if he's alive or dead." Ginzolo and Goddum, still in their first transformations, stood next to Mercutio.

Sistro could sense what the three were about to do.

"Be careful," he said. Mercutio looked at Sistro.

"We might regret what you three do right now," Sistro said.

Mercutio nodded, turned around and looked at Ginzolo and Goddum.

"Ready?" he asked. They nodded. But once they took their first steps, the monster Napoleon blasted out of the rubble.

He walked on all fours. It looked like seven metal spikes were on both sides of his lined vertically, and three on his arms and legs. His skin tan colored fur. His head, like a wolf, a hyena and a jackal fused together with razor sharp teeth, including the molars. His muscles were fifteen times bigger than any human.

And to top it off, he was thirty feet tall.

Six times taller than the horrified Chosen.

"Run!" yelled Mercutio. The beast roared a beast roar mixed with a human's scream and ran after them. Another open door was near the wall where most of the dead Trimals gathered. As they went through, Napoleon came crashing through it, knocking down the wall surrounding it.

"What is he?" Mercutio asked Sistro.

"It is his first madrocellular transformation!" he loudly answered.

"*First?!*" Eviana yelled.

Ginzolo turned his head and saw Napoleon's beast form quickly catching up. He then turned his head back around.

"It looks like his *seventh!*"

As they continued to run inside the sewerway while being followed by a giant horrific beast, Endstra thought of something.

"Sistro!" he yelled. Sistro's attention was turned to his brother, although they were still running. "We can try the disappearance spell!"

"No!" replied Sistro. "We need three wizards for that kind of spell!"

"Mercutio's second transformation *is* a wizard!" yelled Endstra. "He can do it!"

"He's right, Sistro!" said Mercutio. "I know the spell! I can help you!"

"Okay," said Sistro. Mercutio nodded. Everyone stopped and watched as the beast came towards them. It stopped at least fifteen feet away from them. They stared at one another.

"Move out!" Mercutio yelled.

Ginzolo, Goddum and Eviana ran towards Napoleon. Goddum still in his transformation threw rock darts and boulders to his head, then brought out the Grodera, flew to his head and banged the Grodera on top of it. Napoleon felt the piercing of his skin from Eviana's Hydroscepter on his legs. He saw Ginzolo float in front of him, getting ready to give him a giant electrical charge.

Napoleon opened his mouth and his tongue, which was split in two, grabbed both Eviana and Goddum.

He tossed them to the floor.

Goddum transformed to his normal form in a burst of brown light and was getting a headache. Ginzolo, still in *his* first transformation, threw out his great electric attack. Even though it was a direct hit, the metal spikes were a conductor and captured the electricity. He increased it by seven thousand volts more than what Ginzolo threw and Ginzolo could handle. He refired from every metal spike on Napoleon's body.

Ginzolo couldn't absorb it all, even in his transformation. Ginzolo was blasted and returned to his original form in a burst of yellow light. Mercutio, Sistro and Endstra all nodded and put the top of their staffs together.

"Sanitius O' Zulu," began Endstra.

"Alvia ut O' Napoleon," continued Sistro.

"Torovia eskill topaku!" finished Mercutio.

Napoleon's red and black eyes frowned. He saw the three wizards' staff ornaments glow white. He ran toward them.

"Disappear!" the three wizards said in unison. They broke their staff unification; the white light went to the floor.

It disappeared and formed a giant hole.

Napoleon tried to stop at the sight of it, because he couldn't fly in that form.

When he fell in, his paws grasped the edge. Mercutio blasted them with his telekinetic ability. They watched Napoleon fall in an endless black void-listening to his cries mixed with roars and screams. They couldn't see or hear him anymore. The giant hole disappeared.

"Trinity of light," Sistro said, "rid us of Napoleon until another day."

"Is that what you said in that chant?" asked Eviana. Sistro nodded.

"Sistro," said Goddum, "I thought you said a *pure* hearted person could perform a madrocellular transformation."

"I fought Yamalu right after the Last War one thousand seventy-five years ago," said Sistro. "He was able to manipulate the vortex crystal to create the *illusion* of a pure heart. This proves that Napoleon indeed has the powers of the Vortex Crystal."

"But it's not visible," Mercutio added. "If Yamalu *gave* him a piece of the crystal, we would have taken it from him. This proves that the powers are in his blood."

Mercutio looked around.

"We have to keep moving," he said. "Let's go."

"You think you're *so* smart, don't you?" a voice said from the ceiling. Mercutio turned and saw Mascool floating near the ceiling.

Goddum grabbed Ginzolo before he did anything regrettable.

"Do you want another kick to the chin?" asked Mercutio. "If you don't, I would advise you to leave now."

Mascool smirked.

"You won't have a chance once Napoleon knows your ways," he said. "Plus, you'll have *me* to worry about."

"Don't make me laugh," Mercutio said. "The next time you fight us, you'll greatly regret it."

"Just remember," Mascool said. He then looked at Ginzolo, who was struggling to free himself from Goddum's grip.

"This is only the beginning," he finished with a smile.

That broke the straw on the camels back for Ginzolo. He broke through Goddum's grip, and transformed. He flew toward Mascool. As Ginzolo was about to punch him, Mascool disappeared. Ginzolo yelled in anger.

Mercutio forcefully pulled him down with telekinesis.

"You will have your day with Mascool," he said, "but it's not today."

Ginzolo transformed back and nodded in anger.

"I understand," he said. Mercutio looked at the others.

"Let's keep moving," he said as he transformed to his original form.

They kept walking, not knowing what evil *still* awaited them.

The Chosen and the wizards walked down another dark hallway. Mercutio ignited his body so they could see.

"Does anybody know where in the *world* we are?" asked Ginzolo.

"I think we're near the end of the hallway," said Goddum. The flames on Mercutio's body died down until they completely disappeared, which was strange, because he didn't command the flames to die.

They walked into a giant room covered in shades of algae. The room was in-between the hallway, with the tube containing the exit. There was a giant faucet turner in the shape of a steering wheel on the wall to their left. The floor was a giant vent full of holes and was disguised with algae. When Mercutio's flames died, he knew something was wrong with this place.

"Goddum. Ginzolo," Mercutio said. "Try to transform." When they did, it only lasted for three seconds. They tried again, nothing happened.

Ginzolo couldn't make a lightning bolt.

Goddum couldn't make a boulder.

Eviana tried to make a water ball, but nothing happened.

"What magic is this?!" said Ginzolo.

"This is *Yamalu's* magic," said Mercutio. "He made this room take away our powers."

Mercutio went to the entrance of the hallway and put his right hand in it. Outside, he ignited a fireball. He brought it in the room, it disappeared.

"It's a *trap!*" yelled Goddum. Mercutio walked to the middle of the room, a barrier blocked the entrance to the hallway. Goddum tried to break through it. His strength was gone.

"Sistro," said Mercutio, "are your powers gone, too?"

"Unfortunately, yes," he said.

"We are unable to help, kiddo," said Endstra.

"We have to get out of here!" yelled Ginzolo. A really foul sound echoed in the room.

"It came from the other side!" said Eviana. They looked in the back of the other tunnel, four pairs of red glowing eyes appeared. The Chosen took out their weapons as the creatures stepped into the light.

They were Despiratticu. Giant rats the size of a five-foot seven-inch human. These rats had bulging muscles, with tails the same length and white fur. Their two front teeth were razor sharp and yellow as the sun. Their ears were pointed. Their nails looked sharper than their foul front teeth. But what made the Despiratticu the most terrifying animal alive in the Dark World is that when they opened their mouth, there was a human head attached to their long tongue.

The four Despiratticu slowly walked toward the Chosen, showing their tongues in the process.

"Man," said Goddum, "I *hate* these things."

"Don't let your fears get in the way, Goddum," said Mercutio. "We have to kill them to get out of here."

Mercutio cut himself in the palm of his left hand.

It wouldn't heal!

"The room has taken away our immortality," he said, "so be careful." The four slowly backed up.

The wizards stood back.

"Attack!" Mercutio yelled.

They each took one Despiratticu and fought it. The one Ginzolo had immediately attacked. It tried to bite his left side off but Ginzolo's Natunga O' Lioben blocked its two front teeth. It continued to chew on the shield and forcefully pushed him by walking with one hind leg at a time. Ginzolo's strength held the creature at bay. It then revealed its human head tongue.

Ginzolo was startled by the sudden sight of the head. He was hit in the chest with the Despiratticu forehead.

Goddum was having fun. He kept swinging his Grodera with chain at its head. The Despiratticu head was bloody. Each time it showed its human head tongue, Goddum jumped back. A scratch followed. He swung it again and hit its jaw. That made the Despiratticu flip on its back. Goddum repeatedly pounded it with his weapon on its belly until he saw no sign of movement.

The first opportunity he got, Mercutio cut off the Despiratticu's head tongue. After its blue blood gushed out of it, the Despiratticu pounced on him, throwing Mercutio's weapon out of his hand. It grabbed his hands with its two front claws. Even though it's head on its tongue was cut off, the Despiratticu roared a screech. It showed its other fifty sharp teeth, drool oozing from each side. But just when Mercutio thought it was over for him, the Despiratticu felt a pain from its buttocks and responded with a scream-like roar.

It was Eviana's Hydroscepter.

"Back, you beast!" she yelled.

The Despiratticu Mercutio and Ginzolo were fighting immediately came to her. As she turned her Hydroscepter showing it off, she said,

"If you want me, come and get me!"

The two pounced, thinking they had her in their grasp. They looked behind and saw her right there.

"Did you miss me?" she asked. The one with no head on its tongue attacked first. It tried to scratch her in the face, but she did a back flip and cut off its left claw in the process. The other tried to scratch her, too, but she blocked it with her scepter. It then showed its human head tongue. She twirled the Hydroscepter and twisted its tongue in it. She then tossed it all the way to the other side of the room.

Mercutio, Goddum and Ginzolo, who were badly injured, watched Eviana fight the two Despiratticu. The two slowly circled her. One was limping because it was tossed to the other side of the room, and the other was on three legs because its other claw was cut off. They stopped, faced her and repeatedly showed their tongues. The two then charged, hoping to paralyze her legs. But Eviana did a front flip at the last minute and landed out of range. The two Despiratticu rammed each other, killing themselves.

Ginzolo clapped in amazement. Goddum nodded at her.

"Good job, Eviana," he said. Mercutio looked around the room.

"Weren't there *four* of these things?" he asked.

Suddenly, another Despiratticu bit Eviana in the side and took her into the darkness of another tunnel.

"Eviana!" yelled Mercutio. Everyone was worried, including the wizard brothers who watched.

Everyone feared the worst for Eviana, until the Despiratticu that bit her came flying back in the room. A water blast sent it to the wall. It continued until the Despiratticu took its last gasp for air. It stopped when it drowned. Then, the Chosen saw a believable sight.

Eviana was in her first madrocellular transformation!

She was amazing. She was in a one piece blue silkened dress. It had no sleeves with a long split on each side. She had blue sandals and one blue and white glove on her right hand. Her physique was everything a man dreamed of a woman. Her blonde hair met her shoulder blades. Her eyes navy blue and her lips ruby red. She wore sapphire earrings and a dark blue bandana over her head. A silver necklace held her blue medallion.

"Wow," said Mercutio. Eviana raised an eyebrow.

"Is that all you have to say?" she asked. The others were speechless. They haven't seen beauty in a very long time.

"I thought so," she said as she lowered herself to the ground.

"As you know," she said, "the exit is just up the tunnel there. You should regain your powers and immortality when we get there."

Sistro and Endstra walked forward.

"Well then," he said, "let's be off."

As Mercutio followed the two wizards down the tunnel, the others soon joined them, hoping that was the last obstacle in the sewerway.

"*Damn it!*" Yamalu yelled in anger. He amazingly picked up his five hundred-pound chair and threw it out of the giant window.

"*How?!*" he yelled "I created a room in that sewerway that would make them normal, and they *still* destroyed all four of the beasts!"

"We have greatly underestimated these four," said Mascool. Yamalu faced him with a frown.

"Underestimated?" he said. "*Underestimated?!* Those four are nothing but wizards with one power! I can easily destroy them with one snap of a finger!"

"According to the prophecy, you *can't,* my lord."

"And why is that?!"

"Because they are not wizards," said Mascool. "Since they are a godsend, they are defined as devinits; Divine beings. And a godsend cannot destroy *another* godsend."

Yamalu looked at his Vortex Crystal, then looked at Mascool with a frown.

"This," he said, "is *not* a godsend. This is a curse!" He picked up Mascool by the throat with one hand.

"I never *asked* God to use me for his doings over two thousand years ago! I never asked to live this long without disease or infection or human comfort! Men were the reason for that pre-Armageddon and God shall *pay* for creating them! He *and* man created greed, yet he blamed *me* for it!"

He choked Mascool tighter.

"This is not a godsend," he said louder. "This is God's *end!*"

Mascool struggled to get out of his monstrously strong grip, but as he tried, his grip got tighter.

"Unlike the Chosen, he said, "*you* are not a devinit. So the next time you wait to tell me something very, *very* important, I will have a very enjoyable time *killing* you."

Mascool was struggling for air.

"Am I clear?!" he yelled. Mascool nodded. Yamalu dropped him to the floor.

"Get out of my sight!"

"Ye-ye-ye-yes, my lord," he said gasping for air.

Yamalu looked at the broken window. He closed his eyes, and like a rewind button, the chair he threw through the window came back inside, in its right position followed by the broken glass. Yamalu walked to his throne and sat down. He closed his eyes and smirked.

"So many questions," he whispered. "So little answers."

He opened his eyes.

"For the people in this world are beguiled by my attendance. As I was young, I dreamt of winning my parent's love and affection, not their money. God took that away from me along with what would have been my future. For my enslavement of men and the world is only part of my vengeance. They say revenge is a dish best served cold. My cold heart is enough to serve at least seventeen men who also seek revenge.

"My path is set in the stairs of madness. Every step I take turns the world *I* created into a jigsaw puzzle. No, a Mosaic. I decide what pieces to use to create a beautiful masterpiece, of a horrific death frame. To destroy the Chosen would be the closest thing to destroying the Almighty himself! The world is mine. Mine to command! Mine to control! I am not compared to any criminal or terrorist mastermind in my era! I am Yamalu! The Mountain of Chaos! The greatest being in the universe! God cannot touch me! God cannot equal my power. Humph. I *am* God! And I shall rule the entire cosmos with fear and horror! I am everywhere! I am everything!

"Know my name in fear. Know my name in horror. My onslaught of this universe has yet to begin. The people on this earth think I'm just a hateful dictator that must die. Once thy see my true self, they will know they're dealing with God! Once my reign reaches other planets, *they* will also behold my mighty hand! My reign will be great. Men and others shall fall to their knees and worship me, and so will God!

"But the Chosen must die. They must be torn apart like paper. And the only way to do this impossible deed is to destroy the cities their powers originated from. Camenstra will be first, then Yalutar. God's warriors and God himself shall know my fury. And know I am king!"

Mascool entered the throne room once again to ensure Yamalu of something.

"My lord," he said, "I have urgent news."

Yamalu rose from his throne slowly and turned his head to Mascool.

"What is it?" he asked.

"They have found the exit and are heading towards it as we speak."

Yamalu turned his head the other way.

"Where is my son?" he asked. Mascool took a deep breath.

"Trapped in the sewer by a disappearance spell. Mercutio transformed into a wizard and helped Sistro and Endstra perform it."

Yamalu nodded once.

"Reverse the spell," he said. "Free him and teleport him out of there."

Mascool frowned.

"Yes, my lord." He walked out the throne room.

"So," began Yamalu. "Mercutio's going to kill Napoleon in six different ways? I just like to see him try it."

Back in the sewerway, Mascool appeared next to a giant black bubble. It was holding Napoleon. Mascool placed his right hand on the bubble.

"Napoleon trishua replaco magicionlatish piazza O' disturablu!" The bubble erupted into black ooze. Mascool created a force field to protect himself. Napoleon was in his normal form, covered in the black ooze he was contained in. He swatted his hands and wiped his face.

Then he saw Mascool.

"This is the second time they've contained me to get away," he said. "I do not like being contained!"

Mascool smirked and nodded.

"I have orders from your...father," he said. "You must trap the Chosen and yourself inside the Devil Cave Tunnel in the country of Trim. There you settle your score with the Chosen."

Napoleon walked towards Mascool and sniffed him.

"Why do you lie?" he asked.

"I *never* lie," said Mascool.

Napoleon nodded. "Fine," he said. "If my father says it, I must obey."

Napoleon stepped back. The ooze slid off and his outfit was clean. He then flew up and went through the roof of the room. He continued to blast through them until he escaped from the Toxic Sewerway. Mascool smiled and disappeared.

As the Chosen and the wizards continued to the end of the tunnel, Eviana and Mercutio were walking ahead of the others.

"So you never told me *your* story," said Eviana.

"I thought I did," replied Mercutio.

"Just about your mom," she said. "Come on, there has to be at least one good memory in your life!"

Mercutio thought. "I guess it was when..."

"When what?"

"Ask me later."

"Why?"

"Because I can't think of anything." Mercutio smirked at the face Eviana was making.

"Do you think we'll make it to Manhattan at this rate?" she asked.

Mercutio tilted his head.

"Maybe," he said, "and maybe not. All that matters is that we follow our destiny."

"What happens after we do?"

"I don't know," he said. "But whatever happens, we'll be together."

After that encouraging talk, the Chosen and the wizards saw an opening, but a strange light was coming from it.

"Is that light?" said Ginzolo.

"That's impossible!" said Goddum.

"It must be the city of Tritunia," said Sistro. He looked at Eviana.

"I see your father's invention is very popular here."

Eviana nodded.

"Then let's go," said Mercutio. "If it is Tritunia, we can rest there before we continue."

Soon, the six found the exit and left the Toxic Sewerway. The light was definitely coming from the city of Tritunia that was at least twenty to fifty yards from the sewerway exit.

This city of dreams was glamorous. The buildings towered over others. It looked as if the buildings illuminated half of the city's light with their beautiful white walls.

"Behold the city, Tritunia," said Sistro.

"Even without natural sunlight," said Goddum, "It still is a wonder to see." Mercutio looked at the city, then used his enhanced sense of vision to look closer. He saw a thin layer of glass over the city.

"It's protected in glass," said Mercutio. "And by the looks of it, it seems pretty strong."

"Think it's too strong for *me?*" asked Goddum, kiddingly.

Mercutio smirked. "It might," he said. "C'mon. Let's go."

As the Chosen headed into the city, a traveling rogue wearing a green hood slowly followed them. As he headed into the city, he saw them go through a toll teller.

"Welcome to Tritunia; the City of Dreams," the teller greeted.

The rogue showed no facial expression.

"Are you here for business or pleasure?"

The rogue pulled out twenty silver and gold pieces called Nugrocks and poured them in the tellers' hand. Each Nugrock was worth 2,000.00*.

"Both," he said and continued walking.

The rogue kept a safe distance from the humans and wizards. He noticed they entered a restaurant. After he saw them sit down, he entered and sat at a table by himself at the other end from where the Chosen were sitting. He tilted his head to listen.

The Chosen and the two wizards were sitting in a lounge booth.

"So now what?" asked Goddum.

"We stay the night," said Mercutio, "then we continue on our way to Manhattan." Ginzolo nodded once and looked at the menu. Even though the food looked good and was inexpensive, they didn't bring enough money.

They *barely* made the toll.

The others looked at the menu. They didn't have any money.

"I may be immortal," said Goddum, "but I can't go on without something to eat."

Endstra nodded.

"I agree," he said. "I'm famished."

Sistro shook his head.

"You people are so ill tempered," he said. "You have those medallions for a reason!" Mercutio looked at his circular pendant. He rubbed it and closed his eyes.

"Money," Mercutio said to himself. His medallion glowed red and the jewel in the middle of it shot a beam of red light on the table. Three stacks of twenty-five star bills and fifty Nugrocks appeared on the table.

Mercutio opened his eyes and saw three packs of twenty-five star bills. Each pack had one hundred and fifty bills. So counting the bills and coins, they had a total of 111,250*.

"I guess dinners on me tonight, guys," Mercutio said.

The others were amazed and speechless. Endstra showed no expression.

"I don't know why you three are so amazed," he said. "All of you could do the same thing."

"He's right, you know," said Sistro. "All you have to do is the same thing Mercutio just did for *anything* you need."

"Well," said Goddum, "right now I'm starving. Let's put that money into good use."

Mercutio smirked at his friend.

"Yes," he said. "Lets." The waiter came and took their orders. They had to pay before they got their food, but it was worth it.

"Sistro," said Mercutio.

Sistro turned his head to him.

"Yes?"

"Were you born a wizard, or did you practice magic?"

Sistro chuckled. "My brother and I are the greatest wizards in the world," he said.

"Master wizards always practical their magic techniques."

"What about family?"

Sistro dropped his eating utensil. "F-fa-fa-fa-family?" he hesitated with a cough.

"Yeah," said Mercutio. "Do you have any?"

"Not anymore."

"Long story?"

"Very."

"What happened to them?"

"Each member of my family had their own story of death. I cannot explain it all."

"Same here," replied Mercutio. "My mom was the only family I had. She told me the rest of my family was dead. Nostra was the one who said my father was still alive.

Sistro closed his eyes. "What will you do when you find him?"

Mercutio shrugged his shoulders. "First, I'd tell him that mom is dead."

That caught Sistro's attention.

"Your mother is dead?" he said surprised. Mercutio nodded his head.

"Assassinated by one of Yamalu's soldiers," he said. "The strange thing is that she wanted to die so I could stop worrying about her."

Sistro was shocked to hear of Mercutio's mother. As he continued eating, he put his right hand on Mercutio's left shoulder.

"You'll find your father, Mercutio," Sistro said. "I promise."

As they were walking towards an inn, Eviana felt a chill down her spine.

"Someone's following us," she said. Mercutio nodded to let her know he felt it, too. "Don't look," he said. "He'll suspect us."

"Is it Napoleon?" asked Ginzolo.

"Maybe, maybe not."

"You can give me a better answer than that."

"There will be a time to answer questions, but this is not the time or place, so I would advise you to follow my judgment."

Ginzolo frowned, but obeyed. They walked until they were at a crossroad. When they stopped, the stranger following them stood next to them.

He wore a green cape and hood made of cotton. It and his clothes were dirty. The hood covered his face, so they couldn't tell who he was. When it was safe to cross, the Chosen crossed but the rogue didn't. They went inside an inn called The Aurora. Mercutio went to the front desk.

"We need five rooms," he said. He paid for them and went back to the group.

"Five rooms?" said Goddum. "There are *six* of us."

"I know," said Mercutio. "Eviana and I will share one."

Goddum, now understanding, nodded his head with a smile.

"Fine," said Ginzolo. "Give me my key." Mercutio passed out everyone's keys and Ginzolo left first.

"I'll never understand him," said Mercutio. Goddum looked at Ginzolo as he got on the elevator.

"I don't think he *wants* to be understood," he said. Goddum faced Mercutio again. "I think he just wants to be left alone."

"Well," said Sistro, "how about a good night's sleep?" Mercutio and Eviana chuckled.

"I must agree," said Endstra. "I am a bit tired."

"Then what are we waiting for?" asked Sistro. Mercutio looked through the front entrance window. That rogue at the crossroad was still standing there, watching them. Mercutio couldn't see who was under hood even *with* his enhanced sight.

"Mercutio?" called Eviana to get his attention. Mercutio looked at her.

"What's wrong?" she asked. He looked through the window again-the rogue wasn't there.

"Nothing," he said. He walked towards Eviana. They took the elevator to their room.

Back outside, the rogue appeared like magic to where he was standing.

"Simple fools," he said to himself. "They have no idea what will happen to them."

He took his left hand and pulled off his hood.

It was Napoleon!

He smiled as he thought of the plan he was about to unfold.

"Father," he said. "I need soldiers to attack Camenstra as soon as possible."

<I can't afford to loose any more Trimals, Napoleon, > Yamalu's voice said in Napoleon's mind. <I'm already sending an army of four hundred thousand shadows. Try creating an army yourself for reinforcements. >

"Excellent idea, father," Napoleon said with a smile. "With the Chosen out of the way, the world shall finally be ours. There will be no stopping us."

With that said, Napoleon put on his hood and walked away whistling a tune.

Part Two
The Plot

Chapter Three

Up above the world so high was a flying machine that was preparing to land in the Scorpion Tail Tower's fenced area. Yamalu was outside on top of the tower when he noticed it.

"It's about time," he said.

This machine was not of this world. It was silver, red and black stripes near the thrusters. It was not of this world because the language on the ship was neither English, Demarican tongue nor Lingu. It was not of this world because the shape of the machine was not similar to anything created on earth.

It was not of this world because when Yamalu won the Last War one thousand seventy-five years ago, he destroyed all means of transportation, *including* airplanes and helicopters.

Yamalu floated from the roof of the tower to the strange aircraft.

"You may come out to view me," he said in an unearthly language. Suddenly the hatch of the craft opened. Smoke and steam blasted from inside, making it a little hard for Yamalu to see. When the smoke cleared, two human-like creatures exited from the spacecraft and walked towards the ground.

Their heads were diamond-shaped. They had long necks. Their bodies were thinner than the upper torso of the human body. Their arms long and thin-their legs and feet the same. Their hands twice as any human and their fingers were sharpened to a point. They had feet, but no toes. Their feet were rounded at the point where toes were supposed to be. They had small eyes, no nose, no mouth, and they were black and brown with glowing stones inside them.

"Senators of the planet Eargooth," Yamalu said in their language, "welcome to Earth."

The taller alien stepped closer. <We know how to speak all *three* of your languages, Dictator, > it said with an extreme deep voice inside Yamalu's mind. <Which one do you prefer? >

"English, please."

The alien continued in English. <Very well, > it said. The other in a more feminine voice said, <through the observation of your planet from our ancestors, you have ruled this world under a strict thumb for one thousand seventy-five years. >

"That is correct" said Yamalu. "I being immortal and all-powerful would make me the longest living dictator in the world."

<If it is not rude, > the tall one asked, <can you give us your age?">

"Officially," said Yamalu, "I am one thousand six hundred and fifteen years old."

The tall one nodded his head. <We, > it said, <the senators of our planet do not give rule ship of our planet to just anyone. >

"I didn't *ask* you for kingship of your planet," said Yamalu with a grin on his face, "I *demanded* it."

Even though you could not see it in their faces, the two alien senators were getting angry.

<Are you *challenging* us, human? > said the one with the tall neck.

"It depends," said Yamalu. "If you wish to leave without any negotiation planned, you will not have a home planet to go home to!"

<You're bluffing! > yelled the shorter necked one. Yamalu pointed up. The senators saw that he was pointing to the full mood. When they looked at him, the finger he was pointing with started to glow purple. A beam of light shot out of it and headed straight for the moon. The senators watched as the purple beam successfully went through the earth's atmosphere and split the moon in half!

The senators were baffled. If he could do that to the moon, imagine what he would do to their *planet!* The alien senators looked at Yamalu in fear.

"That was just *finger* food," he said. He raised his left palm to the sky. A ball of purple energy formed around it.

"How about the *main course?!*" he yelled. He blasted the ball of energy toward the moon, now split in half. The ball reached it and destroyed one *half* of it!

"Do you need *more* proof?!" he yelled with a menacing smile. "Or do I have to take it by force?!"

The senators were speechless. They had never seen so much power from a single man. Soon, the rubble of the moon crashed to earth as meteors and asteroids.

Yamalu smirked. "I will send a representative I have created for this occasion. They will be in charge in my stead."

The alien senators showed no emotion.

"I also want you to tell other planets inhabited by alien life to surrender their planet to me before I *invade* it." He looked at the aliens with an evil gaze. They automatically felt afraid being in Yamalu's presence and were mesmerized by it. The aliens suddenly bowed and looked at the ground, too afraid to gaze upon him again.

<We now declare *Yamalu* as our lord and master of the planet Eargooth, > the short one said.

<Our people shall see the pain, power and energy of thee, > said the long one. <No treasures on our planet can compare to *you*, my lord. >

Yamalu smirked at the fact he could *easily* corrupt the minds of the Eargoothans with a single stare.

"Rise," he said. The aliens covered their eyes as they rose.

"Now that your planet is mine," he said, "you shall receive the same treatment as earth-ruled under evil and fear."

The senators nodded their heads out of fear.

<Yes, my lord, > said the short one. Soon the representative who looked like Yamalu emerged from the dead skeleton pieces that covered all of the ground around the Scorpion Tail Tower. The aliens watched him come toward them in absolute fear. The *real* Yamalu tilted his head and smirked.

"This is the representative I told you about," he said. "Not only does he have my power, but I can possess him and see things for myself."

The Yamalu clone boarded the senator's spaceship.

<We shall now take our leave and tell our fellow Eargoothans the news, > said the tall one.

"Good," said Yamalu, "good." The frightened senators boarded the spacecraft and took off into the night. Mascool stood behind Yamalu as the spacecraft left the earth's atmosphere.

"The Chosen are out of the Toxic Sewerway and are in an inn called The Aurora," he said. "It's 9:00 in the morning-they should be up by now."

"Is my son freed?"

"Yes, my lord."

"What city are they in?"

"Tritunia, the city of Dreams."

"Figures," Yamalu said as he sucked his teeth. He turned around and headed toward the tower with Mascool not far behind.

"Prepare the troops for the massacre at Camenstra."

Mercutio awoke. He was in his bed with nothing on but his boxers and medallion. As he looked around, he noticed Eviana's bed was made. He turned the other way, his clothes were clean and lying on the chair he fell asleep in with a clean pair of socks and boxers.

Eviana came from the bathroom humming.

"I used my medallion to get you another pair of underwear," she said.

"I appreciate that," said Mercutio with a nod, "but how did you take off my clothes and put me in my bed?"

Eviana thought and scratched her head.

"I don't remember," she said. "I remember washing your clothes, but I don't remember if I took them off." She smiled.

"Weird, huh?"

Mercutio sat on the edge of his bed, making sure he covered his lower torso with a blanket.

"Uh... yeah," he said, "weird." Mercutio reached for his pants and the boxers and changed. When his pants were on, he pulled the blanket off and put on the new pair of black socks and shoes. He stood and put on his shirt. He pulled his medallion over the shirt and said, "Clean body." An aurora of red light illuminated him for three seconds. When it disappeared, he checked his under arms and breath.

His body was clean.

"Men," said Eviana. "Always trying to avoid taking a bath."

Mercutio looked at her with a reminding look.

"Oh," she said softly. "Sorry."

"Besides," Mercutio started, "if I *could* take a bath, I would if we had more time." He looked in the mirror next to Eviana.

"Are the others awake?" she asked. Mercutio used his advanced sense of hearing.

"Everyone's ready except Ginzolo," he said.

"I'll get him up."

"You'd do that?"

"A little splash of ice cold water would do it since he's mostly electricity."

"Good thinking."

As Eviana left the room, Mercutio felt a chill down his spine.

"What do you want, Marblus?"

Marblus emerged from the floor off the shadows in the room.

"I want you to access the GF again," he said.

"Why?" he asked. "So I can become evil again and fight the people I love and walk out of my destined path?"

"This *is* your destined path!"

"No, it's not!" Mercutio yelled. "My path is to beat Yamalu and I don't need the Fox to do it!"

"Oh Mercutio, Mercutio, Mercutio," Marblus said as he shook his head. "How are you going to beat Yamalu if you can't even beat *Napoleon*?"

"What?"

"The last time you faced Napoleon," said Marblus, "you made your second madrocellular transformation as the great Wizard of Fire without using the GF. In Cotendra, you were more powerful."

"Are you saying I am *weaker without* the GF?"

"Exactly," said Marblus. "The very first Phoenix lies inside of you. You can be stronger than any being on earth."

"But how can I control it?! When you tempted me in Cotendra, I almost *killed* Ginzolo!"

"Sistro cleansed the GF. Now *you* must learn to control it."

Mercutio walked towards the Demarican.

"How do I control it?" he asked. "Tell me!"

"That you must figure out," he said as his body started to deteriorate. Mercutio didn't question why he disappeared like that. He also understood that Marblus spoke in riddles.

Mercutio *hated* riddles.

Suddenly, he heard Eviana's voice in Ginzolo's room.

"Ginzolo's ready, Mercutio," she said, knowing he had heard.

Mercutio smiled.

"Call me Merck."

Sistro was sitting down with his eyes closed in the dining area of the inn, while Endstra was getting some food. Sistro opened his eyes when Endstra came back.

"Marblus visited Mercutio just now," said Sistro.

"I know," his brother informed. "I'm a *dark* wizard, remember?"

"What do you think he wants with him?"

"I think he wants Mercutio to tap deeper into his powers."

"You mean the GF?"

"I think so," said Endstra, "but I don't think he will. He hasn't since we were in Cotendra."

"What makes you say that?"

"If you really want my opinion," Endstra said with a mouth full of food and pointing a fork toward his brother, "I would say he's *scared* of it."

"He needs to access his final transformation with it to beat Napoleon."

Endstra swallowed his food. "Only Mercutio can beat Napoleon?"

Sistro nodded slowly. "Yes," he told his brother. "If Mercutio can use the GF to create his fifth madrocellular transformation, he could be the strongest being on earth."

Sistro leaned back in his chair.

"Besides," he continued, "I just spoke it into existence, so it's going to happen *regardless*."

With that said the Chosen headed inside the dining area with the two brothers, got some food and sat down.

"So, Mercutio," said Endstra, "where to *now?*"

"We go to the other end of the city and continue west," said Mercutio. "After we get to the other end of the continent, we have to cross the Great Sea. Manhattan would be right there when we cross it."

"What about your fear of water?" asked Ginzolo.

"I'll get over it," said Mercutio. "So, after we eat, we can be on our way."

"Good, because I'm starving," said Goddum. Mercutio laughed and started to eat. But the wizards and the Chosen were unaware that Napoleon, still in his rogue disguise, was watching them from outside. He held out his hand. A yellow jewel appeared. It floated to the ground, protected by an invisible prism only Ginzolo's hand could go through. Napoleon walked the other way, leaving the jewel to wait for Ginzolo.

As the Chosen and the wizard brothers headed outside, Endstra tripped on the invisible force field. The way he fell made everyone laugh, even Sistro.

"Very funny," Endstra said sarcastically. "What did I trip on anyway?"

Ginzolo picked up the yellow jewel.

"You tripped over a diamond," he said. "What kind is it?" asked Endstra. Mercutio heard a voice coming from the jewel and saw it spark.

"Ginzolo!" Mercutio yelled. "Get rid of that jewel!"

"What?!" said Ginzolo. "Are you loco?!"

Suddenly, the jewel formed electricity around it. It zapped through the entire city, came back to the middle of the street and formed a giant electrical monster.

"I *told* you to get rid of the jewel!" yelled Mercutio.

"Don't *yell* at me!" Ginzolo hollered back.

The monster was pure electricity. It stood on its legs and its hands were claws. Its body was thick and strong. Its head was like a Rhinoceros but with bigger glowing eyes and a metal covering the top of its head and over the horn.

"This is no big deal," said Ginzolo. As the monster attacked the city, Ginzolo flew towards it. He transformed to his first madrocellular transformation and pulled his sword. It glowed yellow and the electricity from the monster went inside. Ginzolo absorbed the energy from the monster. The sword blasted all of the energy back outside to the monster. It swatted Ginzolo to the ground like a fly.

He hit the ground hard.

When he slid back towards the others, he unwillingly transformed back and became unconscious.

"I'll take him," said Eviana.

"No!" yelled Mercutio. "Electricity is your weakness. You'll *die* if you try." Mercutio looked at the monster as it headed down the road.

"I'm with you all the way, Merck," said Goddum.

"I know," said Mercutio, "but I must do this on my own." Mercutio walked towards the monster. Goddum and Eviana watched after Ginzolo, in case he woke.

"Good luck," said Goddum.

Mercutio flew behind the monster and shot a fireball. It turned and looked at him. Mercutio was frowning. He performed his second madrocellular transformation and combined his staff with his sword. The monster roared at him, hoping to blow Mercutio away with its foul breath. The only thing affected by the wind was his hair and robes.

Mercutio smiled.

"Cute," he said.

Mercutio raised his staff and sword combination in the air.

"Filibu Dogama, eso tan bo!" he yelled out loud. Suddenly, a volcano in the Far West of the city erupted. What happened next was astonishing.

The Fox Phoenix once again came out of Mercutio, but this time it fused with the sword-staff combination.

"May I present to you Kagi no Hiteshita," he said. "The Key of Magical Fire." The monster roared again. Eviana was worried.

"Mercutio, be careful!" she yelled. The key was long like a sword with flame blades sharper than the Hikulo. The handle was a gold replica of the Fox Phoenix and feather light.

Mercutio's new weapon floated in the air. Mercutio controlled it by telekinetic abilities. The key blasted the monster backwards, causing him to fall, destroying two buildings in the process. As the monster got up, a hot wind blew behind it. Mercutio said a chant in Lingu.

"Serlipitu O' Pioferia," he said, "taliaqua mai O' songina!"

Suddenly, the key shot out numerous fireballs that exploded on the intense hot wind. The explosions revealed a giant red dragon with green eyes.

"A *dragon?!*" yelled Goddum. How can a dragon fit inside of a *sword?*"

"When you have the Fox Phoenix," said Sistro, "*anything* is possible." Mercutio took both hands and grasped the sword handle. He flew backwards toward the dragons head. When he reached it, he went inside and automatically the dragon was under his control.

"Are you ready?" Mercutio said through the dragon. The monster showed no impression, but it punched with its right hand. Mercutio caught it with his left hand and punched it in the gut with his right. The monster curled up; Mercutio punched him with his right hand on the left side of its face. It fell to the ground.

"Is this all you have?" said Mercutio.

"Get up."

The monster got up and bum rushed Mercutio to the ground. It then picked him up by the neck and slammed him to the ground. This monster had some of Goddum's strength; so that told Mercutio this creature was created by one person.

"Napoleon," Mercutio said to himself.

As it was about to punch his face into the ground, Mercutio shot a ray of fire from his mouth. He used this opportunity to power up.

"This is *insane!*" yelled Goddum.

"Mercutio knows what he's doing," said Endstra. "Just let him be!"

Goddum continued to watch his friend fight this monster. As Mercutio attacked nonstop, he grew impatient.

"I had enough of this *game!*" he said. Then something happened that none of the Chosen had expected.

Mercutio came out of the dragon!

He held the Key of Magical Fire in his hand and raised it. The monster was half beaten, but continued to swing his arms at him. Unbelievably, the monsters hands went right through him.

The GF activated again.

After the dragon was transported back into the key, the tip of it glowed. It then shot out an aurora of red light.

"I hope you're right, Marblus," he said to himself.

The light bent and fell towards the ground, covering Mercutio. The monsters blows still couldn't penetrate through the particles.

"What's he doing?" yelled Eviana.

"I don't know," replied Sistro, "but it's something big!"

As the monster roared again, the red shield of light exploded. What came out was tremendous. Sistro smiled as he saw Mercutio combine his first two madrocellular transformations to create his *third* one.

His body was back in Griffin form. The same brown toga covered his waist to the knees. The difference was his beak was black instead of yellow. There were no wings of fire because he didn't need them. He had on a sleeveless wizard robe. It was black with the Demarican symbol of fire in red on the back. The retina of his eyes was red; he was in control. His arms and hands were made of pure gold.

"His third madrocellular transformation," Sistro said. "Pioferia Comaroku; the Fire Master."

At that moment, Ginzolo came around. He woke seeing Mercutio, now in his third transformation. Ginzolo got angry.

It should've been me to transform, not him, he thought. But before he could do anything, Goddum grabbed his ankle with a good grasp. Ginzolo felt Goddum's hand around his ankle and looked at him with a hateful heart.

"Let go!"

Goddum slowly shook his head.

"This is not your fight," he said. "You should have learned that from the *first* time."

Ginzolo frowned; he knew he was right. He calmed down and watched Mercutio from afar.

The monster didn't care if Mercutio had changed. The monster didn't care if his clothes were different. It didn't care that it was in a well populated place and could easily kill someone with a step of a foot.

It was about to change its mind.

"Spawn of Napoleon!" Mercutio yelled out loud. "Your evil deed was to destroy us."

The monster snarled.

Mercutio picked up the Key of Magical Fire.

"And for that," he said, "you must be *punished!*"

With the thrust of Mercutio's right hand, the monster floated in the air, high above the city.

Mercutio flew towards it holding the key with both hands and the blade next to his left side. When he reached it, the tip of the blade glowed and he circled the monster. He circled faster, faster and faster, until it looked like a red ring around the monster. In front of the monster, Mercutio quickly flew, holding the key like a rocket launcher. As the tip continued to glow a bright red, Mercutio hollered,

"Particle Lava Blast!"

Soon the tip of the key glowed even more, then stopped suddenly. After one second, a giant amount of lava and fire blasted from the key.

It covered the monster completely. It flowed on an invisible floor in the sky that Mercutio made when he flew away after he spun around it. When the key transformed into a Hikulo, the lava and the monster disappeared. The only thing left from the monster was bits of energy. Mercutio held out his sword and the energy was sucked inside. It went into his body through his hands and into his head.

As Mercutio floated back towards the group Goddum let go of Ginzolo's ankle-slowly applauding with a smirk on his face. The smirk turned into a smile, then a laugh.

"The bird is back!"

"And better than ever!" smiled Mercutio. As he landed, Mercutio looked at Ginzolo.

"Napoleon?" he asked. Mercutio nodded.

"He's here," he said, "and something tells me he was that character who was following us."

Endstra walked toward Eviana. "We need to leave as soon as possible," he said. "If we keep heading west, we should get to the Great Sea in a week."

But faith would not allow this adventure to go by smoothly. A panicked man came running down a street, looking for someone. When he saw Mercutio and the others, he smiled in relief and ran towards them, tripping over his own feet in the process.

"Are you four, the ones promised by the prophecy one thousand twenty-five years ago?"

Mercutio nodded. "Yes, we are the Chosen."

The man released a sigh of relief. "Good," he said, "because I have a really big problem. I have come a great distance. From the city of Camenstra!"

Mercutio looked at Sistro, then at Eviana. He nudged his head toward the man. Eviana went to him and nursed him ice water. You see, Camenstra was in the lands of the deserts and mountains. He had to cross the mountains guarding the city with the Hidden Death Ocean following it. The desert also guarded the underground city of New Dimbar. As the man drank the water provided by Eviana's powers, he nodded.

"Thank you," he said.

"Now I want you to calm down and tell us what happened," said Endstra. The man stood up and took a deep breath.

"Camenstra," he said. "I have come this distance to tell you all that Camenstra has been overtaken by Yamalu's shadow demons!"

Mercutio looked at Sistro.

Sistro nodded.

"We must protect that city at all cost," he said.

"Then what are we waiting for?" asked Goddum. "Let's go!"

The man felt relieved. "Thank you," he said. "Bless you, all!"

Two days later, the group reached the Hidden Death Ocean, one of the most dangerous places on Earth. It was also the roof and the entrance of New Dimbar, the only city in the world that is underground. The winds were blowing hard, carrying large amounts of sand in the air.

"Follow me!" the man yelled. "I marked a safe route for us to take without the sand swallowing us!"

The Chosen did not hesitate to follow.

"Are you sure this isn't one of Napoleon's tricks?" Endstra asked his brother. Sistro struggled to keep his hood on his head.

"Yes, I am," he said. "I am certain this is real. I have a feeling."

Seconds later, Eviana tripped and her foot hit a sand trap. Ginzolo grabbed her in time with his speed before it swallowed her whole. She stood up, dusted herself and said,

"Thanks."

She then continued with the others.

"I don't see why we can't fly," yelled Ginzolo.

"One," Mercutio started, "our guide can't fly. Two, we have yet to experience the harsh winds like these."

"You talk as if we'll experience *more* like this."

"It is a possibility," said Mercutio. "Now quiet before you drown in this flying sand."

Eviana worked her way up the line, until she was walking next to Mercutio. He noticed her out of the corner of his eye.

"There are some days I wished Ginzolo wasn't immortal," he said with a smirk.

"He saved my life just a few seconds ago."

"You're *immortal,* Eviana. Not even a *sand trap* could kill you."

The sand settled. The stars became visible. Once they saw their guide stop, they ran towards him.

"Are we near the entrance?" asked Eviana.

"We are near the left side of the city," the man said. "If we continue this way, we'll be there in four hours."

The man started walking again, so did the others.

"Let's hope that we aren't too late," Sistro said to himself.

It was 12:00 a.m. when the Chosen reached Camenstra. The mountains that guarded the city were snow topped, but they reached the other side. Mercutio looked at the city-it was calm and quiet. He enhanced his vision and saw shadow demons inside the city, patrolling the premises.

"There are definitely shadows in there."

Mercutio saw something float to the top of the Camenstrian Tower. When it got high enough, Mercutio sensed it was Napoleon. Mercutio used his enhanced hearing to listen.

"My soldiers," he yelled, "you have done a fine job infiltrating this city. Now, by the orders of my father, it is time to show your strength. Burn! Destroy! Pillage this village of mortals. They have sinned against my father by being the ones responsible for giving God the kinetic power inside one of the Chosen!"

The soldiers screeched at Napoleon showing agreement to his words. His smile was demented and menaced. He raised his hand and a small fireball was ignited.

"The time of darkness," Napoleon yelled, "has *begun!*"

He threw the fireball on a haystack.

It spread through the city.

Sistro then remembered a scene from his dream over one thousand years ago.

The city of Camenstra was on fire. He saw buildings collapsing. He saw people on fire and screaming in terror. Sistro then noticed even before the fire that the buildings were aged more than ever.

This was a vision from the future.

Sistro felt a rumbling in the Earth. He turned around and saw a swarm of flying shadow demons. When they reached Sistro they went straight through him and went to destroy the remains of the city. You see, they could neither see him, feel him nor hear him because this was a vision from the future.

Sistro looked shocked.

"Good Lord, what have I done?!"

"You five handle the city," he said. "I have business to attend." As the Chosen and Endstra went to the city, Sistro stood at the line of mountains where the flying shadow demons were supposed to be coming from. He formed his third madrocellular transformation. Like Mercutio, Sistro fused his staff sword and created another key weapon.

The shadows came towards him. When they were in perfect sight, he held out his key weapon.

"Holt!" he yelled.

The shadows unwillingly stopped.

"You may not come any further," he said. The shadows had a hateful look.

"If you wish to face someone," he said, "then face *me!*"

The shadow demons suddenly flew towards him. He flew in the air, but the shadows followed in a cluttered line. As Sistro turned around, he shot light energy blasts at the shadows. Even though they were effective, it wasn't enough to stop all of them.

In the city, Mercutio, Eviana, Ginzolo, Endstra and Goddum were figuring out ways to settle the fires. Mercutio absorbed one section of the city that was on fire through his fingertips. Eviana, of course, sprayed water. Goddum used dirt to suffocate the flames. Endstra used his dark powers to overcome the flames and put them out.

Ginzolo couldn't help.

If he tried, he would just start *more* fires. So he decided to do something even more helpful to the group. He decided to do something that would make *him* worthy of being leader of the Chosen.

He decided to face Napoleon *alone.*

As Ginzolo flew towards the Chosen's strongest foe yet, everyone but Mercutio felt concerned.

"He won't win," he said to Eviana. "Not without us." Endstra came towards Mercutio.

"Then let's go after him," he said.

"Not you, Endstra."

"And why *not?*"

"Because Sistro told you to stay away from Napoleon at all cost," said Mercutio. "He said your life depends on it."

Even though he didn't understand, Endstra respected Mercutio and Sistro's wishes and stayed. He put out the rest of the fires as the others flew toward Ginzolo.

And Napoleon.

Sistro fought every shadow to the last. Each time he destroyed one, a group of at least fifteen either gang up or jump on top of him. Sistro's third transformation was strong, but not enough to handle around four hundred thousand shadow demons. When he killed one, a wave of shadows threw him to the ground. Even though he didn't transform back, he was extremely weak. The shadows returned to the ground and gathered around Sistro.

Suddenly, the shadows that ganged up on him were sucked away.

It was Endstra with his darkness staff.

"Get off my brother, you bothersome *filth!*" As the remaining three hundred fifty thousand shadows came to him, he knocked them out one by one, then sucked them into his staff to recharge his power. Sistro was on the ground, watching with a bloody nose and bleeding cuts from the ground impact.

By the time Endstra sucked up the three hundredth one, the remaining shadows created a giant hand. It had the imitation of sharp fingers. Almost like bird talons. It smacked him a few feet away from the battlefield, but he landed on his feet. As he ran back, he saw the remaining fifty thousand shadow demons form other body parts. Now there were two complete arms connected to a body. There were no feet, only a tail. The sides of the head formed two erect horns. But even though it was made of fifty thousand shadows, it opened its eyes. It opened glowing white eyes. It had a mouth with sharp teeth and a corroded tongue. Its lips were stitched through with a thick dirty string that extended every time it opened its mouth. Endstra looked at the shadow demon; it floated from the ground to the air with only its tail touching the ground. He could only say one thing.

"Oh."

Ginzolo landed in the dark of the city so he could hide from the others. As he saw them fly past, he smiled and continued toward the Camenstrian Tower. Once he reached it, he saw Napoleon floating in the air with his back facing him. Napoleon knew Ginzolo was behind him and smiled at the fact *he was so stupid.*

Ginzolo released a thunder bolt directly at Napoleon's head, but before it reached him, he flew up, did a front flip and punched the air, resulting in a very strong telekinetic punch that sent Ginzolo falling into the Camenstrian Tower.

Napoleon, upside down with his arms folded, smiled.

"You really don't think you can beat me, *do* you?"

Ginzolo got out of the rubble from the building.

"You sound like Mercutio," he said. Napoleon spun right side up, shaking his head.

"I sound like *you*," said Napoleon. He disappeared, then reappeared behind him and elbowed Ginzolo in the neck with Goddum's strength, breaking it.

As Ginzolo's neck healed, Napoleon said, "I am as fast as you are."

Ginzolo frowned. He sent a right punch to his gut. Napoleon dodged and swung a left kick to his ribs.

"I know every move you will make."

"You have the vortex powers in you," said Ginzolo as he gasped for air and drooled blood.

"Oh, it's much more than my father's powers," he said. He grabbed Ginzolo with an extended left arm and threw him to the ground.

Ginzolo slowly recuperated his strength, stood up and performed his madrocellular transformation.

"When you were a babe," said Napoleon as his hand went back to normal, "you were captured by Yamalu, my father. His servant, Mascool, who is your friends' murderer, took a DNA sample of you that contained your power and special ability. He then put the raw material in me when I was an embryo. Same with Goddum. I was nursed in a liquid containing some of all my father's powers. As I grew, so did they."

It then all made sense to Ginzolo; Napoleon's origin of his super speed; Mascool's monologue before he killed his best friend. The reason why Napoleon had his abilities was because a piece of himself was inside Napoleon feeding him his powers.

"Are you saying," said Ginzolo with a frowned face, "that you have my DNA?!"

"Yes," smirked Napoleon. "And Goddum's as a matter of fact."

Ginzolo flew toward him as he took out his sword and shield.

"I'm gonna *kill* you!" was the last statement Ginzolo said before the major fight. As Ginzolo swung his sword at Napoleon, he dodged every blow. He swung again. Napoleon stopped the blade with his index finger, then blew his breath which sent him hurtling backwards. Ginzolo, in control of himself, flew back.

Napoleon raised his right hand in the air and a sword with a gray blade appeared.

"Your lion transformation is nothing compared to my normal stature," he said. "It looks like the only Chosen who is worthy enough to fight me is *Mercutio*."

Ginzolo was *real* mad, now. He flew toward Napoleon, but was soon blasted back by telekinesis. With a smile of wickedness, Napoleon yelled in a morphed voice.

"Let me show you a *real* lion transformation!"

His muscles bulged again.

"Great," whispered Ginzolo.

Napoleon's shirt and pants were ripped off. His body sprouted light brown hair again. The only part of his pants that remained on his body was his lower torso. His hands turned into giant claws. His nails were sharpened and curved downward. His hair grew extremely long on his head. His face changed into the shape of a lion with a black snout, drooling mouth razor sharp teeth and a crazed look on his face.

"LET'S PLAY."

Endstra was in awe of the thirty-seven foot shadow demon made of fifty thousand regular shadows.

"Now that's something you don't see everyday."

The giant shadow roared a screech and attempted to scratch the wizard. Endstra dodged.

"You wanna play?" asked Endstra. "C'mon, then."

The demon's eyes glowed and shot a ray of light at Endstra. His staff reflected and blinded it for a while.

Endstra flew up and twirled his staff in a martial artistic way. He threw it at the monster's face. When the staff hit, it spun around and came back to him.

"You're gonna pay for everything that you've done to my little brother," Endstra said as he caught and raised his staff. Endstra yelled at the top of his voice. The black jewel on the top of his staff glowed. It sent an aurora around Endstra covering his entire body. The aurora erupted when Endstra stopped yelling, which was also when it finished its course.

Endstra was in his first madrocellular transformation.

Like Sistro's third, Endstra was in an outfit like the Chosen, just black. His shirt was a long sleeve silk shirt with a V-neck collar. His pants were black sheer with a black belt holding them. The buckle was a black icicle-shaped crest, which was the shape of his pendant.

His shoes were *very* rare; Twenty-second Century Stacy Adams. Black, of course.

His mustache was cut and lined. Unlike the other Chosen, Endstra had stylish black leather gloves.

Endstra pulled out a three bladed sword. The one in the middle was erect and the other two were curved downwards like banana peels. The giant shadow slowly backed up. Endstra smiled. The demon retreated.

"Oh," he said, "you're not going anywhere." The shadow turned and bum rushed him quickly. Endstra was surprised but not hurt. The monsters mouth suddenly inhaled air. It inhaled so much, it acted as a vacuum.

It tried to suck him inside.

Endstra forcefully held his ground, but couldn't resist it for long. Already he was slowly headed toward its mouth. Soon the giant shadow stopped inhaling and blew out the air. The air turned into fire! Endstra flew around trying to avoid the fire, but it was always near him. While the monster annoyingly followed him with its fire breath, Endstra aimed and threw the triple bladed sword at what he thought was the throat. It twirled back, because the two blades acted like boomerang ends. The shadow choked a little. It gave Endstra time to perform his second madrocellular transformation.

After Endstra went through the process again, his appearance was completely different. His black hair was longed and permed. He had no facial hair. His nails were long and painted black. His clothes were black and of thirteenth century-London. Endstra's eyes were completely black. When he smiled, his carnivore teeth were sharper than any human.

His second madrocellular transformation was a vampire.

Endstra raised his right hand. A black energy came around it when he put it in the form of a fist.

"Let's go."

Ginzolo was frightened out of his mind. He had seen Napoleon transform into a stronger and eviler lion form more powerful than he. But even though he was scared of Napoleon, Ginzolo didn't show it. He just frowned and tightened the grip on his sword his transformation gave him. Napoleon still had the sword with the gray blade in his right hand. He licked the blade with his tongue

"You're going to die by *my* hand, Napoleon," he said.

"WE SHALL SEE."

The battle was on. Ginzolo crashed his body into Napoleon's chest. It knocked the wind out of him but he regenerated. Ginzolo thought he was regaining his power, so he flew towards him. What he didn't know was that Napoleon was playing possum, if such creatures still existed. He turned around and slapped Ginzolo's face with his sword. His wound was bad, but quickly healed. Ginzolo quickly flew toward the villain. They clashed swords. They continued until Napoleon knocked Ginzolo's sword out of his hand.

Ginzolo flew to catch his sword before it fell to the ground. Napoleon followed and shot energy bombs. As Ginzolo ducked and dodged, Napoleon was right behind him. Ginzolo caught it. He turned around, held out his sword, and rammed it into Napoleon's heart. Napoleon was surprised and curious as to how he could get close to him in the middle of physical combat. He looked at the sword that went through his heart to his back. Then he looked at Ginzolo who evilly smirked.

Ginzolo twisted the sword vertically.

"Die," he whispered.

Ginzolo let go of the sword and flew back some. He transformed into human form. But, this battle was not done.

Napoleon, still with a surprised look, slowly pulled out the sword -inch by-inch. Napoleon tilted his head to his left as he pulled out the sword-covered in his blood. Because Ginzolo was no longer in transformation, the sword disappeared. Napoleon looked at his flesh. The gory wound to his heart quickly healed along with the internal structures. Remember, Napoleon is still in his lion's transformation. Napoleon looked at Ginzolo with a sinister smile on his face. He rose is right index finger and waved it back and forth.

"UNGH, UNGH, UNGH..."

The shadow demon roared at Endstra, who was in his second madrocellular transformation. Endstra smiled and blasted the black energy from his right hand at the monster. It circled continuously and drained it of its powers. It then retreated to Endstra's right hand. As he gathered the dark powers, the shadow became weary. Endstra flew to its face and swung-kicked it. The demon flew backwards and fell to the ground. Endstra saw the demon was regaining power. Endstra blasted it back to the monster and stole its regained powers again.

"You're a tough little monster, are you?" he said. The monster frowned and once again regained more power.

That shadow demon is made of at least fifty thousand shadows, Endstra thought. *They each have a power supply that's feeding this monster. But how do I get to that power supply?* Suddenly, he got it. Since he was a creature of the night, he could just suck it out of him!

After all, he *was* a vampire.

But it was easier said than done. Before he could strike, the demon released a giant energy blast from the front of his body! Endstra tried to absorb all the energy he could. He dodged the rest of the attack. When it was over, the shadow was out of energy.

This was Endstra's chance.

He flew to the shadow and landed on its neck. He dug his fingernails into its skin and bit into its vein like a mosquito.

The demon felt the nails and the bite of Endstra's vapirisimic teeth. It tried to shake him off. Endstra's nails were in too deep to be shaken out. They and his teeth were attached to its skin. Endstra sucked the energy through his mouth and absorbed it through his nails. The monster tried to shake him off. Its power was slowly decreasing.

After at least ten minutes of holding on to the shadow, Endstra finally gathered all of the demons dark energy. He let go and flew away. The demon turned gray. Its left claw grabbed its neck and became imbalanced. Unfortunately, Endstra had gathered its powers.

He didn't *kill* the demon.

The demon's gray body turned black again.

The demon's glowing white eyes frowned at Endstra. It stood tall. A purple aurora came from inside the beast. It roared and released two legs and demonic wings.

Endstra tilted his head to the right.

"A back-up energy source," he said. "Cool."

Endstra once again flew towards the monster, hoping to do the same thing he had done but with better results. But this time the monster couldn't be fooled. It quickly flew upward and tossed a blast. It caught him off guard and hit him to the ground next to Sistro.

"Having fun?" Sistro sarcastically said to his older brother.

Endstra got up.

"I'm just getting started," he said. He flew towards the monster. But as he was flying, he transformed into a black ball and hit the demon back to the ground. When the ball exploded, Endstra was in his third madrocellular transformation!

He was wearing a Japanese rice hat outlined in black string and a black cotton Japanese robe that extended to his ankles. The sleeves were long. He wore black socks with wooden sandals. His pants made of cotton. The only thing white on him was the belt tied around his waist.

The creature snarled at the new Endstra. It flew towards him and pulled out its claws. Endstra prepared a giant aerial attack. When they collided, Endstra's first attack was a high strung kick to the jaw. After the demon recuperated from the attack, it spun its claws around, hoping to slice this annoying pest out of existence. As Endstra ducked and dodged the swipes, he released small, but powerful blasts of transformed energy beams from his fingers. As the beast attacked, more beams came.

When the demon stopped, Endstra socked the left side of its jaw with his new strength. It took the shadow right out of the air, but didn't kill it. It once again attempted its ultimate attack; a giant energy attack from the front of its body! But before it performed it, Endstra threw three pressure point needles at the palm of its hands and the top of its forehead. When it did the attack, Endstra unbelievably stood in front of it without blocking!

The beast smiled to see its opponent was such a fool. But when the attack was over, the demon came to realize the acupuncture needles on itself.

Endstra was still alive!

The needles on the shadow allowed him to absorb *all* of the energy from the blast. He changed in the blast. He had wings attached to his arms. His body, covered in dark brown fur. His hands were claws. His body was muscular. He had no shirt, only pants and two belts. He had no shoes, because his feet would not fit any. But what was shocking was his head, which was the same as a bat-a bat with glowing red eyes.

His fourth madrocellular transformation.

The Bat Beast.

Ginzolo couldn't beat Napoleon. Not without the others. He knew this before he left them behind. Napoleon giggled at the last attempt Ginzolo had made to destroy him. Ginzolo flew towards him in anger and fought without any thought. That made it a lot easier for Napoleon to bring Ginzolo down and use him for his *real* purpose.

Napoleon beat Ginzolo every time, even transformed back to his self, he beat him. Ginzolo was weak and had only enough energy for at least one more electric attack.

"This is getting very old very fast," said Napoleon. He pulled out his sword with the gray blade.

"It's time to end this!"

With that said, he threw the sword with amazing speed through Ginzolo's stomach. Even though immortal, it still hurt.

Ginzolo slowly but painfully pulled the sword from his belly. The gray blade turned to dust.

Napoleon was shocked.

"Impossible!" he yelled. "That was supposed to *kill* you!"

Ginzolo threw the handle to the ground. His wound started to heal. For the first time, Napoleon was angry with Ginzolo. He flew towards him-Ginzolo quickly formed a giant ball of his remaining electrical energy.

"Thunder Rage!" Ginzolo yelled. He threw it at Napoleon. Baffled by the power of the once-thought weakling, the ball exploded. A white light covered the entire city for at least five seconds, then imploded.

The Camenstrian Tower - destroyed - along with the other buildings.

No sign of Napoleon, whatsoever.

Ginzolo smiled and took a sigh of relief.

He did it!

He defeated Napoleon single-handedly!

Holding his broken right arm, he closed his eyes and fell to the ground. His bones mended. From the fall, a smoke suddenly emerged from the soil and entered Ginzolo's wound the gray bladed sword left.

Ginzolo suddenly opened his eyes.

Sistro gained enough strength to stand. As he transformed to his regular form, he saw his brother in his fourth form of power gaze down at the giant demon. Sistro knew Endstra could beat this creature on his own. You see, even though it didn't seem like it, Endstra was really stronger than Sistro. Endstra could perform all five of his transformation.

Sistro could only perform three.

Plus, he was always prepared for anything.

"Good luck," Sistro whispered.

He flew off to aid the Chosen.

The demon roared at Endstra. He replied with an ear-shattering bat screech. The shadow swung its claws at him. Endstra dodged both attacks, flew under it and uppercut punched it in its belly. It tossed it in the air, but it caught the wind and flew to Endstra's sky level.

"Just because I'm a bat," Endstra began, "doesn't mean I'm blind."

The demon snarled. It then quickly flew towards him and punched him to the ground. Endstra landed on one foot, one knee and one hand, flew towards the beast and head-butted it. It landed five feet away from him.

"I've grown tired of this game," he said as his left hand formed raw black energy around it. His right hand imitated the same energy. They formed to two red glowing balls with black spectacles inside them.

"Charging Frenzy!" he cried. He threw them, they formed pure light energy. Both balls hit the demon and exploded. After the collision, half of the left wing was gone, along with its left arm and a bit of its left side. Its right leg along with the right side of its upper torso was gone.

It was mutilated.

Endstra smirked. "You put up quite a fight," he said. "I'm really impressed."

Paralyzed by the attack, the shadow showed a face of shock and fear.

"However," Endstra said wiping the smirk from his face, "this is where it ends!"

Endstra quickly flew towards the demon and powerfully elbowed it to the ground. Still paralyzed, the giant horrifically looked at Endstra in the sky. He was about to perform one last attack.

Endstra aimed the right palm of his hand at the monster as it started to glow. Once the giant black, red and white glow consumed Endstra's entire hand, he winked at the demon.

"Die," he whispered. "Dark Horde!"

With a push of the same hand, a gigantic triangle-shaped blast of energy came from Endstra's hand. In five seconds after it covered the demon, Endstra stopped. A giant hole was in the area of the demon.

The battle was over. The monster was done for.
Endstra transformed to his original form and smiled.
"Well," he said, "*that* was fun."

The celebration in Camenstra was held in one of the main halls. You see, the Camenstrian Tower was annihilated by Ginzolo's attack. The main halls were underground. The king retreated to them in times of peril with his people. Sistro was completely regenerated. Endstra was given a metal of honor for willingly protecting the city from harm. Goddum, Mercutio and Eviana were present, but were concerned for Ginzolo. He had not been seen ever since the fight against Napoleon.

The king silenced the people of Camenstra, who were half-drunk and half-stoned.

"Order! Order!" he demanded. He raised his glass to the Chosen who were at the party. "To the great warriors of the Dark World," he yelled. "We thank you for your aid, and may your quest of quests be blessed!"

Mercutio and Goddum smiled and banged their pints of brew as the people of Camenstra cheered for them. With a smirk on her face, Eviana crossed her arms and shook her head.

"Men," she said as the smirk turned into a smile.

After it looked like Mercutio was over his drunkenness, Eviana and he snuck out onto the surface.

"Any trace of Ginzolo yet?" asked Mercutio.

"He's somewhere in this city, I know that," she said. "But you and Goddum only cared about getting drunk."

"I was not drunk!" Mercutio said with a giggle.

"Then explain the hangover you had thirty minutes ago."

Mercutio tried to think of a logical explanation, but couldn't. Eviana laughed.

"Was it something I said?" he asked.

"No," she answered. "No it wasn't! That's the *point!*" Mercutio thought about it, then laughed, too. Then there were seconds of silence.

"You're in love with me, aren't you?"

That got Eviana's attention.

"Well," she stated, "I was under the impression that we were just friends."

Mercutio shook his head.

"I think it's deeper than that."

"How can you tell?"

"Well," started Mercutio, "you were the only one I could connect with when the evil of the GF controlled me in Cotendra."

"Okay…"

"Then, we always talked and found we have a lot in common."

"Strike two…"

"And to top it all off," he said loudly, "you're the only person on this earth that can *kill* me!"

He then smirked.

"Well, until I can master the GF in its entirety."

"So," she said as she came closer to him, "you really think it's destined for us to be together?"

"I don't think," he said. He touched her face with his left hand and put his right hand around her waist. "I know."

Eviana smiled. She put her body close to his.

"You want to know something else?"

"What?"

"It's about to rain."

"*What!?*"

Eviana grabbed him.

"It's okay," she cooed, trying to calm Mercutio down. "Trust me," she said. Her soothing voice erased all fear from Mercutio's mind. Mercutio looked up and saw the first rain drop come toward him, but it didn't land on him. Instead it rolled by him. Eviana was protecting him. She giggled.

"You are amazing," he said. The rain poured harder.

"This field is one hundred percent waterproof," she said. "I guarantee no water will get in here or-"

Mercutio put his index finger on her lips.

"Be quiet and kiss me."

And indeed they kissed. They lip locked and hadn't noticed they were spinning around in the air, slowly. It was a dream come true. They had finally found their lovers.

But for one person who was out in the rain watching, his dreams ended. Ginzolo sobbed. He lost the only woman he cared about to a man he had to take orders from and hated so much. With everything lost but his pride, Ginzolo walked, away from the lovers' sight.

Eviana let go of Mercutio's lips.

"I felt him, too," said Mercutio, "but...there's something else. Something... familiar."

Eviana looked at her new boyfriend.

"He's in the halls," she said. "Let's go see where he's been."

"Ginzolo!" said Goddum with his arms outstretched. Ginzolo gave him a friendly hug.

"Where have you been?" he asked after he let go. "The king awarded you with a metal of bravery for defeating Napoleon."

"I don't want it," he said.

"That still doesn't explain what happened to you," said Eviana as Mercutio and she entered the hall.

"I needed to recuperate," he said. "It took all the strength I had left to beat him."

Mercutio sensed very quickly that something was wrong with Ginzolo but couldn't point it out.

Sistro walked by and sensed it, too.

"Is everyone all right?" he asked. Ginzolo nodded.

"Fine," he said, "everything's fine. I'm ready to leave whenever they are."

"Then let's leave," said Mercutio. "We have a lot of ground to cover." Ginzolo nodded and walked pass Mercutio. As Ginzolo left the hall, Mercutio chuckled.

"What's so funny?" Endstra asked. Mercutio began to calm down.

"Remember when Sistro told Napoleon he was gonna die six different ways by *my* hand?"

"What's your point?" said Goddum.

"Well," Mercutio said, "I learned that all wizards have a gift to actually speak things into existence. For example, the prediction about Napoleon."

Eviana put two and two together. "Oh, I see."

"I wish *I* could," said Goddum. He sat and put his chin in his right hand.

"Don't you see?" said Mercutio. "When Sistro said that, he changed the future."

"Meaning," interrupted Sistro, "that Ginzolo never killed him."

Goddum and Ginzolo had certain looks on their faces. Goddum's was anger. Ginzolo's was blank. "Are you saying that-"

"Yes, Goddum," said Sistro. "What I am saying is that Napoleon is still *alive*."

Ginzolo folded his arms. "Then where is he, old man?" Sistro looked at him shocked.

"What did you call me?" he said in a normal tone of voice, which intimidated Ginzolo a bit.

"I mean," he said with a shrug of his shoulders, "no one could've survived that blast, even if they tried."

"I don't think it's that simple," said Mercutio. "Remember we're dealing with an immortal that has Goddum and Ginzolo's powers and one-fourth of Yamalu's powers, which I might add could be more than all of our powers combined."

"Well, since you're the one who's gonna kill this thorn on our sides," Ginzolo said as he walked towards Mercutio, "why don't you now?"

"He's not ready yet, Ginzolo," said Sistro.

"I asked the leader," Ginzolo said to Sistro without moving an eye off Mercutio, "not the Wizard of Light."

Sistro was baffled once again. Even though Ginzolo had the guts to confront Sistro, he never did it before.

"He's right, Ginzolo," said Mercutio. "I'm not ready yet." He looked around at the others.

"And I *won't* be if we *stay* here. Now let's go. We're behind schedule."

As the group prepared to leave Camenstra, Ginzolo noticed Eviana giggling at something Mercutio was telling her. Ginzolo closed his eyes and shivered a little.

He headed toward the exit of the halls.

"I sent five hundred thousand shadows to aid my son's army of two hundred fifty," said Yamalu in a whisper. "What you are saying is that those shadows were beaten by that loathsome wizard Endstra, even after the survivors formed *both* Legion transformations?!"

Mascool did not reply.

Yamalu grabbed him with his telekinetic ability, swung him in the air at least fifteen times, shot him out of the main window and watched him fall to his tenth death.

Yamalu took a deep breath and turned the opposite way from the windows.

"I feel better," he said for the third time. He sensed Mascool hovering back to the throne room. He apologized by saying, "Believe me, my lord. I had ho idea how powerful Endstra had become."

Yamalu frowned.

Without looking at him, he once again threw Mascool from the throne room window and didn't smile until he heard him hit the ground.

By the time Mascool reached the window, he had learned to keep his mouth shut. Yamalu sensed his sudden silence.

"Mascool," he said, "when you freed my son, what did you tell him?"

"I gave him valuable information about the Chosen's whereabouts."

"You also lied to him," said Yamalu with a serious face as he sat on his throne. "You lied to him *twice*."

Mascool was caught and knew it.

"Please explain this to me, my lord."

"First," Yamalu explained, "you told him to lead the Chosen off-course to the Devil Cave Tunnel and said I commanded it. I said no such thing."

Mascool felt a cold chill down his spine.

"My lord, please forgive-"

"I'm not done," Yamalu said with a firm voice. "The second lie you told him was that you *never* lie. That itself," he said with a soft chuckle, "was a lie."

After feeling fear all over his body, Mascool dropped to his knees and begged for mercy.

"Please forgive me, my lord!" he said with a woeful voice. "I let jealousy get in the way! I'm sorry!" Yamalu looked at Mascool in disgust, then smiled.

"Very well," he said, "you are forgiven." Mascool rose from the ground.

"Thank you, my lord!" said Mascool in relief. Yamalu rose from his throne and walked toward the giant window.

"However," he began, "your jealousy of Napoleon might be useful."

"I don't understand, my lord."

"There was never a plan to lead the Chosen to the tunnel," he said, "but there is now."

"Yes, but the question is this," Mascool said. "Can we pull it off?"

Yamalu smirked. "Of course!" he said. "It's nothing but child's play! Send as many Trimals we can afford to get rid of to the exit of the tunnel in Africa."

Mascool nodded and attempted to leave.

"Before you leave, Mascool," Yamalu said, "tell me this." Mascool turned around and looked at Yamalu, awaiting his question.

"Where is my son?"

Mercutio started a fire on the ground in front of them while Eviana fell asleep on his right shoulder. Goddum stood behind Mercutio, looking at the night sky.

"I just don't understand how we got off course," he said.

Mercutio agreed with a shrug of his shoulders. Yes, it was true. For the first time ever, the Chosen had no idea where they were.

"I can't believe it either, Goddum," he told him as he put Eviana's head on his lap. "We were supposed to go west all the way to the Scorpion Tail Tower, but I don't know what happened."

Goddum looked at Mercutio with a serious face.

"It was the earth."

"What happened, Goddum?"

"When we left Camenstra," he said, "we were only two miles past the city. When I couldn't see the city anymore, I felt the ground move at least three times after we left."

"I didn't feel anything," interrupted Ginzolo.

"Well of *course* you didn't. I'm a biokinetic, and a biochemist. I'm *one* with the earth." Trying to forget about Ginzolo's unwanted comment, Mercutio continued to talk to Goddum.

"So what do you think is happening?"

"I think Yamalu's trying to throw us off-course."

Mercutio thought.

"Do you have the power to do this, Goddum?"

"Yes, but I didn't."

"I didn't say you did."

Mercutio thought. Then his face brightened up with the idea of a culprit.

"But *Napoleon* could!" he said. "He has your power of Biokinesis! It's *Napoleon* who threw us off-course."

Mercutio looked and saw Ginzolo sitting down. His attempt to prove Goddum wrong was humiliating.

"The only question is where *is* he?"

A black owl and a white owl, landed at the campsite. The white one landed near Mercutio and the black one on Goddum's right shoulder. A few seconds later, they flew near Ginzolo. The black one suddenly transformed into Endstra. The white one turned to Sistro soon after.

"How was your flight?" asked Mercutio.

"As smooth as the sand," said Endstra. "Made me wish I had night vision earlier!"

"Did you find out anything about our location?" asked Sistro.

"We found out who *led* us out here," said Goddum.

"Who?" asked Endstra.

"Who do *you* think?" asked Mercutio.

Endstra knew by that sarcasm that it was Napoleon.

"If it was Napoleon," said Ginzolo, "then where *is* he? Invisibility isn't one of his powers."

"But that's the main thing about Napoleon, Ginzolo," Sistro said. "We don't know *what* he's capable of."

"Besides," said Mercutio, "if he could turn invisible, I could easily find him with my sense of smell."

Ginzolo chuckled. "Do you really think he's that stupid that he wouldn't know about your five enhanced senses, Mercutio?" He looked at Sistro.

"This is *Napoleon*," he said. "The son of Yamalu, the person we are trying to destroy."

Everyone was speechless.

"You might have the power to speak things into existence, Sistro," Ginzolo continued, "but I put all I had into that attack." Ginzolo got up and put his shield behind him.

"If I couldn't kill him," he said as he walked into the darkness, "then none of us can."

"You think he's coming back?" asked Goddum. "I mean, it's been three hours already."

"He's probably just blowing off some steam," said Eviana as she woke from her sleep. "You know how Ginzolo is; always self-centered." Sistro looked around the camp in the dark.

"What's wrong, Sistro?" asked Mercutio. Sistro was paralyzed in thought. The night air flew past the campsite. It had a stale odor of seawater and essences of smoke. They then heard a maniacal laugh in the same wind. Sistro showed an emotion he had never shown before.

He felt fear.

"Something is terribly wrong."

Ginzolo returned while the wind was still blowing. The laughing stopped, but the wind got more ferocious.

"What's going on?!" yelled Ginzolo.

"I don't know," replied Mercutio, "but we have to leave now! This wind is too strong to stand. We need shelter!"

"I know somewhere," he said. "Follow me!"

So the Chosen and the wizards followed Ginzolo for almost one and one half-hours. The wind died down a little, but still strong. The wind left a taste in Mercutio's mouth. He asked, "Where are we going, Ginzolo?"

"We're almost there," he said. After a few more steps, Ginzolo stopped and pointed forward.

"There," he said.

Spikes came from the ground with a dirty brown color on them. They were large and everywhere. One was as tall as Mt. Fuji used to be. They surrounded what looked like a giant open mouth with teeth as sharp as the spikes on the ground. Its eyes were shut in pain and anger. Even though it was made of the earth, its skin looked burned and scarred. Its nose was pointed upward.

This was definitely *not* a holy place.

"*This* is the shelter you found?!" Mercutio yelled at Ginzolo. "This looks even *worse* than the storm itself! I rather be captured at Yamalu's lair than go inside this demented place!" Mercutio looked at the terrifying sight again.

"What *is* this place, anyway?" he asked.

"Satara ni Bularis," said Sistro. He frowned at Ginzolo.

"The Devil Cave Tunnel!"

Ginzolo started to breathe hard. "I-it was the only place I could find!" he said. "I had no idea what this place was!" Sistro looked at the demented entrance.

"This place is *evil*," he said. "We enter death as soon as we enter the tunnel." Mercutio looked at Goddum.

"Where does this tunnel lead?" he asked. Goddum closed his eyes to become one with the earth.

"It goes to North Africa," he said. "If nothing else gets in our way," he said as he opened his eyes, "we can cross the ocean to Scorpion, Manhattan."

Ginzolo butted in. "It sounds like a good plan," he said.

"Let the leader decide," he said. Mercutio looked at him. "Mercutio?"

He made the decision Sistro hoped he wouldn't.

"We'll go through the tunnel."

Sistro closed his eyes and took a deep breath.

"So be it."

And so the Chosen started into the forest of giant spikes to get the entrance of the Devil Cave Tunnel.

"These spikes are cold," said Ginzolo as he touched one. "That's because these spikes are rock ice," said Eviana.

"Rock ice?" repeated Mercutio.

"Yeah," Eviana said. "Rock ice gives an illusion that it's made of rock, but it's really ice, so don't touch anything, Merck." Mercutio swallowed and nodded in acceptance.

"Were almost there," said Goddum, using his power to be one with the earth.

"Then let's keep going before the windstorm comes back," said Mercutio. After another hour of walking through the Spike Forest, they came to the giant head entrance. There was a tongue connecting the entrance to the spike jungle. The only problem-underneath the bridge was a moat of black acid bubbling in heat.

"Well, that's something you don't see everyday," said Ginzolo.

"This is boiling acid," said Sistro. "Be very careful."

Sistro and Endstra crossed the bridge first. Eviana followed with haste. Ginzolo flew over the bridge with an ignorant grin on his face and his hands in his pockets. Goddum, because of his weight, also flew to the entrance. It was Mercutio's turn and for the first time, he was scared stiff.

Oh man, he thought. *I'm immortal and I <u>still</u> don't like this.* Goddum noticed him still at the bridge entryway.

"Hey, Merck!" he yelled. Mercutio looked at his friend. "You need some help, man?" Mercutio swallowed, then shook his head. "No," he said. "I'll be fine." Ginzolo shook his head in humor.

"Some leader," he said. "He can't even cross a *bridge* without chickening out."

"Shut your mouth, infidel," Sistro said. "At least Mercutio has enough courage to *walk* across the bridge."

Well, that shut Ginzolo's mouth. But as he was about to get on Goddum's case, he said, "The bridge wouldn't have sustained my weight. That's why *I* flew. You have no excuse."

Once again, Ginzolo was speechless. All of his attempts to humiliate Mercutio were washed down the drain. He folded his arms and watched Mercutio walk across the tongue-shaped bridge over a pool of bubbly hot acid.

Mercutio took his first step, trying to keep his balance. The bridge was spacey and sturdy, but he wasn't taking any chances. He didn't know why he was so scared. He was never afraid of bridges before. He only feared God and water and *this* was no water. Fear was in his face. Everything he thought he knew about courage leapt out of his now brittle body and dissolved in the acid.

His second step.

He huffed a sigh of relief as he continued his third.

Suddenly, a force pushed his legs to the left of the bridge. His feet slipped off but he grabbed the other end of the bridge.

His feet were in the acid.

"Mercutio!" Eviana cried as she ran to him. Mercutio slipped again in an attempt to return to the top and grabbed the edge of the tongue-like bridge.

His body from the waist down was in the acid.

Mercutio yelled painfully as the acid ate his legs and groin. The pain was unlike any he had felt before.

If Eviana did not grab his hand in time, he would've been completely dissolved.

Eviana pulled Mercutio back on the bridge. His entire lower body was gone. She pulled him into the entrance where the others were waiting. With his hands, Mercutio leaned against the inside cheek of the head entrance.

"How is everything?" Sistro asked Mercutio. He looked at his lower half as it started to quickly regenerate.

"I'll be fine," he said. He started to stand up.

"Thank you," he told her.

"You would've done the same for me."

"I would?"

Eviana smiled.

Suddenly the earth started to shake. The Chosen saw the rock ice burst into rubble with the force coming towards them.

"Time to go!" yelled Ginzolo. The force caught up to the head entrance. It split in half and closed the entrance. But while running, they fell through a giant hole and slid down with the rubble of the earthquake soon falling behind them.

"We have to move faster!" yelled Mercutio. *"Fly* down the chute!" Everyone, of course, listened and flew down, leaving the rocks and boulders behind them.

"I see a light!" yelled Endstra.

"Keep moving!" replied Mercutio. By the time they reached the light, they were thrown out of the chute and landed on the ground. Mercutio landed safely and helped everyone else up.

Unfortunately, the boulders caught up. There were so many, the wizards had to create a telepathic shield. Mercutio transformed to his second madrocellular transformation with the GF to increase the force fields power. When the spillage was over, the wizards broke their field and gazed at the wall of stones covering their only exit. Goddum tried to penetrate it.

"It's impossible to move!" he said surprisingly.

They were trapped in the Devil Cave Tunnel.

Chapter Four

Like a diamond in the sky was the doorway entrance to the actual tunnel. It was on the wall behind the heroes. It was at least six stories tall, and the only way to the entrance was a long stairway connected to the wall. It was on the right side of the wall on the right side of the cave.

"We now have one choice," said Sistro. "We must pass through the Devil Cave Tunnel."

Mercutio created a flame in his hand for sight.

"Be on your guard," said Mercutio. "Napoleon could be anywhere." The Chosen and the wizards started up the long stairway. Ginzolo was once again isolated and smiled at the rest of the group.

Goddum noticed and alerted Mercutio.

"Hey, Merck," said Goddum, "I think there's something wrong with Ginzolo."

"You just figured *that* out?"

"I'm serious, man," said Goddum. "I'm not psychic, but something tells me Ginzolo *wanted* us to come this way."

"Come on, Goddum," said Mercutio playfully. "Ginzolo's a lot of things, but he's not a traitor."

"Even though he may not be," interrupted Sistro, who was behind the two friends, "there is still something terribly wrong about him."

"What do think it is?" asked Mercutio.

"I don't know," said Sistro. "Only time will tell. But right now, we must attend to the situation at hand."

After climbing the murderous staircase, they were finally at the entrance of the tunnel. Mercutio looked at the doorway. It was an ancient black marble door with insignias and hieroglyphics.

"What's the language on the wall?" asked Eviana.

"It's a form of Lingu written in fire," he said.

"The Camenstrian people," said Sistro, "were the founders of this tunnel. It would only be right for them to leave their mark."

Mercutio quickly madrocellularly transformed his second form and read the text.

"Ti vios O' legadi vi copato," he said in Lingu. "Ti genista O' pioferia ivs forvadt to entracidu."

Mercutio was terrified the moment he finished the passage.

"What did it say?" said Eviana. Mercutio turned and faced everyone.

"The lives of tales are certain," he said. "The beginning of fire lies beyond these doors!"

"The GF!" gasped Endstra.

The doors opened.

Mercutio transformed to his third transformation, just in case there were any kind of danger. He was the first through the door. But what he saw bewildered him. The others came behind him. The sight stunned them.

The tunnel was gigantic. At least twenty times taller than the Chosen. It was made of black rock in a circular form. The tunnel appeared to have no end because it was pitch black to the normal eye. But the eye catcher was this;

the tunnel illuminated by diamonds, were connected to the walls, ground and the ceiling.

"It's beautiful," said Goddum. Sistro walked up front.

"Looks can be deceiving," he said.

"Stick together," said Mercutio. "A guy could get lost in a place like this."

Since the tunnel was so wide and long, the Chosen's trek was not even halfway in one day. The tunnel had twists. The scenery did not change. The sound of water from outside alerted them. They were in the ocean. For at least five days they were in the tunnel. It wasn't until the next day one of their biggest plots commensed.

It was five o' clock in the morning when Ginzolo awoke. Everyone else was asleep, including the wizards. He looked at everyone as they were sleeping, but spent most of his time gazing at Eviana. She was dead asleep as Ginzolo stroked her head. He felt her satin silk blonde hair and smiled at her radiant beauty.

"You're *sick*," said Mercutio without opening his eyes, "you know that?"

"How did you know I was awake?" he whispered.

"Well," Mercutio said, "I heard you wake up and wander around the place."

He opened his eyes and stared right into his face.

"Even smelled your morning breath."

Ginzolo showed no emotion. Those enhanced senses of his were really annoying him. He scowled at Mercutio as he sat up.

"Step away from Eviana," Mercutio said with a hand gesture.

Ginzolo stood still.

"Get away from her," he said louder as he stood up.

Ginzolo stood there, smiling.

At this time, Mercutio's voice awoke everyone. When Eviana awoke, Ginzolo grabbed and squeezed her neck.

"Ginzolo, what are you doing?" asked Sistro.

"Put her down, Ginzolo" said Mercutio.

"I told you something was wrong with him!" said Goddum.

"Yeah," replied Mercutio, "you're right. And I think I know what it is."

Ginzolo smiled and sniffed Eviana's hair. She was in tears, knowing he could easily kill her because of the elemental rule. Mercutio walked in front of Ginzolo with a stare he all too well remembered.

"Aren't *I* the one you want?" Mercutio asked. The others looked confused.

"I'm the one you're afraid of," he said. "Not Eviana."

"You really think I'm afraid of *you*?" Ginzolo said with a laugh. "Your *nothing* compared to *my* power!"

Sistro suddenly realized what happened to Ginzolo.

Mercutio used his third transformation and accessed the Kagi no Hiteshita.

"You think you're so smart, *don't* you?" Mercutio asked. "It was *you* who threw us off course with your Biokinesis to lead us to this tunnel."

"Ginzolo doesn't have Biokinesis…" Goddum whispered to himself.

"You probably made that windstorm and made me fall off the bridge," Mercutio continued.

Goddum shook his head in confusion. "He can't do *any* of that," he said.

"And after you trapped us here, you would finish us off - one by one." Mercutio frowned.

"Isn't that right, *Napoleon?!*"

"Of course!" said Endstra. Sistro smiled at Mercutio's confirmation.

"But how?" asked Goddum.

"I don't know," answered Mercutio, "but I think it happened in Camenstra during the fight."

Ginzolo laughed. "I'm surprised," he said. Then he grinned evilly.

"I'm surprised you didn't figure it out sooner."

Mercutio's Hawk face didn't show any emotion.

"Let her go, Napoleon."

Ginzolo threw Eviana to the ground. He then folded his arms.

"I threw a gray blade in his belly and made him think it was to kill him so he could gain the initiative," he said. "What the blade *really* did was make an opening for me to enter and possess his body whenever I wanted."

He smiled.

"I decided to let him think he won the fight before I took over."

Ginzolo punched the level three Mercutio to the nearby wall with Goddum's strength. Mercutio quickly regrouped.

"Let me see how far this body can go before I leave it!"

Napoleon pushed Ginzolo's body from madrocellular transformation level one to level two in mere seconds.

The sight was mesmerizing.

Ginzolo had on white cotton pants, yellow socks and yellow Japanese sandals. He had a long yellow silken Japanese robe-the sleeves extended to his knees. He had a white silken ribbon around his neck and waist. A yellow square hat tilted over his forehead and two yellow ribbons hanging around and from the sides. An aurora of yellow light glowed over him with shocks of lightning around him. Ginzolo looked at himself and shrugged his shoulders.

"Acceptable," he said.

Mercutio raised his Kagi no Hiteshita and attacked Ginzolo's body in full force. Ginzolo's new strength along with Napoleon controlling him made him just as powerful as Mercutio's level transformation *with* the GF. Mercutio swung the key, knowing Ginzolo's body would dodge every swing. He knew Napoleon would tire at a certain point. He tried to get him to his resting point early. Mercutio got him to his tired point; he kicked him in his ribs and sent him flying to the rock.

Mercutio's GF in his level three transformation gave him strength that matched Goddum's first transformation.

That's enough strength to move *mountains.*

He was stuck to the wall, until Napoleon used his strength to burst out of it. Ginzolo took out a yellow whip that crackled electricity; he whipped it around Mercutio's right hand. The end of the whip turned into a cobra head. It showed its purple fangs contained of black venom.

"Hito blades!" said Sistro.

The snake was about to bite his right arm. Mercutio grabbed and pulled it off him. While the snake was still in the air, Mercutio shot a red ray from each eye. It burst into flames.

"Is that the best you got?"

Ginzolo ran around Mercutio with both his *and* Napoleon's speed combined! Mercutio couldn't keep up. Ginzolo punched and kicked Mercutio fifty times faster than the speed of light. Eviana and Sistro felt his pain every 0.01 second. Suddenly, Ginzolo stopped in the kicking position, but Mercutio was nowhere to be seen. Goddum looked on the ground and saw a very deep ditch line at least five feet deeper than the tunnel underwater. Mercutio was at the end, buried in the rocks and diamonds. Ginzolo's kick was fast, Mercutio was kicked back two yards before the others could blink.

"Pathetic," Ginzolo said.

Eviana suddenly performed her level one madrocellular transformation and flew towards Ginzolo. Napoleon was too busy gloating over his victory in Ginzolo's body that he didn't see the waterfall-sized blast Eviana sent out. It took Ginzolo's body to the nearest wall and continued to pound on him until there was nothing left.

"Get Mercutio," she said. "Hurry! Before he regenerates!"

Goddum also transformed while flying to Mercutio. When he got there, he sucked all of the rocks and diamonds off him through his left palm. He grabbed Mercutio - who was knocked out but still in his level three transformation - by his back and leg joints and took him to the others.

Ginzolo's body regenerated as soon as Goddum came back. Napoleon was completely in control this time. He saw Goddum nurture Mercutio to health.

Eviana stood in front of them.

"You want 'em?" she said. "Come get 'em."

Napoleon smirked.

"Lucky for me," he said, "I'm no gentleman!"

Napoleon made Ginzolo's left hand grab a weapon in his robes. It was a samurai sword of some sort. He swung it at her, but she ducked and tripped him with her Hydroscepter. He attempted to stab her five times, but missed. The sixth attempt she flipped over him; stabbing him with the blade of the Hydroscepter. Mercutio woke up and saw Goddum in his level one transformation.

"Where's Eviana?"

"She's fighting Napoleon."

Mercutio stood and walked towards the two fighters.

Ginzolo raced around Eviana until she flew upwards and froze the ground around him. He slipped, bounced off the walls so fast, the tunnel started to shake. He caught himself and faced Eviana.

Mercutio was behind him with a glowing red right hand.

Ginzolo blew Eviana a kiss.

She was angry, now.

With both hands, she formed one of her most powerful attacks yet.

"Tsunami…" she said as her hands glowed blue, "Wave!" A giant blast of water formed at least half the size of the tunnel. Ginzolo smiled as he saw the wave head toward him. Mercutio was about to shoot the Particle Lava Blast with the aid of his glowing right hand so the water could cool with the lava, trapping Ginzolo inside.

Ginzolo *knew* Mercutio was behind him.

With the water at least five inches in front of him, he moved with the combined speed of himself and Napoleon's. As Mercutio's tip of the Kagi no Hiteshita started to glow, he noticed Ginzolo vanished.

Unfortunately, he noticed it right before the water hit him full force.

"No!" yelled Goddum. He looked at Ginzolo, who had his back turned to him. Goddum punched and a line of rocks formed in the air. When Ginzolo turned around, the line of rocks had formed a sledge hammered top and knocked him at least fifty feet further into the tunnel.

"Bastard!" he yelled.

Eviana was in shock. She looked at her hands.

How did this happen, she thought. Suddenly, she heard breath on her neck.

Eviana took Ginzolo's neck and threw him over her on the ground face first. He got up and the bruises on his face - of course - rejuvenated. He walked backwards and suddenly stopped.

"I think I had my fun in this body for long enough," he said. He closed his eyes. Ginzolo's body started shaking. Ginzolo's eyes suddenly opened. His pupils were black and bigger. It looked like he was in pain. He yelled painfully when this black gas suddenly was ejected from his body. The gas formed into a black skeleton.

Ginzolo fell on the floor, unconscious.

The skeleton stood still, then turned its head to Eviana. It walked toward her and its organs started to form, along with inner tissue. The incomplete body touched her face with its hand.

"Say hello to Mercutio for me," it said, "if he ever wakes up."

The body then developed skin and clothes.

"Napoleon," said Eviana, "touch me again, and you'd wish you *were* mortal!"

He ran down the tunnel in Ginzolo's speed.

He ran where they had to go.

Eviana picked up Ginzolo, who was still unconscious, and flew to Goddum. They flew to where Eviana accidentally blasted Mercutio. Sistro and Endstra were next to his body. Sistro saw the two come towards them.

"How's Ginzolo?" asked Endstra.

"He's alive," said Goddum. "He's just unconscious." Eviana gasped at the sight of Mercutio's body.

He in regular form was wrinkled from the water, cold and barely breathing.

"I don't know how long he can live," said Sistro, devastated. "We need to find a source of fire; otherwise his soul could leave any moment."

Eviana put Ginzolo's body down and went to Mercutio. His rich black skin he once had started to fade.

"I'm so sorry," she said to him. Tears ran down her face. She held his cold, wet hand and put her free one on her chest.

"Forgive me," she said. Sistro was crying. He looked at Ginzolo, and at an instant, he broke out of his coma.

Ginzolo opened his eyes.

"What happened?" he asked as he stood up. He looked around the tunnel.

"Where are we?"

"Napoleon possessed your body and lured us to this place," said Goddum. "It's called the Devil Cave Tunnel."

Ginzolo looked at his clothes. They were different.

"I transformed?" he said with gladness.

"Napoleon pushed your body to your second madrocellular transformation," said Sistro. "But, unfortunately, as you can see, he through you made Eviana attack Mercutio with a very powerful water attack." He showed Mercutio's body to Ginzolo.

"Unless we get him to a source of fire," he said, "he will likewise perish."

Ginzolo looked at his half dead body, then smirked.

"I never liked him, *anyway*."

That was the last straw for Sistro. He stood up, took his staff and swung it like a baseball bat. He hit Ginzolo's knees, which sent him spinning into he air, then kicked him while *still* in the air.

Even in his second transformation, Sistro was way too strong for Ginzolo to handle.

"Keep your tongue in your mouth, you leech!" he yelled at him. "By the time we get out of here, you will learn to respect this man as leader and as *family!*" As Ginzolo stood up, his anger and hatred for Mercutio and Sistro overfilled in his cup. But he realized that in order to get to Mascool, he must listen to his leaders.

Even if he wasn't one of them.

"There's a way to start a fire," said Goddum as he pulled a leaf from his back pocket.

"Where did you find that?" he asked.

"I found it in the sewerway," Goddum said. "Something told me we might need it."

"That was the Lord's voice," Sistro replied. He looked at Mercutio. "He knew this would happen."

"What does a leaf have to do with starting a fire?" asked Ginzolo, walking back to the rest of the group.

"Like paper," said Goddum, "leaves are flammable. Anything can produce fire can make this catch on fire if it's close enough."

"But what can we use to produce a fire?" asked Endstra.

"The same thing that starts God-made forests fires," said Eviana.

Everyone turned to Ginzolo.

He sighed.

"Electricity," he said depressingly.

"Listen," said Goddum as he stood up. "I don't care if you don't like Mercutio. I don't even care if you don't like anyone in this tunnel besides Eviana. But if you're ever going to avenge your friends death," he said while pointing in his face, "you're gonna have to do things you don't like."

"Goddum's right," said Sistro. "Mercutio is your brother, let alone your leader." He started to walk toward him. "You must learn to trust, for that is the meaning of family." Ginzolo put his hands on his hips.

"Since when did *I* become the bad guy?" he asked. "You expect me to save the life of someone who never gave a damn about me?!"

"Because you never gave a damn about *him!*" Goddum yelled. "You ever heard of the Golden Rule?!"

Goddum was angry. His best friend was about to die and the only person who could save his life wouldn't even volunteer.

Ginzolo thought about what Goddum said. He was right. He couldn't get to Mascool without Mercutio.

"I can't here," he said. "We need to get further into the tunnel."

Goddum nodded. "Understood," he said. He picked up Mercutio and put him over his left shoulder. Sistro and Endstra walked towards the Chosen.

"Then lets go," said Sistro. As they walked, Endstra said, "Be careful. Napoleon could be anywhere."

Yamalu was outside. The stench of slaves and work filled the air. He saw his statues around his tower in perfect alignment. He heard screams of helpless mortals about to die because of rebellion and disobedience.

He loved it.

<Father. >

It was Napoleon.

It was his son.

"Are you out of that 'Ginzolo' person?" he asked.

<I was able to use him to lead the Chosen to the tunnel. >

"How are they?"

<Their leader is down, > he said with a chuckle. <The water girl sprayed Mercutio with a giant water attack by mistake. He could die at any moment. >

Yamalu smiled at the good news. "Good work," he said. "One down and three to go."

<Exactly. >

"What about the wizards?" he asked. "Are they still alive?"

<Mercutio found out my identity before I could get to them. >

Yamalu closed his eyes in disappointment. "Just make sure you kill them," he said.

"And start with Endstra."

<Yes, father. >

The tunnel was dark.

Pitch black.

Not even Sistro's *light* could penetrate it.

They stopped and rested. Goddum put down Mercutio. Sistro looked at his staff.

"I hope this works," he whispered. He bounced his staff. And for the first time after entering the dark tunnel, Sistro's staff finally penetrated the darkness. They were near the entrance of a shrine made of black granite and diamond veins. It was suspended with chains.

Under it was an eternal fall.

Goddum created a rock and threw it over the cliff. He waited, waited, and waited.

Not a sound came from the rock.

"Forget it, Goddum," said Sistro. "That fall is endless. The rock will never reach the ground." Sistro put his hands behind his back.

"We shall rest here."

Ginzolo nervously looked at Mercutio. He paced back and fourth trying to make up his mind.

Save his life or let him die?

"I believe you have a job to do," said Goddum. Ginzolo looked at Goddum's emotionless face.

Goddum handed him the leaf.

As Ginzolo reached for it, his hand was shaking. When it was near, Ginzolo sent a medium-sized shock.

The leaf caught fire.

Goddum released a sigh of relief. He carried the torched leaf, placed it on Mercutio's chest and closed his eyes.

"Let's just hope were not too late."

Where am I? I had *no* idea where I was. It looked like I was in my third transformation. It was black all over. I couldn't see a thing. As I created a fireball in my right palm, I saw a wall. It had some kind of writing on it. As I felt it with my left, my body started to feel cold. I increased the light and saw a door with the Demaric symbol of fire on it. I looked under it and saw the symbols of water, earth, and lightning. All four of them were different in this weird way.

All of them had a gazing pair of eyes.

I felt the fire symbol and the eyes glowed red. Suddenly, the door opened to reveal this white light.

I was blinded by its shine.

I don't remember what happened next, but I opened my eyes to a remarkable sight.

Sunlight!

I saw natural sunlight! I haven't seen this since I was in Cotendra. The sun showing, the sky blue.

It was *blue!*

I saw clouds and felt heat down my back. I was standing on fresh green grass and saw a building of gigantic proportions.

The temple was of Greek descent with a mixture of ancient Egyptian. There were two pillars next to the entrance, and there was a pathway made of stunning black gold where I was standing. As I walked toward the temple, I started to feel something strange. When I entered it, my powers – fully regenerated.

The doors of the temple slammed shut.

I didn't care, unbelievingly. I just kept walking. Torches on the walls lightened the tunnel. The walls - a light brown – were aged to perfection. As I felt them with my right hand, I saw a ghostly appearance of Eviana floating around me. She touched me with those perfect hands.

"*I love you,*" she whispered in my ear. I closed my eyes in joy. I opened them. I was in this ballroom. Eviana was standing right there. She had on a stunning blue dress. I was in this red and black suit. It almost matched my medallion and Hikulo.

A song play from the early Twentieth Century called "Life is But a Dream".

We started to dance.

With my right hand, I gently put it around her waist.

"You look beautiful," I said. Eviana smirked.

"I never heard *those* words come out from that mouth before."

"You want to hear some more?" I said with a grin. Eviana chuckled and put her head on my left shoulder.

"I'm sorry, Merck," she said as she let out her breath. "I didn't know you were behind Ginzolo."

I put my left hand on her beautiful head of blonde hair.

"It's okay," I whispered to her. "I needed a bath, anyway." Eviana smiled, then chuckled. She wrapped her arms around my waist. "I'm just thankful I'm still alive."

Eviana held her head up to look at me.

"*I love you,*" she whispered. Even though I heard her say that a few moments ago, I still was touched. As the song was about to end, we snuck in one last kiss.

Suddenly, I was back in the hallway in my third transformation. I had no idea whether I was headed to the door or further into the tunnel. I used my enhanced sight to check the ways. The door was in front of me, so I headed the other way. After about thirty seconds, I saw a double-hinged door of red gold. It had the Demaric symbol of fire with gazing eyes.

But that was the only symbol.

I pushed it open. I was in a giant shrine room. It was ancient Egyptian, complete with giant statues of birds and tomb guardians. They were as high as the tombs twenty-five foot ceiling. In the middle of the tomb, a small pool of gasoline. Two stand-up torches were on each side of the table-sized bowl full of the gas. The walls were of hieroglyphs and Lingu writing.

I walked and looked around the room. The Egyptian translation was "Look no further. The beginning of fire is within your grasp."

I heard a bird screech.

I turned around; I saw a statue behind the bowl of gasoline I did not see before.

It was a replica of the Fox Phoenix!

Its wings were opened; its talon feet were firmly planted on the ground and its head over the bowl. It was made from regular and red gold, but the eyes looked as if they were made of black diamonds.

I started on my way to the bowl of gasoline and looked at it. I stared at the Fox Phoenix's eyes. I took my attention off the statue and looked at one of the torches. I took the torch on my right, picked it up and put it in the gas.

It put the fire out.

"Weird," I said. I put the pole back. I looked at my hands. The Demaric symbol of fire suddenly appeared on them.

"The beginning of fire is within your *grasp*," I whispered. I stepped back and put out my left hand.

"Well," I said, "here we go." I sprayed fire from my fingertips on the gasoline. The gasoline was ignited. A giant flame waved back and forth under the head of the Fox Phoenix statue.

As soon as I held out my hands, it glowed red. The flame rose with my hands. I thought, smiled and sent the fireball colliding with the statue. It broke into hundreds of pieces, but that wasn't it. It turned out the statue was hiding an entrance to a bigger temple. It was dark. A line of fire on the floors was its only source of light. The wall across from me had the same Demaric symbol in a fluorescent red.

I smiled when I found out where this was going.

"What's the point of bringing me here, Marblus?"

Marblus appeared from the ground as shadows in front of me, like Mascool appeared in the sewerway.

"You are too wise for me," he said. "You have definitely grown mentally and physically."

"Cut the crap," I said seriously. "Why am I here?"

"To show you your *true* power," he said. "This temple is the shrine of the Spirit of Fire."

"What does this have to do with me?"

"There is an artifact in here that you need to further your abilities."

I chuckled. "I have too many already, thank you." As I was about to head the other way, he said,

"An artifact to summon one of the most ferocious fire beings on earth next to the Fox Phoenix."

I faced him again.

"What is it?"

"Ti Strongata Ghorita O' Pioferia; the Mighty Spirit of Fire. It's the strongest fire being next to the Fox Phoenix."

I was intrigued by this offer.

"Sistro said in order to unlock the GF's full potential, you need the help of fire creatures."

"Are you trying to bribe me?"

"Of course not, Mercutio." I looked at him suspiciously. "All I want in return is your *medallion*." He opened his right hand. It was red with sharpened fingers. His palm was pitch-black with imprinted tattoos.

"Let me see the artifact."

"As you wish," he said. Suddenly a wind came. His body turned to dust.

He's such a showoff.

There was a staircase in front of me that lead to the artifact. Even with my enhanced vision, I couldn't see the top. As I walked up an endless flight of stairs, I could only wish this were worth the walk. I finally reached the top. I saw it. The sphere made of ruby. The Demarican symbol was on the front of it outlined in twenty-four karat gold. Next to the artifact were two stand-up torch lights, much like the ones in the shrine I had just seen moments ago.

"So," I said, "the artifact that holds possession to the Spirit of Fire."

I sensed Marblus behind me.

"Yes, it is," he said. "There are two ways to use this element spirit. You can either fuse with it to create your fourth transformation, or use the spirits real form. If you do, only you will it listen to. You will be the only one to understand it when it speaks."

"Is it possible for me to use it both ways at the same time?"

"You control the Fox Phoenix," replied Marblus. "For you, *anything* is possible."

"I guess you're right," I said with a sigh.

"So," he said as he once again held out his Demaric hand. "Do we have a bargain?"

This was going to be tough. Give up my medallion for the strongest fire spirit next to the Fox Phoenix. But, I knew what to do.

I put my right hand in my pocket, then looked at Marblus. I snatched the medallion off my neck and put it in his hand. Marblus closed it. His long sleeve covered his hand as he lowered it. I picked up the giant ruby.

"Congratulations," was all I heard. Marblus was gone.

I used my senses of sight, sound and smell to ensure me Marblus was really gone. I grabbed my *real* medallion out of my right pocket and put it around my neck. I held the ruby with both hands and uttered something in Lingu.

"Strongata Ghorita O' Pioferia," I said, "uma togu ti Filibu Dogama ne zi ka xa isulu nepapu siblarita!"

Suddenly, the giant ruby glowed. It glowed brighter and brighter until it started to crack. Since I was in my third transformation I had hawk eyes; I wasn't blinded by the light. The ruby started to shake as it glowed even brighter and the crack started expanding. Then a red ribbon-like flow of energy started to flow around me.

I could tell what I had said was working.

"Togu isulu!" I yelled. "Nikae so ti ka zoe maxi ti stregou of caribu noe ot ti realiku zonita!" The ruby burst into thousands of pieces and out came a giant blast of fire at least ten times bigger than I.

The flame formed into the Mighty Spirit of Fire.

I heard elemental spirits either took the form of the element or an animal that represents the element.

The spirit was in elemental form.

It was like a wave of fire forming in front of me. Suddenly out of the wave came two arms. The hands were claw-like, which wasn't surprising to me. The flames were shaped like an eleven-foot man, but what looked like the head remained a wild flame. It wasn't until it opened its red eyes that I felt his power.

"Who are you," he said even though he had no mouth, "to wake me from my slumber?"

"I am Mercutio," I said, "the leader of the Chosen and possessor of the fire element. I have summoned you for a great importance."

"And what importance is that?"

"Join me and fuse with my powers," I said, "so I can lead the Chosen to victory!" The spirit looked at my handprints and nodded.

"I sense your powers are mixed with the Fox Phoenix. I have no choice but to serve you."

"Very well, then," I said. I once thought the Fox Phoenix was the only power source I was supposed to have. When I first saw the Mighty Spirit of Fire, I felt no emotion.

Just his power.

This spirit with the GF will make me even *more* powerful. I pulled out the Kagi no Hiteshita and pointed the tip at him.

"I accept you, Mighty Spirit of Fire!"

The red ribbon-like flows of energy first came out of his eyes and entered the tip of my sword. By the time *that* flow of energy was finished, a dead silence was in that temple for at least one second. Suddenly, the spirit burst into flames and moved all around the temple like an out of control comet. Then as it came towards me, I grasped my sword with both hands to get ready for impact.

The flame hit me like a ray of light. The fire was on the other side of the temple. It stretched over to me. As I gathered the flames in the Key of Magical Fire, I felt like I was a mortal falling into the earth's atmosphere and surviving! The pressure of the power was hard to fight but I held my ground. I felt the spirits power inside me as it was fusing with the GF.

"Yes!" I yelled. "This is it! I have the beginning of fire!" As the last of the fire entered the sword, a sound explosion came from the key. From the sound explosion came a white light that started at the entrance of the temple. When it came to me, not only was it blinding, but also I was blasted through the wall behind me. As I was flying backwards going only God knows where, I felt my heart beat.

It hurt.

Then it beat again, and again, and again. It hurt so much I grabbed my chest; I screamed so loud, it could have destroyed the world.

Mercutio opened his eyes.

"He's alive!" Goddum yelled. "He's alive!"

Sistro was relieved to hear the news, but he sensed something was not right.

"Get away from him," he said. "Now!" The others moved out of his way, Mercutio uttered grunts and jerked his body at random times. Even though Mercutio was alive, this was definitely not normal.

Suddenly Mercutio rose in the air in the horizontal position. Goddum was shocked. So was Ginzolo. Eviana was worried, but Sistro smiled.

He knew what was happening to Mercutio.

Mercutio started to shiver spontaneously to replace the random jerks. Soon he was yelling an "ah" sound.

"What's happening?" asked Eviana. Sistro looked at her with a grin on his face.

"The GF has fused with another power of fire," he said. "He is about to perform his fourth madrocellular transformation!"

Mercutio's body was set on fire from the leaf. Even though he was shivering, he reacted to the heat. The fire covered his body and he started spinning. He spun faster, and faster, and faster until all you could see was a blur of red and yellow light. It grew brighter, and brighter, and brighter until it blinded everyone who was watching. It even blinded Endstra.

When it suddenly stopped, Mercutio was in his fourth madrocellular transformation.

He floated in the air with his arms open. He had the Demaric ritual mask of the Fire Lord on his upper head. His black shirt had the insignia of the Fox Phoenix with two red eyes surrounding the tail. He had his bright red dress pants, but wore a red Demaric robe. It had slits in the elbow joints to show wisdom and extended sleeves on the bottom to show power and spirituality.

Sistro smirked. "May I present to you, Ti Pioferia Loridos," he said. "The Fire God."

Mercutio looked at himself. His palms had the Demarican symbol of fire. He felt the mask on his face and the extended sleeves on his robe. As he realized what happened, he smiled.

"It worked," he whispered. He looked at the others, who were on his immediate right. Goddum was glad to see Mercutio alive and so was Eviana. Sistro and Endstra watched him.

Mercutio lowered himself to the ground and smirked.

"Hey."

Eviana couldn't take it anymore. She ran toward Mercutio, grabbed him around the waist and laid her head on his chest. He rested his head on the top of hers.

She burst into tears.

"I'm sorry, Merck," she said as she cried. "I didn't know you were behind Ginzolo."

He put his left hand on her beautiful head of blonde hair.

"It's okay," he whispered to her. "I needed a bath, anyway."

Eviana smiled and came out of her depression. Mercutio smiled.

"I'm just thankful I'm still alive."

He paused. Something was wrong.

Didn't this conversation happen in his dream?

Goddum walked to the couple. "We thought we lost you!" he said.

"Are you *crying,* man?"

Goddum felt his face and wiped the tear away. "No, no," he said, "of course not. You know how I am."

Mercutio smiled. "Yeah, you're right," he said. Goddum gave Mercutio a brotherly hug and cried.

"I love you, man!" the heart-filled Goddum said. Sistro was also crying. Endstra smirked. As they went toward him, Sistro let out a sigh of relief and smiled.

"Welcome back to the land of the living!" said Endstra as he prepared to hug Mercutio. Sistro put his right hand on Mercutio's left shoulder. Mercutio put his hand on his.

"There's something about Marblus that is very dark-sided," he told Sistro. Sistro's smile slowly turned into a stone silent serious face.

"What happened?"

"When he showed me where the power of the Mighty Spirit of Fire was, he asked for my medallion in exchange." Sistro was shocked.

Endstra wasn't surprised.

"I knew he couldn't be trustworthy," he said out loud.

"Why would he want your medallion?" asked Eviana.

"I don't know," said Mercutio. "I gave him a fake one, though. I don't know if he found out if it was a fake yet."

"Only the Chosen," said Sistro, "can use the medallions. Which brings up the question why did Marblus want your medallion? He gave them to me to give to *you*."

"We can't answer that question right now," said Endstra. We have to keep moving. The only reason we stopped was to revive Mercutio."

"Endstra's right," said Mercutio, "we have to keep going. Like I said before; Napoleon could be anywhere."

Sistro nodded. Even though Marblus' possible treachery disturbed him, he couldn't let this show on his infinite list of burdens.

"I agree," he said with the same nervous stature he had about Mercutio's mother.

Mercutio looked at the temple. "Where does this lead to?" he asked.

"Possibly, to Hell," Endstra said. "We've been everywhere else, so I wouldn't be surprised if it did."

Sistro smiled at his brother's sarcasm.

"It leads to the second half of the tunnel," he said.

"Second?" said Ginzolo. "It feels like we've been through this thing five times already!"

"That's one of the reasons Napoleon lead us here in the first place," said Mercutio. "If this is the entrance to the rest of the tunnel, then let's go." Goddum and Ginzolo nodded. Eviana stood next to her man. Sistro and Endstra stood behind him.

They walked into the temple.

Down at the Scorpion's Lair, Mascool led Yamalu to the chamber where the army was waiting. But before they entered, Yamalu stopped Mascool.

"Now I said any Trimal force we can afford to get rid of," he said. "What group are you sending over there?"

Mascool smiled. "During their births," he said, "there was more than expected."

Mascool opened the door.

What was shown was amazingly terrifying. Yamalu, Mascool and *Napoleon* put together couldn't figure out how this mistake happened.

There were at least twenty-five thousand tiger Trimals below, roaring, snarling, and almost fighting each other. They were so overfilled with energy.

"How did this happen?" Yamalu said with an amazed sound.

"During the process," said Mascool, "the tigers were impregnated. They produced five times as many pregnancies than the first time."

"How many did each tiger produce?"

"Fifty cubs per tiger."

"How many were there?"

"Five hundred," said Mascool. "I forced the cubs to mate as soon as they hit puberty through shock treatments."

"Send half of this army into the tunnel," he said. "Send the others to the tunnel exit."

Mascool bowed. "Yes, my lord." He went through the blast-proof doors. Yamalu looked at his massive army and grinned.

"Their days are numbered."

"Sistro!" yelled Mercutio. "Ginzolo! Endstra! Where are you?!" Eviana walked towards Mercutio.

"They're not over there," she said.

"Not over here, either," said.

"How did they get lost in the first place?"

"It must be when we were around the first part of the temple," replied Mercutio. "This is a very good place to get lost in. I told you that."

Soon, Eviana started to see an exit from the temple.

"Hey, Merck," said Eviana.

"What do you see?" he asked.

She shook her head. "I thought I saw an exit," she said, "but I can't see it now. It's too dark."

Mercutio put his hand in front of them and a fireball at least three times as big as Mercutio's fist formed.

"Better?" he asked playfully. Eviana laughed as she nodded her head. The light from the fireball illuminated the hallway.

Goddum went to Mercutio and Eviana.

"Did you find them?" he asked.

"No," said Mercutio, "but we found an exit."

The door was the same as it was in his dream.

Double-hinged doors. Red gold. Demaric symbols of the Chosen's elements.

This was *not* coincidence.

Mercutio looked at the imprints of the symbols on his hands. He knew his dream was related to reality; otherwise he wouldn't be in his fourth transformation.

Let alone alive.

The three Chosen walked to the door. Mercutio raised the fireball up over his head with his telekinetic ability. As he grabbed the handles to the doors, he looked at Eviana. Then Goddum. He looked at the door again, and pushed them.

They wouldn't open.

"Let me try," said Goddum. He grabbed the handles and attempted to push the doors open.

Nothing.

He attempted to push them open again.

Nothing.

"Oh, come on," said Eviana. "Anybody knows that you have to *pull* these doors open." She went to the doors to pull them open.

Nothing.

"Any more ideas?" asked Goddum sarcastically. Mercutio didn't understand. The door opened perfectly in his dream.

What was he missing?

Suddenly, he got an idea.

"Transform," he said.

"Why?" asked Goddum.

Eviana knew what Mercutio was saying. "If we send our strongest blasts of energy," she said, "we might be able to open the doors."

Mercutio nodded. "Something told me you were a genius," he said.

"Well, I try."

"Okay," said Goddum, "let's try it." Goddum and Eviana transformed into their first madrocellular transformation. The trio put up their left-hand palm up and their right directly behind it.

"Ready?" Mercutio asked. Each responded by nodding their heads. Mercutio looked at the door.

"Fire!"

Beams of light blue, brown and red hit the door with the red beam in the middle and the blue one on the red beams left. The brown one was on the right. Mercutio, Goddum and Eviana couldn't even make the doors twitch.

"Put more strength into it!" yelled Mercutio. "Give it all you have!"

At the same time, the three beams increased in dramatic size, with the red one being the biggest.

The doors wobbled.

"It's not working!" Eviana yelled. Mercutio suddenly got another idea.

"Goddum! Eviana!" he yelled. "Cross your beams into mine!"

"Are you sure?!" Goddum loudly asked.

"Yes!" yelled Mercutio. "Do it! Do it *now!*"

Goddum and Eviana crossed into Mercutio's red beam, and suddenly the beam grew as big as the door.

"One…" said Mercutio as the doors waved back and forth.

"Two…" said Goddum as the sweat from his furred head rolled down his cheek.

"Three!" yelled Eviana.

"Now!" yelled Mercutio. Eviana, Mercutio and Goddum added a stampeding force of power to the beam. The hallway-sized beam was too overwhelming for the doors perfect lock.

The doors were blasted off the hinges.

The three exhausted Chosen stopped blasting and rested. Mercutio looked at Eviana.

"You all right?" He asked her.

"What?" she said. "Just because I'm a woman means you have to check on me?"

"I knew you were fine," he said. "It's just human nature."

Eviana smiled. "Thanks for asking." Mercutio chuckled.

Goddum rolled his eyes. "Yeah, I'm fine, too!" he said playfully. Mercutio looked at his best friend.

"Goddum, I didn't know you needed attention," he said. "I thought that was below you."

"Yeah," he said as he transformed back. "But it wouldn't hurt once in a while." Mercutio laughed. Then suddenly, Goddum and Eviana started to glow. Goddum glowed brown and Eviana light blue. They glowed for at least seven seconds, and when it stopped, Goddum and Eviana were in their second madrocellular transformations!

Eviana was in an outfit worn in the Amazon Clan. A blue cloth wrapped her breasts and tied around her back. She had a long skirt that was split in four areas. She had her hair in a ponytail and blue Atlantacorian tattoos on her face cheeks and around her navel. In her left hand, a water-like sword that somewhat resembled Mercutio's Hikulo. And to top it all off, her physique was better than her first transformation!

"What're you looking at?" said Eviana to Mercutio, who was staring and admiring her physique.

"Nothing! Nothing. Why do you ask?"

Eviana laughed. Mercutio joined in. He turned around and saw a miraculous sight. Even Eviana stopped laughing.

Goddum's second madrocellular transformation was an Elephant!

Goddum kept his muscular physique, but his body was at least two times bigger than his regular size. His tusks and ears were pierced, like his first transformation. Of course, his body was upright, but even though he had hooves for hands, they still looked very powerful. He had on a sleeveless robe that was multicolored with gold trimmings. On the top of his head, right between his ears, was a beaded headpiece with different colored beads that matched his robe.

This was one of the most fascinating animal madrocellular transformations next to Mercutio's first.

"Wow," was the response from Eviana and Mercutio's mouths.

"Is that all you have to say?" said Goddum.

"I fold," said Eviana. She put both weapons in one hand and raised the empty one. Mercutio chuckled.

"Do you think your strength increased?" he asked. Goddum created a medium-sized boulder and threw it at the wall next to him. The boulder blasted through all of the walls and was able to dig at least fifty miles as soon as it hit the wall of the main tunnel. Mercutio and Eviana looked through the hole it made in the walls. Eviana nodded her head.

"Impressive," she said.

"Well," said Goddum trying to show off his physique, "what do you think?"

"I think you have a lot of growing to do before you try to show a sign of arrogance, Goddum, possessor of Biokinesis," said a familiar voice.

"Who said that?" asked Goddum panicking.

"It sounded like Sistro," said Mercutio.

Eviana looked at the entrance the doors were blasted off of.

"I think it came from in here," she said.

"Of course it came from in here. That's where we've *been!*"

Endstra and Ginzolo came out after getting the okay from Sistro.

"How'd you get in there?" said Mercutio with a confused look on his face.

"We fell through a trap door following you," said Ginzolo. "It took us to this room-"

"That lead to the exit," continued Endstra. "We knew you would find us. That's why we stayed."

"Besides," said Sistro, "we didn't want to *leave* you."

Mercutio walked towards Sistro.

"Where's the exit?" he asked. Sistro pointed at the carved out exit port.

"This doorway," he said, "leads back to the tunnel if we head southwest."

Mercutio nodded. He looked at Eviana, Goddum and Ginzolo, in *his* second transformation.

"If that door's the exit, then that's where we'll go."

So the Chosen left the shrine, unknowing about Yamalu or Napoleon's next trick.

Sistro and Mercutio gazed at the new point of the tunnel. It was confusing to find it like this.

The tunnel was split into two entryways.

"There always has to be something..." said Mercutio as he shook his head.

"It wouldn't be an adventure if it weren't," said Sistro. Sistro and Mercutio turned to face the others.

"It looks like we have a dilemma on our hands," said Mercutio. "One of these tunnels leads to the exit in North Africa. The other tunnel may trap us in here forever."

He looked at Goddum.

After a few seconds of meditation, he shook his head.

"I can't tell which leads to the exit," he said, "but one *is* a trap."

Ginzolo sighed. "So you mean to tell me," he said, "that we'll be stuck here forever if we take the wrong tunnel?!"

"It doesn't get any better than this," said Endstra. "How will we know which tunnels the right one?"

"There's only one way." He turned his head away and looked at them serious.

"We have to split up."

"What?!" yelled Sistro. "We can't split up! None of us can stand a *chance* if we're separated!"

"If we *all* go down the *wrong* tunnel, we'll *never* get to Manhattan!" Mercutio yelled back. "At least *two* of us will make it out of here!"

Sistro was furious. He stepped forward and angrily stared at him.

"You almost *died* in this God-forsaken place!" he said.

"But this isn't about *me!*" replied Mercutio. "We have to get out of here one way or another!"

Sistro knew he was right. After all, he *was* the leader. Mercutio faced the others. He transformed into his regular form and pulled out Hikulo.

"Here's how we will be splitting up," said Mercutio. "There will be a wizard for every two of us. That means two Chosen and a wizard. Who wants to go with Sistro?" Goddum and Ginzolo raised their hands quickly. Then they walked toward him as Eviana closed her eyes in relief. Mercutio sighed with the same impression.

"Well," he said, "I guess were together again."

Endstra looked at the two and shook his head.

"So," Sistro said as he interrupted. "Which tunnel shall each party take?"

"My party will take the one on the left," replied Mercutio. "Yours can take the right one." Sistro nodded. A tear fell from his right eye.

"Are you all right?" asked Mercutio. Sistro wiped away the tear. "Yes," he said, "I'm fine." Mercutio looked at the Chosen and walked towards them.

"Remember," he said as he looked at each of them. "We are not a fellowship."

He put his left hand in front of them.

"We are family."

Eviana put her hand on Mercutio's.

"Family," she said.

Goddum put his hand on Eviana.

"Family," he said.

Ginzolo thought he would never hear that phrase again, but put his hand on top of Goddum's.

"Familia," he said with a smirk.

The Chosen broke the unification. They went to their assigned wizards.

"One last piece of advice," said Mercutio. "In order for us to communicate with each other, you have to transform. We can talk to each other through our minds that way."

Then they went in the tunnels.

As Endstra, Mercutio and Eviana moved closer into the tunnel, Eviana started to worry.

"I don't like this, Merck," she nervously said. "I don't like this one bit."

Mercutio grabbed her by the waist and kissed the top of her head.

"We're fine," he said. Eviana cuddled on Mercutio's chest, as a child would hug a teddy bear sleeping in its bed.

"Endstra?" said Mercutio. Endstra turned and gave Mercutio his attention.

"Do you know what's wrong with Sistro?"

Endstra shrugged his shoulders. "I don't know," he said. "Sistro's been acting differently ever since we started this journey. As a matter of fact, he always starts to act weird when he's around you, Mercutio."

"Why me?"

"I don't know," replied Endstra. "I guess there's something about you that makes Sistro a lot prouder. Stronger, in a way. Personally, I think God chose the right person to have the power of Pyrokinesis."

Mercutio smiled. "Thanks, Endstra," he said. "You're all right yourself."

"I know," he said jokingly.

As the three laughed, a voice came dragging towards them in the wind.

And *this* tunnel carried no wind.

"What was that?" asked Endstra.

"Whatever it is," said Mercutio, "I sense it's not here to help us. Run!"

So the lovers and the wizard ran until the tunnel widened. They ran into a six-story wall with doors all around it.

"Dead-end!" Endstra yelled.

The voices came closer, followed by two lights.

The Chosen walked back to the wall, and transformed. Mercutio and Endstra was in their fourth and Eviana in her second. What came out of the tunnel were Tunnel Phantoms; ghostly creatures of the Devil Cave Tunnel.

Tunnel Phantoms were covered in a gray cloak. They had no legs, and looked like they had ho hands on the fact that their sleeves were very long. Inside their hoods was an eerie circular white light that covered as much ground as a Twentieth Century searchlight. These were rumored to be the lost souls of the miners of Camenstra who died creating this tunnel to North Africa. Their source of their power was in their light. Wanderers who were unaware of these creatures are caught by them and sucked dry of their energy to replenish their power, which lies in their light. Now the Chosen figured out their powers was in the light.

They just didn't know how to get rid of it.

The phantoms moved closer to the group. Mercutio took out Hikulo and transformed it to the Kagi no Hiteshita.

"Move out!" he yelled. Eviana went to the left, Endstra went to the right and Mercutio went down the middle.

They were facing *two* of these creatures.

"Don't let them touch you!" Mercutio yelled. At that moment, one of their hands almost grabbed him. He dodged, then sprayed a blast of fire from his mouth on the hand.

The fire on its sleeve stopped. Its light grew brighter.

"Don't use energy attacks!" yelled Mercutio again. "They'll just absorb it and become stronger!"

"Then what are we supposed to do?!" Eviana yelled as she dodged the phantoms blows. Eviana tripped and was about to be grabbed by the phantom she was fighting; Endstra flew in and slashed its hand off with his bat-like claws.

"Fight!" he yelled.

Mercutio felt warmth inside of him. Suddenly the warmth turned into a glow. This attracted the two phantoms.

"Mercutio!" yelled Eviana. "Mercutio, don't do it!"

But Mercutio ignored her call and continued to illuminate.

"Mighty Spirit of Fire!" he yelled. "I summon you to reality!" A blast of fire burst out of his rib cage and mouth. It took human form – as tall as the six-story wall – eyes glowing red when it opened them.

The Mighty Spirit of Fire folded its arms.

"The phantoms have a craving for energy," said Mercutio. "Let's give them a lifetime supply."

"As you wish, master," the spirit said.

The phantoms came closer.

In unison, Mercutio and the spirit prepared to attack.

"Pioferia," they said in unison, "Angrivoto!" The spirit and Mercutio sent out a burst of energy. Even though the Tunnel Phantoms absorbed it, it was too much for them to handle.

Their lights burst and the phantoms exploded.

The Mighty Spirit of Fire entered Mercutio's body the same way he left. Mercutio almost collapsed on the floor, until he caught himself. He stood up, wearied, and transformed to his regular form. He walked to Eviana and just hugged her.

She pushed him off.

"Don't you *ever* scare me like that!" she yelled.

She hugged him.

"You could've *died*," said Endstra, "you know that?"

Mercutio nodded. "It had to be done," he said. "I had enough energy to give those creatures so they couldn't have anymore to store."

Mercutio looked at the doors in the walls. "One of these doors leads to the remainder of the tunnel," he said.

"I'll help you look," said Endstra.

Mercutio started at the bottom while Endstra flew to the top. Mercutio moved upward and Endstra downward, the doors lead to small caverns in the wall.

No portal to the continuation of the tunnel.

At least not yet.

All the doors were checked except for one in the middle. Mercutio and Endstra were at this door.

"You open it," said Mercutio.

Endstra reached out and grabbed the knob. He twisted it and opened the door.

Nothing.

"Follow me," he told Endstra. They flew down to Eviana.

"We're leaving," he said, "now!"

But before they were about to exit the way they entered, a wall suddenly blocked the exit.

"No!" Mercutio yelled as he flew to the wall. He banged, sliced and burned the wall.

Not a single pebble fell.

"Guys," said Mercutio, "I don't think this is the right tunnel."

Part Three
The Climax

Chapter Five

"Twinkle, twinkle little star," a voice in the tunnel said. "How I wonder where you are." Suddenly a hideous laugh filled the tunnel Sistro's group was in. They wondered where the voice was coming from.

"Too bad Mercutio picked the wrong tunnel," it said. "I really looked forward to facing him again." Sistro knew the voice.

"Napoleon," he said.

"Good job, Sistro," Napoleon's voice said. "Usually, Mercutio's the one who figures out where I am just by listening to my *breathing* pattern!"

"This is your *last* warning, Napoleon!" yelled Sistro. "Go back to Yamalu, or-"

Napoleon appeared right in front of Sistro and grabbed his neck.

"Or what?" he yelled. "You're going to send your *watchdogs* after me?" Ginzolo in his second transformation took out his sword and cut off Napoleon's hand at the speed of light.

"That," he said, "was for taking over my body!"

Napoleon watched his hand grow back. Once it grew, he punched Ginzolo all the way to the tunnel entrance.

"That was for being stupid!" said Napoleon.

Goddum transformed into his second form.

"You wanna punch?" he asked Napoleon. *"I'll show you a punch!"* Even though Napoleon blocked it, Goddum's elephant punch sent him crashing to the tunnel ceiling and to the ground at the same speed.

Napoleon attempted to get up. Goddum kicked him in the jaw, which sent him flying further into the tunnel. Ginzolo flew back to his party; and the three flew deeper into the tunnel to find Napoleon.

He found them first.

In a split second, Napoleon appeared in front of them and roundhouse kicked all three in the jaw at the same time. Only Goddum showed no pain. He landed on his feet, ran towards Napoleon, formed a giant boulder in his hand and attempted to smash Napoleon with it.

He missed.

Goddum continued to slap the ground with the boulder and Napoleon continued to dodge it, until he kicked it into hundreds of pieces with his right leg.

Goddum threw out a punch that formed a line of boulders like the one that punched Napoleon previously. He dodged it, only to confront *another* punch from the *other* hand! The punch sent Napoleon flying in the air, but he stopped himself before he hit the ceiling again and floated in the air.

Napoleon felt his mouth with his left fingers. He felt blood and wiped it off. He looked at Goddum with an evil glance, then suddenly smiled. At the blink of an eye, Napoleon sent out an aura blast that hit Goddum head-on. It plummeted him to the ground and was turned back to his first transformation. He stood with a frown on his face and pushed in his right dislocated shoulder.

"*Please*," said Napoleon as he shook his head. "Spare me the responsibility of having to beat you! Just give up now, and I will say you fought a good match!"

But what Napoleon didn't know was that Ginzolo was behind him with a Hito blade!

Goddum smiled. "I may not be able to beat you," he said, "but I guarantee you this:

You will not see the outside of this tunnel!"

Ginzolo sent the sword through Napoleon's heart until the blade was visible.

As he saw the blade through his heart, blood flowed out of Napoleon's mouth. Ginzolo let go of the sword. Napoleon fell like a ton of bricks.

Ginzolo floated down to the ground and checked Napoleon's pulse.

"Got you *this* time," he said as he rose. "*Bastard*," he said in Spanish. Sistro walked to the two Chosen.

"We have to keep moving," he said, "we have no time to waste."

Goddum responded to the wizards' advice quickly and moved forward. Ginzolo kept going; he had one thought in his head:

Napoleon is dead.
I killed him for <u>real</u>.
I saw him die, and he's never coming back.

As they continued down the tunnel, Sistro looked at Ginzolo. He was transforming back to his original form.

"You showed a hatred for Napoleon that exceeded your hatred for *Mascool*," said Sistro. Ginzolo gazed at Sistro through the corner of his eye, but continued to look forward.

"Nobody controls my body but *me!*" he said with a frown.

"Well," Sistro said with a sigh, "you *did* buy us some time. If we move quickly, we'll be back at the main tunnel in no time."

Ginzolo nodded and smirked a little. Goddum transformed to his second transformation.

"That was a nice trick," he said. "How did you get that sword?"

"I stole it from Napoleon when he punched me," said Ginzolo.

Goddum forgot Ginzolo had super-speed.

"Do you think Mercutio and the others can get out of that tunnel?"

"If Mercutio can't," said Ginzolo, "then we're *all* in trouble."

Napoleon's body laid in black rock and dirt – pale – cold – the sword still through his heart. The blood that oozed out of his mouth dried on the edge of his bottom lip. His eyelids were opened and the pupils were rolled back. The whites of his eyes were showing. His fingers stuck in a seizure position. His mouth open, but no breathing was being performed.

He was *dead.*

Lifeless.

But was it *possible*? Here, the man that stood in the Chosen's way through so many events. Their first encounter with him, his hideous madrocellular transformation in the Toxic Sewerway, taking control of Ginzolo's body as he foolishly fought him in Camenstra. The victory he almost had when Eviana attacked Mercutio with a water attack.

A very *powerful* one, at that.

So how come he died at the hand he called a fool numerous times, and controlled with no resistance whatsoever?

How come he let *Ginzolo* kill him?

Was it his carelessness that made him think he could easily beat him? Or maybe he was so arrogant he didn't notice his sword was missing.

Either way, he was *still* dead.

But there was a reason why Napoleon's soul was released from his body. Only this could answer the question of how a predator could be killed by the hands of its prey.

It was all planned.

With a blink of his eyes, Napoleon gasped for air and took a breath. He started to shake like one would in a seizure and his body suddenly formed a fetal position. The color in his African based body suddenly came back. The dried blood on his bottom lip liquefied and entered his mouth.

With the sword still through his heart, it started beating!

As soon as it started beating, Napoleon, out of his seizure, stood up.

He was alive.

Alive!

His face showed no emotion as he surveyed the scene of his death. He sensed the group went further into the tunnel.

An animal always trusts his instincts.

"They're a waste of my time," he said after he sucked his teeth. He looked at the sword, grabbed the handle behind him and pulled it from his heart slowly.

For a regular being, pulling a sword from their body that slow would be even more painful than the actual piercing. As the blade slid out of his heart, the wound healed rapidly. So did the flesh wound. He licked the blood from the Hito blade and smiled.

Why was he alive? A Hito blade was supposed to *kill* an immortal! Is there something *else* that makes Napoleon eerily unique?

Yes, there is something. Something that passed from father to son.

The power of the Vortex Crystal.

When Napoleon was an embryo in his tube of birth fluid, he was injected with Goddum's Biokinesis and strength when Captain Solara, one of Yamalu's best soldiers, captured him in Dimbar. When Goddum escaped from the secret military base in Dimbar, he attempted to destroy the embryo by punching the tube open, sending the fetus outside and leaving it for dead.

He failed.

Mascool discovered the fetus and brought it to Yamalu.

Soon after that, Napoleon was injected with Ginzolo's DNA, which consisted of his Electrokenisis and speed. Mascool took the sample of Ginzolo when he was a baby. Mascool injected Napoleon when Ginzolo first used his powers. But the main source of his powers came from the Vortex Crystal. Yamalu chipped off a small piece of the crystal and put it in the substance Napoleon was being nursed in. With the vortex crystal, you are not just an immortal.

You are perfection.

Nothing could kill you.

Not even a *Hito blade.*

After licking both sides of his sword, he put it up and cracked his neck.

"Well," he said softly, "I guess it wouldn't hurt."

He started walking towards the group, then floated towards them. Suddenly he disappeared, blending into the tunnel.

Sistro decided to rest for a while. Goddum and Ginzolo sat down.

"We shall rest for now," he said as he sat down.

Napoleon was on the ceiling, still invisible to their eyes.

"I'm so glad that we don't have to face Napoleon again," said Ginzolo as he put his hands behind his back.

Goddum smirked. Sistro shook his head.

"I told you," Sistro said, "that you bought us some time. That was not our last encounter with Napoleon.

"What?" Ginzolo whispered. "How could you say that? Napoleon is *dead*! I *killed* him!"

"Of course you killed him," said Goddum, "but it doesn't mean he isn't *dead*."

"You're not making any kind of sense, Goddum," yelled Ginzolo. "He's *dead*! I *killed* him! I checked his *pulse*!"

"*Shut up!*" yelled Sistro.

Ginzolo became silent.

"Now," he continued, "you already know that Napoleon was given a small piece of the Vortex Crystal that was put in his blood stream by Yamalu in his nursing liquid."

He looked around.

"That one small piece is as powerful as all *six* of us in our *third* transformations put together. Not only that, but of course it gave him immortality."

He leaned closer.

"That's not all. According to legend, if you have the crystal, whether it's a fragment of it, a piece of it, a shard of it, you're a *perfect* immortal. Not even a *Hito blade* can kill you."

Ginzolo's mouth opened as he heard this tale.

"B-but, his pulse!" he yelled.

"The blade *did* kill him," said Goddum, "but the powers of the crystal overcame death and resurrected him. It took some time because it was his first time dying from a Hito blade."

Goddum stood up.

"Besides," he continued, "Sistro spoke it into existence; *Mercutio* would be the one to destroy Napoleon. Even if he *didn't* have any of the crystals powers and a regular immortal like you and me, he *still* wouldn't die."

Ginzolo once again felt a sign of depression. This was the second time he thought he had killed Napoleon and found he was still alive. This was just as depressing as when he saw Mercutio and Eviana kiss in the rain in Camenstra after his *first* battle with Napoleon.

"So," Ginzolo whispered, "It's all up to Mercutio to save the day."

"Your time to show yourself will come," said Sistro. He put his hand on his shoulder. "I promise you that." Sistro then stood and picked up his staff.

"Well," he said while stretching, "I think we've rested enough. Let's keep moving."

As the group traveled into the tunnel and out of regular visual range, Napoleon became visible and floated off the ceiling. He landed on the ground feet first with a smirk on his face. He turned the other way and flew to the entrance of the tunnel. He looked down the tunnel. Mercutio's group was in. He immediately knew they were trapped.

How lucky for him.

Napoleon hovered in the air and flew into the tunnel with haste. He knew this was the wrong tunnel, but that didn't bother him.

It just gladdened him.

Besides, there was someone in that tunnel he had to destroy first. Someone his father told him to destroy once he left Ginzolo's body.

Endstra.

Mercutio was trying to open the wall that trapped them inside this place. He tried fire attacks so he could weaken the wall to break it.

Nothing.

He tried using the Hikulo and the Kagi no Hiteshita for a powerful combination that could possibly destroy it.

Still nothing.

"Forget it," said Endstra in his original form. Unless you're trying to pass the time, it's impossible to get out of here!"

Mercutio hit the wall again, again, and again a little slower. The last time he hit it, he dropped the sword and fell on his knees with his head lowered.

"Were never gonna get out of here," he whispered.

"Don't you threat," Endstra said as he stood and walked toward him. "We need you more than ever. And keep trying. Only *you* can break the wall."

Mercutio got off his knees and looked at Endstra out of the corner of his eyes.

"Is that a fact?" he asked.

"*Now* it is," answered Endstra. "Wizards speak things into existence, *remember?*"

Mercutio nodded, remembering the truth about the Wizard race of humans.

"How's Eviana?" Mercutio asked. She was sleeping on the other side of the room.

Endstra smirked. "She's doing what I think *we* should be doing."

Mercutio yawned, followed by a small chuckle. "I guess you're right," he said and blinked his eyes. Endstra looked at the ceiling and saw small ledges. He transformed to his fourth transformation and flew to the ledge of the ceiling. Just like a bat, Endstra clung his feet to it and hung upside down.

Mercutio laughed at Endstra's behavior. He never acted like the creature his transformations allowed him to be.

"I'll see you in about a few hours," said Endstra loudly. Mercutio waved his hand in approval. Endstra fell asleep. Mercutio sat on the ground and just thought.

Even *if* Endstra spoke it into existence, how was he going to break this wall?

"I haven't even mastered the *GF* yet," he whispered to himself. He lay on the ground, having perfect visual contact with Eviana and Endstra.

His eyelids became heavy.

As he surrendered slowly to the control of a useful sleep, his last words before it were,

"If only I could find him…"
Mercutio fell asleep.

Napoleon was at the wall that trapped the other three. He touched it with his left hand. It sent a wave like a ripple in a pool of water. Then he put his entire left hand in the wall. As he pulled it out, it came with a truthful rule.

You can come in, but you can *never* come out.

Napoleon was about to break that rule.

Napoleon stepped into the wall and came out on the other side, which was the room Mercutio, Eviana and Endstra was in. Napoleon looked on the floor. Mercutio and Eviana were fast asleep. He looked up and saw Endstra hanging upside-down sleeping like a bat.

"Amazing," said Napoleon shaking his head. He flew towards his upside-down face. He reached in his pocket and pulled out a round crest of Yamalu's about three inches high. He placed it on Endstra's chest gently in-between his upper abs.

It glowed purple.

"I guess I can have a little fun before I kill you," Napoleon whispered in Endstra's right bat-shaped ear. Napoleon pulled out another and flipped it to the ground. It landed on Mercutio's chest face up and *also* glowed purple.

Napoleon smiled. He knew without looking that the crest landed on Mercutio.

He went back to the wall and unsurprisingly found it solid as a rock. He put his right hand on it, and sent such a force of electrical energy through it, that it had no choice but to let him through. But before he went through the portal, he snapped his fingers.

And the rest was only a dream.

The dream started with Mercutio walking in this desert. The sun was exposed with no darkness to bind it.

It was free.

Mercutio, who of course is used to extreme temperatures of heat, kept walking until he saw Endstra, who was face down in the sand.

It didn't look like he was breathing.

Mercutio ran to Endstra and got his head out of the sand. He was alive but barely breathing. He soon awoke from his deadly trance.

"Where are we?" he asked Mercutio.

"Somewhere in the middle of the HDO," said Mercutio as he helped Endstra up. "C'mon," he said, "we have to find the entrance to Dimbar." Endstra looked at the many sand traps that surrounded them. Then he noticed one looked like sand seeped into the ground.

"That one!" Endstra pointed. Endstra and Mercutio ran to the trap door, almost being swallowed by a sand trap in the process. When they reached the entrance, they fell through the trap door like they were supposed to.

But something was different.

When the two slid down the tubes, the tubes cut off. Mercutio and Endstra caught themselves and floated in the air. There was something wrong. In the part of the city they were it, there was no light. As they flew, they were terrified of what they saw.

The city was in ruins. The glass of the buildings were broken and on the ground. There were dead bodies almost everywhere. The means of transportation that were recovered and restored for use were destroyed. The entire suburban area was wrecked with collapsed roofs and destroyed houses. The roof of the city had hundreds of holes in it, letting the sun shine its light in the dark, unlit city.

"My home..." Mercutio whispered to himself.

"C'mon," said Endstra, trying to calm him down, "let's look around. We might find something we need."

So they flew towards the city that was once the city of New Dimbar.

When Mercutio and Endstra reached the destroyed city, they immediately started to search for survivors. So far their mission was failing because everyone they found was *dead*.

"Everyone's dead!" yelled Endstra. Mercutio met Endstra and they walked in front of the kings' tower.

"Stop," said Mercutio as he held out his hand. Endstra stopped and looked around.

"What is it?" he asked. Mercutio enhanced his hearing – footsteps – coming from the tower.

Mercutio looked up.

"We are not alone."

Suddenly, a man jumped out of the window from the top floor of the kings' tower. As he fell closer to the two, he pulled out a sword and started laughing maniacally.

"Napoleon!" said Mercutio. He came closer.

"Move!" Mercutio and Endstra moved out of the way. Napoleon landed on his left knee, with his left hand on the ground. Right after the glass from the jump hit the ground, Napoleon suddenly jerked his head and faced the two men.

Napoleon slowly stood with that evil trademark smile on his face. Mercutio looked at him with a hatred he only had when the evil of the GF took over him. But something *more* was fueling his anger. Something that *involved* Napoleon and gave him this raged anger.

He destroyed his home.

He did it with no remorse, whatsoever.

In a raged yell, a red aurora suddenly glowed over Mercutio. He took out the Hikulo, flew towards Napoleon and attacked out of rage. Even though Mercutio wasn't thinking when he was attacking, he was *still* strategizing. Every time Napoleon dodged an attack, Mercutio always plotted one following the previous attack. Once Napoleon got tired, he blasted Mercutio into a building with his telekinetic ability.

"Enough!" yelled Napoleon. "You're not the one I'm after!" He then slowly turned his head and faced Endstra.

Endstra tossed his staff on the ground, and stood in a martial arts stance.

"Oh, really," Napoleon sarcastically said as he threw his sword on the ground. Napoleon charged at him with a bull's speed, but Endstra suddenly disappeared when Napoleon reached him. He looked up and saw Endstra one second before he punched Napoleon in the face and sent him into another building. Within four seconds, Napoleon burst out of the rubble of the building. He stared Endstra down. Endstra transformed into his second madrocellular transformation.

"Let's go."

Napoleon flew towards Endstra with a sword in his hand.

Endstra pulled out his.

Their swords clashed and almost destroyed *both* blades. Mercutio recovered from the blast Napoleon sent and was about to join the fight, until he realized he was trapped inside an invisible box by Napoleon.

He was forced out of the match.

The two immortals continued to clash swords. They floated upward. Napoleon tried to stab Endstra in the head, but Endstra *grabbed* the blade, twisted it off, uppercut punched him in the jaw and slapped him with the sword handle. Because of reflexes, Napoleon responded to the slap by punching Endstra in the stomach. It sent Endstra flying into the kings' tower, but instead of going through it, he put his feet on it. Napoleon sent so much force in his punch, all of the remaining glass shattered from the entire building when Endstra kicked off. Endstra flew towards Napoleon, skipped his third transformation and went straight to his fourth. They prepared to punch. When they met, the force behind their punches sent Endstra and Napoleon in separate directions!

Endstra caught himself, but Napoleon was hurtled into a building on the other side of the city. Endstra breathing heavily, and stared at the spot Napoleon landed. After Endstra caught his breath, he floated near the crash site.

Endstra reached Napoleon's landing point, he tried to find him. Mercutio, released from the telekinetic box, flew next to Endstra.

"Did you find him yet?" asked Mercutio.

Endstra shook his bat-shaped head. "Not yet."

"Well, even though I think it's a trap, I think we should go in and look for him.

Endstra nodded. "I think you're right," he said. Mercutio transformed to his fourth form and created the Kagi no Hiteshita. Endstra made sure each of his claws were sharpened. Together, they entered the building.

They searched through the inside of the darkened building. They at first saw nothing but columns used to support the building, dried cement with metallic wires coming from the inside them and failing light systems flickering continuously, but annoyingly. Mercutio took a step and suddenly saw movement in the darkness, but when the light came on, nothing was there.

"He's using the darkness as a cloak of invisibility," said Endstra. "Be careful."

"Just attack anything that moves," replied Mercutio as he prepared to enter the darkness. Endstra nodded and went to the other side of the room. Mercutio was definitely on his guard as he created a ball of fire in his left palm. He walked until he came to a wall. He stood still once he reached it and closed his eyes. He was used his enhanced sense of hearing and smell. Napoleon was right in front of him. Once Mercutio opened his eyes, he grabbed the fireball to put it out. Then he yelled and suddenly flew forward very quickly and grabbed Napoleon in the process. Once they were in the light, Mercutio threw Napoleon to the ground.

Endstra heard the voice and immediately flew to the lightened area. He smirked when he saw Napoleon lying on the ground.

"Nice job," he said with a nod. Mercutio replied with a nod and said, "thanks." As Napoleon attempted to get up, Endstra and Mercutio looked at each other.

"Let's finish this," said Endstra.

"Let's."

Napoleon stood up, his appearance – very strange. His eyes were bleeding. Cuts were all over his face and body. He held his left arm like it was dislocated. He was breathing hard. Mercutio scaled him up and down. He immediately sensed feelings he had never sensed in him before.

He was scared.

He was weak.

Even *Endstra* saw something different.

Mercutio realized why Napoleon was acting this way.

He *wasn't* Napoleon.

Napoleon was more strategic than this. He wouldn't let himself be tossed around by a six-foot bat. Nor would he *ever* turn down a fight with Mercutio. But what threw it off was Napoleon would never stand in front of him if he was hiding in the darkness. This had to be an imposter.

Or at least an imitator.

But still, this imposter was very convincing. Jumping from the very top of the kings' tower was very much like Napoleon. It did all of the sarcastic comments he said to Endstra during the fight. So who would know so much of Napoleon's ways and motives to the point where they could imitate him almost perfectly?

How could this imitator be immortal if he wasn't a wizard? Mercutio could only think of one person who could mimic Napoleon almost perfectly.

That person was Napoleon.

There was only one conclusion.

This was a copy.

But even if Mercutio's hypothesis was correct, this *copy* was a nuisance like the real Napoleon. It was time to get rid of him. After the copy pushed in his dislocated shoulder, both Mercutio and Endstra punched him out of the building and into the air. Even though he caught himself and floated in the air, the copied Napoleon was dazed. The fact that he was a copy came more into effect when he saw Endstra and Mercutio float towards him

He was scared out of his mind.

Endstra and Mercutio stopped at the same time, the copy jumped. Endstra knew then it wasn't the real Napoleon, but a copy. Suddenly, Endstra raised his left hand and Mercutio his right. They were next to each other. But something happened. Something weird, new and that never happened before in either Endstra's or Mercutio's life.

Their hands were merging together!

This was starting to scare the copy to death, let alone Mercutio and Endstra. Suddenly, they came together moderately slow, until they were completely aligned. A red light mixed with a black light engulfed them and blinded the copy. In three seconds, the light suddenly stopped, and another man was seen instead of Mercutio and Endstra.

He was black with a tapered mustache, texturized hair with curls on the sides. He was slim, muscular and wore a burgundy sleeveless compression shirt with a mock neck. His pants were black dress pants and black shoes with a very thick sole. He had two black dog collar wristbands on his left wrist. He wore a pendant that was half of Mercutio's and half Endstra's in his first transformation. But what made this person strange was the retina of his right eye was black, and the other was red! When two flames of black fire appeared in both of the man's hands, the Napoleon copy was shocked in awe.

"Mercutio?" the copy asked.

"No," the man said with a combination of Mercutio and Endstra's voices. "I am Hikoi," he said, "the merged combination of Mercutio and Endstra." Hikoi smirked and took out the Hikulo. He stared at the copy as the swords outer blades straightened out and turned burgundy.

"It's time to end this," he said as the sword caught on fire from the ones in his hands.

The copy frowned, and flew towards the combined forces with a ramming speed, until Hikoi shot a red ball with black spectacles from the transformed Hikulo. The ball was similar to the attack Endstra made when he finished off the legion of shadows back in Camenstra. The copy didn't see the attack in time. When the ball reached him, it stretched itself and wrapped around him.

He couldn't move.

Hikoi put the Hikulo away, and held out both hands. In his left hand was a wild flame and in his right was a black energy acting as wild as the flame. As the Napoleon copy helplessly watched Hikoi, he showed a look that was photographic.

If cameras still existed.

As both energies grew to a very large size, Hikoi smiled with a show of teeth.

"Good-bye," he said to the copy.

He then clasped the elements together with a clap from his hand. "Energy Merge!" he yelled. They merged into a giant energy beam and totally dissolved the copy when it reached him.

And in that same light that illuminated from the blast, everything disappeared.

The glowing purple pendants on Endstra and Mercutio exploded. Suddenly, Mercutio and Endstra awakened and both gasped for air. He clung from the ceiling, flew to the ground while transforming to his normal form in the process and helped Mercutio up.

"You all right?" asked Endstra.

"Dimbar," said Mercutio softly. "Napoleon. Hikoi…"

"You had the same dream?" Endstra asked amazingly.

"You were in mine!" said Mercutio.

"You were, too!"

"We're having connected dreams?"

"It happens," replied Endstra. Mercutio rubbed his neck.

"Well," he said, "if we had the same dream, can you explain what happened to us when we became Hikoi?"

"We merged," Endstra replied. "Hikoi is the person from both of our energies."

"Can we do it in real life?"

Endstra smiled.

"Only one way to find out."

Endstra put out his left hand and Mercutio his right. They drew their hands together and merged into one!

They quickly pulled their hands apart.

"Weird," said Mercutio.

"Very," Endstra replied.

Suddenly Mercutio regained hope and confidence. He took out the Hikulo.

"Wake up Eviana," said Mercutio. "We're getting out of here!"

To Mercutio, everything was making sense. His spirit was renewed by a single illusion. He now realized his dream was surrounded by self-pity and grief. The only way to reach reality was to drop these burdens and step into reality.

The dream was over.

Reality had just begun.

Napoleon already knew the dreams failed. After all, he didn't want to *kill* them.

Just amuse them.

He was sitting on the ceiling trying to figure out where this new source of power that Mercutio and Endstra demonstrated in the dream had come from. He had never felt energy like that besides his own. It didn't make sense how this power was controlled.

He had to possess it.

"Napoleon," a voice in the tunnel called out. He looked around and saw no one.

"Napoleon!" it said louder.

Napoleon floated to the ground, still upside-down in his sitting position, turned his body around and landed on the ground, still sitting. He stood up and walked down the tunnel. When he stopped, he felt a chill down his spine that was cold as ice. He knew someone was behind him, but didn't know whom.

Napoleon turned around to see Mascool.

"What do *you* want?" he asked his father's servant.

"Something that should've been mine since you were created," Mascool said with a hateful tone. Napoleon grinned at Mascool's tone of diction.

"And what might *that* be?"

"Your blood."

"My *blood?!*" Napoleon said with a surprised look on his face.

"Your blood is the only way I can gain enough respect in my master for him to notice me," he said. "Because believe it or not, I am the one Yamalu notices."

"That's because you're in his *face* twenty-four seven!" he sarcastically said.

"*I* will be the one to destroy Endstra *and* Sistro," replied Mascool. "That is how I will be declared the most powerful wizard-like being on earth.

He stared at Napoleon's veins of blood in his neck.

"And I need your blood to do it."

Napoleon figured out that he wanted his powers. He used that blood speech to try to throw him off. He stared Mascool down from head to toe; he wondered why he was so eagerly trying to impress his father. Even though he had at least three-fourths of Yamalu's spirit, Napoleon was his own person with his own personality. It was pitiful through his eyes that this "dog" wants to prove to his "master", his father that it had more dominance.

Napoleon chuckled in his face.

Mascool suddenly felt intimidated. A creature *he* basically created just laughed in his face. He frowned and lowered his face. He had never been laughed at before. Maybe ridiculed, talked about. Probably even embarrassed.

But *never* laughed at.

Suddenly, Mascool punched Napoleon with a left hand transformed into a metallic two-foot wide and two-foot long box that almost sent him back to the trap entrance!

Napoleon stood up from the powerful punch with a broken jaw. He quickly put it back into place with no pain and moved it back and fourth. Napoleon frowned as Mascool's hands formed two metallic blades.

"If it's a fight you want," Napoleon said angrily, "then it's a fight you'll get!"

Napoleon took out his sword and flew toward Mascool with haste. Mascool got ready for impact, using his blade hands as a crossed shield. As soon as Napoleon was in striking distance, Mascool used both of his blades to attack him, but it wasn't effective, he thought.

Napoleon slammed into Mascool and both went to the area of the tunnel where it split.

Mascool got up from the charge; he heard his rib cage mend. But when he looked at Napoleon, he saw his attack was effective.

He sliced off both of his arms.

Not that they wouldn't grow back, but at least he could *touch* him. Mascool transformed his hands back. Napoleon grew new arms. He reached for a weapon, but couldn't find one. So he did what he always did when he needed a new weapon.

He *made* one out of pure thought.

As Napoleon grabbed his new weapon from the air, Mascool pulled out a dagger. He ran to slit his throat, but Napoleon blocked it with his sword, spun around and slit his stomach. Mascool healed and attempted several more times to cut him in numerous places, but Napoleon ducked and dodged every attempt. He did a back flip and kicked the dagger out of his Mascool's hand. It landed on the ceiling with the blade stuck inside a diamond.

Mascool grabbed Napoleon's head, punched it five times, head-butted it once, and thrust it into his left knee with a bone crushing force. He spun-kicked the left sides of his face so hard, it sent Napoleon hurtling into the nearest wall. After the dust settled, Napoleon was stuck in the wall.

Mascool walked up to him and closed his eyes. He put his hands in front of him and a ball of black energy formed in them.

When he opened his eyes, they were pitch-black.

He then blasted a giant energy attack that created a *third* tunnel! As the dust settled, Mascool walked down the newly created tunnel, looking for any traces of Napoleon. He was only halfway down the tunnel when Napoleon came out of the darkness and punched Mascool with Goddum's strength. Mascool bounced off the walls while hurtling out of the tunnel.

Mascool stood up. With a wicked smile, Napoleon walked towards Mascool. When he came close enough, Mascool punched him with his right hand. Napoleon dodged it and kicked him while flipping backwards. It sent Mascool at least five feet in the air, but before he landed on the ground, Napoleon punched him to the nearest wall. He flew toward Mascool, thrust his left foot through his stomach, grabbed his shoulders and threw him over his head. When he landed, his stomach wound healed, he came face to face with Napoleon's left fist. The punch sent him at least seven feet from Napoleon, but Napoleon's left arm stretched abnormally, grabbed his neck, tossed him around and threw him on the ground head first.

But Napoleon didn't let go. With his extended arm, Napoleon spun Mascool around, making him scrape his head on the diamond-infested walls. When he did let go, Mascool crashed into a wall. He bounced off and skid backwards on the ground. After all of his wounds healed, Mascool stood up and started to breathe heavily.

"I'm ashamed," said Napoleon. "You are my father's servant who has a *major* ego problem. You challenge *me* to a fight, but *you* end up losing."

He shook his head.

"I must say," he said, "that I am very disappointed."

"I will kill you," said Mascool softly, "if it's the last thing I do!"

Mascool suddenly ran towards Napoleon.

"Please," he said as he put his hand forward. Mascool stopped. He tried to move, but all of his joints were frozen.

He was paralyzed.

"Go back to my father," Napoleon said as his hand glowed pink. The energy shot off his hand and formed a giant glowing pink circle on the ground under Mascool. Suddenly the circle shot out enough energy that it looked like Mascool was inside a glowing pink tube. With a growing scream, he dissolved into the energy. Once he was completely dissolved, the energy went back to the circle in the ground. It then disappeared and left the universal insignia of Yamalu's crest.

"Complete waste of my time," said Napoleon.

Napoleon put the idea in Mascool's mind that he could beat him, even though it was a lost cause. It started with the laugh. That told Mascool to fight right from the beginning. It gave him the impulse to mold his fist and punch Napoleon with it.

The laugh *told* him to fight Napoleon.

He basically sent mind control with the laugh. It probably whispered in his ear,

"You're not gonna let that human laugh in your face, are you?"

The idea of killing Napoleon was already in Mascool. Napoleon just turned the idea into an act.

It was like clockwork.

Even though Mascool's appearance was not planned, it was still programmed perfectly.

Then there were the hits Napoleon took after he eliminated the dagger. Napoleon let him damage him *that* much so he could have his fun.

That's what he called strategy.

But taking over Ginzolo's body through an open wound after making him think he won the battle wasn't strategy.

It was fun.

Moving out of the way of Eviana's water attack so Mercutio would be hit wasn't strategy.

It was fun.

Making Ginzolo think that he killed him when he rammed that Hito blade through his heart wasn't strategy.

It was fun.

Napoleon's sick, demented way of seeing the world was that he was the *only* one worthy to be the second strongest being in the world.

Not *Mascool*.

That's why Yamalu told *him* to kill Endstra. If Mascool were to kill Sistro and Endstra, then take their powers, Mascool would probably be powerful than Yamalu!

Napoleon wasn't taught, but he wasn't *stupid.*

But one thing that caught Napoleon off-guard prior to this brawl with Mascool was the energy source he felt when Endstra and Mercutio were fighting the copy of him in their dream.

What was it?

What did those two do to get it?

Napoleon put his mind on this matter as soon as he sent Mascool back to his father's palace. Then he thought of the one person who might know of the power and how to get it.

"Sistro," he said to himself.

Napoleon floated in the air – in tremendous speed – flew down the tunnel Sistro's group went down once again. The fiend smiled. He figured out what he was having.

Fun.

Goddum in his regular form tried to keep up with the others. Being an elephant for three hours can be very stressful.

"Can you contact any of them yet?" he asked Ginzolo. Ginzolo in his second transformation shook his head.

"They must be in their normal form," replied Ginzolo. "I can't get in touch."

Sistro shook his head. "I think we have taken a toll for the worse."

He stopped and sat down.

"Without Mercutio, there is no hope."

Ginzolo sat next to him, finally feeling guilty. He nudged him with his shoulder.

"How's it going?" he asked. Sistro laughed, and then sighed. Ginzolo looked at Goddum, who was sitting on the opposite side.

"You know," started Ginzolo, "when we started off on this journey, I was very cocky. I mean, with everything that happened when I was sixteen, I had to be. My best friend was murdered right in front of me!

"That's the reason I wanted Mercutio's place as leader. I wanted to be the person in the tale that everyone knew. The person that mattered the most. But that doesn't matter now. What matters is getting out of this tunnel and back on course." As Ginzolo was speaking, both Sistro and Goddum were amazed to hear these words from his mouth.

"I understand what you are trying to tell me," Sistro said as he slowly nodded with a smirk, "and I forgive you."

Ginzolo thought about what he meant, then thought about what he was going to say and chuckled.

"You're okay, Sistro," Ginzolo said.

"I know."

Sistro, Goddum and Ginzolo got up and stretched.

"Let's moved," said Sistro. "We have no time to waste."

As they kept moving, Goddum suddenly felt the earth change once again.

"Something's wrong," he said.

Suddenly, the ground five feet ahead collapsed into a black abyss. An entire section of the tunnel plummeted into an endless fall of a black void.

"He's here," Sistro whispered.

A cold wind blew fiercely through the remainder of the tunnel. The three tried to resist the wind as they wondered what was happening.

Then, they saw him.

It was Napoleon.

Even though Ginzolo knew he wasn't dead, he was still surprised to see him alive.

Napoleon grinned evilly. He took out his sword – dove into the ground and burrowed toward them. The three took out their weapons. Ginzolo and Goddum transformed into second form.

Napoleon burst out of the ground.

Goddum attacked first. He swung the Grodera to his face, stomach and kneecaps. It hit his face and stomach, but he jumped to dodge the attempt at his knees. Goddum swung his right hand at Napoleon's face, then swung the Grodera near his feet. He did these three times straight with Napoleon blocking. The fourth time, he punched again, but this time Goddum spun around and made the Grodera trip him. When Napoleon fell, he flipped up and flew upwards. Goddum created a medium-sized boulder and threw it. Napoleon, off-balanced, started to fall; but as he fell, he tilted sideways and spun around with his sword in his right hand. He landed on his right knee, quickly jumped upward, sliced Goddum's belly and the middle of his head with the Hito bladed sword. While they were still in the air, Napoleon kicked Goddum with his own strength, aided by his telekinetic abilities.

Goddum then fell on the edge of the newly formed cliff, unconscious.

Ginzolo and Sistro charged in side-by-side. His sword and staff armed Sistro while only a sword armed Ginzolo. They reached Napoleon, and put their swords on top of his to force it out of his hand. Napoleon pushed the weapons from his, and spun around with his sword clashing with theirs. He clashed with Ginzolo's at least four times before blasting him off with telekinesis. He faced Sistro, who attempted to slap his face with his staff five times. Sistro flipped his staff around, he spun around, quickly stabbed him once and hit him in the chin with his staff, making Napoleon fall backwards.

As Napoleon quickly rose, he also performed tricks with his weapon. He spun around, flipped and twirled it every time Sistro defended or was injured by it. Ginzolo suddenly came to and rushed to aid Sistro. When he reached Napoleon, he attempted to stab him. He dodged it while dodging one of Sistro's attacks. Then he tried to cut off his head, but Napoleon ducked, elbowed him in the stomach and punched his head into a wall. He fell to the ground, unconscious.

Sistro was the only one left. He knew he would be. Goddum and Ginzolo couldn't beat Napoleon by themselves. It wasn't because he spoke it into existence.

He was just too strong for them.

But the thought of death continued to circle in Sistro's mind. Something that gave him a way past his own fortune telling.

Death and defeat were two different things.

"I beat your father," Sistro said, "and I will defeat you!"

Sistro transformed into a heavenly creature. It was no animal. No beast of the earth, whatsoever. It was madrocellular, but it was something he was already. He showed off his new biceps and abs. He had on black sandals. The lower portion of his white robes did not change. He had on white wristbands on each wrist and a ring on each hand; a diamond of the left and a cream-colored stone on the right. His staff was gold with a giant diamond on the top of the rod. His facial hair – cut off. His hair was longer. But the most noticeable thing about this fourth madrocellular transformation was that behind him was a glowing circle of yellow light that would follow him everywhere.

"Nice," replied Napoleon. "A lot better than *Ginzolo's,* anyway." Napoleon charged toward Sistro. He blocked with his new staff when Napoleon attacked him. Napoleon attacked wherever he could, but Sistro blocked with his staff with a speed that almost matched Ginzolo's! After one final attempt from Napoleon, Sistro threw him halfway out of the tunnel with his telekinetic ability.

Sistro didn't *move* after he transformed.

He didn't even break a sweat.

When Napoleon came back, Sistro was in the same position.

"Give it up, Napoleon," he said with a majestic voice. "Good always triumphs over evil."

Napoleon smiled. He put his left hand behind his back and formed a dart.

"Not today," said Napoleon. He threw the dart at Sistro, but he blocked it with a twirl of his staff. It bounced off the wall, to the ground, in the ceiling and in Sistro's neck. It immediately sent a potion into his system. After he reacted to the sting, he turned back to himself and fell asleep after he collapsed.

"I win," whispered Napoleon.

"Particle Lava Blast!"

"Tsunami Wave!"

"Dark Horde!"

All three attacks went straight to the wall they tried to destroy. They even crossed the attacks into one giant attack!

Nothing.

Not even a rock.

Mercutio, Eviana and Endstra were out of breath. Those attacks took a lot out of them.

"Let's take a break," said Mercutio. "We'll try again later." As the three separated in the room, Mercutio noticed Eviana use her powers to fix a drink of water for Endstra and herself. Even though he desperately wanted ice cold, crisp and refreshing water, Mercutio *knew* he couldn't drink it. He could drink anything *except* water.

Mercutio couldn't understand it, either. His body would take in anything but Hydrogen Monoxide.

"Mercutio," said Eviana as she walked toward him. Mercutio transformed from his fourth form to his original and looked into her sapphire blue eyes. That's where one of his passions for her was. Those eyes sent a message of peace and love within the air. Breathing it instantly gave the lucky person a blessing that could only come from God; as if he were saying you never had to worry about *anything* anymore.

Mercutio *loved* that message.

Mercutio lay on the wall; Eviana put her body on his and laid her head on his chest. Mercutio put his chin on her head and started to pet her beautiful blonde hair.

"You just don't know how you make me feel," he whispered. Eviana smiled.

"Ditto," she whispered back. Mercutio smiled. Eviana suddenly raised her head from her private personal pillow.

"Where do we go from here?" she asked.

Mercutio wasn't prepared to answer that question. He never thought about their relationship going further than what it was already. Until Mercutio could fully control the GF, this would have to be where their relationship would take them.

Because of his problem, he couldn't love her fully.

But knowing what the answer to her question was already, he answered her in three words:

"I don't know."

Eviana knew the answer he would give her. She heard it so many times she answered the questions. But it didn't matter to her; as long as she heard the three words that *really* mattered.

Mercutio once again looked into his lovers beautiful sapphire blue eyes.

"I love you," he whispered.

Those were the words. She kissed him tenderly, and Mercutio replied by wrapping his hands firmly around her waist, and held on for an eternity and a day.

As she kissed him, Eviana suddenly remembered Nostra's promise.

He'd kept it.

Because she found her true love.

Mercutio suddenly heard a buzz in his ear that was extremely high pitched. Eviana quickly removed the weight of her body from him when he reacted to the irritating sound. He walked to the middle of the room with his hands over his ears.

"What's wrong?" asked Endstra. Soon, he started to hear it, too. Eviana couldn't make out what was happening. She felt so scared and confused that she didn't know what to do. She stood back and watched, suddenly frightened.

<Mercutio, > a voice said in Mercutio and Endstra's head. Suddenly Eviana heard it, too.

Mercutio frowned, knowing this voice.

"What do you want, Napoleon?"

<Did you enjoy my little pretend brawl? > he asked. <I bet it took no time to see through it, yes? >

"You have no idea," said Endstra.

Eviana had no idea what they were talking about.

<That's just what I wanted to talk to you two about, > said Napoleon. <You and Endstra demonstrated a power in the dream that I never witnessed before. What was it? >

"That's for us to know, and for you to find out," Endstra said with a smirk.

"Mercutio, what's he talking about?" Eviana asked.

<Oh, but you *are* going to tell me, > Napoleon said in an eerie voice.

"And how do you know that?" asked Mercutio.

Suddenly the giant room transformed into a platform that showed Sistro, Ginzolo and Goddum trapped. Mercutio saw them paralyzed on the ground. Endstra looked around, scanning the area. Eviana stood next to Mercutio, wondering what happened.

They were soon once again back inside the room.

<The time is four o' clock, a.m., > said Napoleon. <You have twenty minutes to get there and tell me how you got that power. >

Mercutio frowned as he heard Napoleon chuckle.

"Damn you, Napoleon," said Mercutio.

<I'll be waiting, > said Napoleon. The buzzing suddenly came back, and this time *everyone* heard it. When it stopped, Mercutio suddenly heard a ticking sound that only he could hear. It ticked annoyingly as it chimed every second.

Tick. Tick. Tick.

Mercutio realized this wasn't just some irritating noise that took refuge in his head.

It was a timer.

They were being counted down.

"We have to break that wall now!" said Mercutio. Eviana transformed to her second transformation and prepared to attack, until Mercutio stopped her with his hand.

"I'll do it," he told her. Mercutio stared at the wall. He frowned at the obstacle that was keeping his group hostage. He closed his eyes with the frown still on his face. After three seconds, he suddenly opened them and they caught on fire.

He placed his right hand to the side of his body, and did the same with his left.

"Strongata Ghorita O' Pioferia," he said in Lingu, "nikae mop umi papu stregou kaitu repolin!"

Out of his fingertips blasted fire so hot that even *water* would get burned.

"Help me break this wall!" Mercutio yelled.

The flames once again formed the unbelievable sight of the Mighty Spirit of Fire. As it opened its eyes, it immediately folded its arms.

"I am *yours,* master," it said with its deep voice.

Mercutio created the Kagi no Hiteshita and floated in the air. Just like he did with the dragon in Tritunia, he floated backwards and entered the spirits head.

He took control of it.

He put his hands on the wall and stepped back. Endstra and Eviana quickly stepped out of the way before they were stepped on. Mercutio pushed the wall with the strength of the Spirit of Fire. As he pushed, the room filled with fire. The flames exploded. It knocked Endstra and Eviana off of their feet. After that, Eviana saw that the room was destroyed. Small flames all over the place. The wall was destroyed. Rocks were everywhere.

The *wall* was destroyed?!

As Eviana stood up, Endstra saw the wonderful sight, also. Eviana looked around and saw everything except for the one who started all of this.

Mercutio.

Endstra and Eviana saw a human shadow on the other side of where the wall once was. When the dust cleared, the shadowy figure was Mercutio.

He was in his fourth transformation without his mask. His arms were plated in regular and red gold. The fire in his eyes slowly died down with every step he took. He stood directly in front of Eviana. After a few seconds, they kissed like they haven't seen each other in years. Endstra smiled at the couple. As their lips separated, Mercutio looked at Endstra.

"Let's get out of here," he said. "We have no time to lose."

Endstra nodded. He transformed to *his* fourth transformation and took flight. Mercutio floated in the air facing the tunnel. Eviana flew next to her lover.

"Let's move!" yelled Mercutio.

And they flew down the tunnel to save their friends.

Chapter Six

"How I wonder where you are, Mercutio," Sistro whispered to himself as he lay on the cold ground. He was forced to look at the black ceiling that seemed to go on forever; the only thing on Sistro's mind was that Mercutio found a way out of the tunnel and was on his way to stop Napoleon for good.

But was it *possible?*

Speaking of the devil, Napoleon suddenly popped in Sistro's face, surprising him.

"Boo," he said.

Sistro frowned as Napoleon formed his trademark grin. Napoleon looked at each and every one of the Chosen he captured.

Even though he only captured two, he was very proud of himself.

"Its 4:03," Napoleon said with that grin still on his face. "You *sure* Mercutio will come and save you in time?"

"He'll be here, Napoleon!" yelled Ginzolo. Napoleon immediately turned to him.

"Just wait," he continued, "Mercutio's no punk like *you*. He'll fight you straight. He doesn't have to take over your body to try to win a fight!"

"Isn't this cute," said Napoleon. "You're finally taking up for Mercutio."

Napoleon quickly wiped the smirk off his face.

"I wonder how long this will last?"

"I finally realized how much of a fool I was," said Ginzolo. "I had to find out the hard way that people have their own destined path to walk on, and that you have to *follow* before you can lead. Crawl before you walk."

Napoleon sucked his teeth.

"What's the world coming to?" Goddum said with a chuckle.

Napoleon raised his hand, making Ginzolo float upward to face him directly.

"Didn't you *want* to destroy Mercutio?" he asked. "Didn't it feel good to make the only woman you had feelings about attack the man who stole her from you? Your spirit is a weird one, Ginzolo. And until you get what you want, you can never be *complete!*"

Ginzolo spat in Napoleon's face.

"Fuck you, *ese*," he said. "This battle will be the *last* one you will ever have with any of the Chosen."

Napoleon licked the spit off his face. Then he smirked with an evil look.

"I know," he whispered. "I'm *counting* on it."

4:05

Three hundred seconds past the fourth hour.

They had fifteen minutes to get to the location shown to them.

Eviana, Endstra and Mercutio flew out of the tunnel and into the other one about one thousand miles slower than Ginzolo usually flies.

Ginzolo is five hundred thousand times faster than the speed of light.

But as soon as they entered the other tunnel, an axe that was spinning as fast as the three were flying, dug right into the flesh of Eviana's back. With the speed that both she and the axe were traveling the force of it hit her and knocked her into a wall, then the other, then the ceiling, and landed face first into the ground, leaving a trail of black dust from the rock.

"Eviana!" cried Mercutio. He flew down to her and removed the axe. He looked at the weapon.

No Hito blade.

"Thank God," he said relieved.

As he helped Eviana up after she revived, Endstra heard something with his bat-ears that were just as good as Mercutio's

"Oh, *guys?*" he said. "I think I hear the culprits."

Mercutio looked down the way the tunnel with his enhanced sight.

He saw a massive force of Trimals.

Tiger Trimals were walking their way.

"Beautiful," said Mercutio.

The tiger Trimals snarled, growled and roared. They wore battle armor with the sign of Yamalu on their breastplates. The ones with helmets were similar to the gorillas in the sewerway. Only elbows were protected with armor instead of their joints. Their groins were protected by an elastic metal of some kind and behind them a hole for their tail to go through that connected with their groin plate. Connected to that was a white string inside of their behinds to hold the armor in place. By the looks of it, these weren't just mutants.

They were freaks.

And they were all *male*.

"We don't have *time* for this," Mercutio said. He took out Hikulo and transformed it into Kagi no Hiteshita.

"Tell me about it," said Endstra, who suddenly pulled out his claws. "How many do you count?"

"Twelve thousand five hundred," Mercutio said. The army came into normal visual range. "Let's do this with haste."

The army ran towards them. The three took fighting positions, with Mercutio and Eviana holding their weapons. When they met, the army immediately covered them. They were of course outnumbered. But almost four seconds after they were covered, the three sent off a burst of energy that blasted them.

It also destroyed about three-fourths of the army.

"What's the count *now?*" asked Endstra.

"One hundred sixty-six," said Mercutio. "*Now* we have a fighting chance." The remaining Trimals started on their way toward the three, Mercutio yelled,

"Move out!" The three went to different places in the decreased ocean of mutant tigers.

Eviana was up against fifty-six of the creatures. She transformed into her second madrocellular transformation and took out the Hydroscepter. She twirled it around her side, neck and legs, cutting and slicing the Trimals in the process. But suddenly, about ten ganged up on her and punched her in the face, causing Eviana to fall on her back.

She transformed and became unconscious.

"Eviana!" yelled Mercutio. He quickly flew towards her, but was detoured instantly when a group of fifty-five Trimals ran in front of him. Mercutio took the Kagi no Hiteshita and instantly sliced through the group with one swipe, leaving a trail of fire. Mercutio reached Eviana; a Trimal jumped on his back, dug its nails in his skin and started biting his flesh.

Mercutio yelled in pain as the creature dug deeper in his flesh. He ran around and banged the Trimal on the wall at least five times before it let go. As Mercutio's skin started to heal, he grabbed the Kagi no Hiteshita and sliced off its head.

He then went to Eviana.

Her forehead showed that it bled a bit. Endstra ran toward Mercutio's direction, shooting energy blasts at the surviving soldiers.

"New count?" said Endstra.

"About a hundred," replied Mercutio. "Eviana's out. It's just you and me."

"I hate to admit it, but I hate it when you're right."

"I do, too."

As the tiger Trimals came closer, Mercutio suddenly was struck with an idea.

"Let's merge," suggested Mercutio. "Let's summon Hikoi." Endstra looked at Mercutio, then at the wave of Trimals slowly coming towards them, then at Mercutio again.

"Are you *serious?*" he asked.

"Yes!" yelled Mercutio. "It's the only way we can beat these things and *still* get to the others before 4:20."

Endstra looked at his left hand, then at the army.

"Then let's do it."

Mercutio took his right hand and put it in front of him. Endstra did the same thing with his left. In a unison movement, their hands merged into one, shooting out a black and red light. The red and black light consumed the entire tunnel. When it stopped, the leader of the Chosen and the Master Wizard of Dark Magic, combined into the being Hikoi.

The tigers were baffled as they saw him. Neither his clothing nor his attitude had changed since the dream Mercutio and Endstra had.

Hikoi folded his arms and smirked.

"This should be fun," he said sounding like Mercutio and Endstra put together. The Hikulo's blades straightened and turned burgundy.

Hikoi flew towards the army to eliminate them one by one. With either a slice of the sword, a punch of the fist or a kick of the foot, Hikoi destroyed them until there were about fifty left. The tigers were afraid, but to them it was a good thing.

Because it kept their adrenaline up.

"Fifty," said Hikoi surprisingly. Then he smiled.

"My favorite number."

Hikoi raised the burgundy Hikulo in the air. He allowed the creatures to get at least four feet in front of him when he tossed the sword in the air.

The blades glowed.

"I think it's time I made my leave," Hikoi said as he rose in the air. "But before I do," he continued, "I have a parting gift for you." Hikoi grabbed the glowing sword; it extended further than the blades. It then turned into a burgundy beam. A burgundy aurora descended over him.

"Sword of Might!" he yelled. Hikoi flew over the Trimals. The blade beam did its work. As soon as it hit a Trimal, it exploded. The survivors tried to run, but Hikoi formed fire energy in one hand and a dark energy in the other. When they grew to the right size after his first attack, Hikoi used his *favorite* one.

"Energy Merge!" he yelled. He combined the energies with the clap of his hands. The elements turned into a twelve-foot wide, twelve-foot long blast that annihilated all of the surviving Trimals, and made another tunnel in the process.

The Trimals were gone.

Good riddance.

Hikoi flew to the ground and let out a sigh. Mercutio and Endstra stepped out of Hikoi's body, and Hikoi disappeared.

"Well," said Endstra, "that was fun."

Mercutio nodded in agreement. He looked behind him and saw Eviana was coming around. When she stood, Mercutio immediately ran to her side.

"You okay?" he asked. Eviana nodded and saw that every single Trimal was dead.

"H-how did you-"

"It doesn't matter," he said as he put his index finger over her mouth.

"Let's go."

"Yes, sir," Endstra replied.

And the three continued toward Napoleon.

4:15

Everyone including Napoleon was surprised. He was expecting the three to beat those Trimals ten minutes ago.

"He should've been here by now," he said. "I guess Mercutio is no longer the warrior I thought he was."

"Never underestimate the power of the Chosen," Sistro said. "He'll be here on time and put you in your place!"

Napoleon gazed into the hole in Sistro's face called a mouth. That was Sistro's power. His words could either bring someone higher than mountains or below the depths of Hell.

Napoleon didn't like it.

He pulled out his sword and put the end of it to Sistro's throat.

"I will kill you now," he whispered, "so I can show Mercutio I am *serious!*"

"Now is that really necessary?" a voice said from afar. Napoleon turned to his left and saw Mercutio and the others floating over the cliff leading to the platform. Napoleon put his sword blade on his shoulder.

"It's about time," he said.

Mercutio, Endstra and Eviana looked around to make sure this was the right place. After they saw the three lying on the ground defenseless, they automatically clarified that this was the right location.

"It's only 4:17," said Mercutio. "A little too eager don't you think?"

Napoleon smiled. "Yes," he said. "I am *very* eager to kill you."

Napoleon suddenly forgot about the power and focused on Mercutio.

Only this would *really* satisfy him.

The three entered the force field, knowing they couldn't escape.

"Release them," demanded Mercutio. "This is between you and me."

Napoleon raised his hand to release his hostages. Then he waved it to move everyone except Mercutio out of the way.

"Yes," he said. "Let this be our *final* battle!"

Mercutio took out Hikulo. Napoleon smiled and raised his sword in the air. Then he pointed it at Mercutio.

"You're gonna *die* tonight!" said Napoleon.

Mercutio shook his head.

"I do not think so."

Napoleon attacked first He swung his sword to try to cut off Mercutio's head. Mercutio dodged the attack with his Hikulo, then spun around and attempted to stab Napoleon in his head. Napoleon dodged it by moving his head back; he thrust his right fist into Mercutio's stomach.

Then he sent an uppercut to his chin.

Before Mercutio could regroup, Napoleon picked him up and threw him in the force field, which sent him bouncing off another one. He headed toward Napoleon, punched him to the ground face first.

Mercutio immediately recovered and punched Napoleon repeatedly with his free hand and twirled his sword to blind him. After taking about nine punches, Napoleon caught Mercutio's sword with his left thumb and kicked him in his ribs.

Mercutio caught himself in the air, quickly flew toward him and kicked his head in by back flipping and having his right foot impact with Napoleon's head. As soon as he regrouped, Mercutio sent a fire blast. It hit the force field; the blast sent Napoleon bouncing all over the platform. When he landed on the ground, he saw Mercutio in his first madrocellular transformation walking towards him through the flames of the last attack.

Napoleon hovered over the ground and flew to Mercutio to clash swords. They clashed about seven times before Mercutio flew back and shot navigational fireballs at him. Even though every one hit Napoleon, he still was coming toward him like he was dodging them. When he reached Mercutio, he spun around and attempted to stab him in the stomach. He missed, and Mercutio back flipped and kicked Napoleon with his bird talon feet.

Then with his wings of fire, took off into the heights.

Because of his wings, Mercutio was able to fly twenty times faster than Napoleon. Mercutio turned around and nose-dived toward Napoleon. He sent out energy blasts of a great number, but Mercutio swatted them like flies. When he met with Napoleon, Mercutio forcefully punched Napoleon into the platform of rock.

Mercutio retreated back to the air and shot Napoleon with a fire blast. He recovered. Napoleon counter-attacked with an energy blast of his own. Both forces kept the blasts and energy going and circled around the platform in the air. They suddenly stopped, took different positions and shot again. Napoleon dodged Mercutio's attack, and shot numerous amounts of black blasts from all over his body.

Mercutio tightened his grip on Hikulo, flew around the room deflecting the blasts with his sword or dodging by the single movement of his body. When he reached Napoleon, he punched him in the face, then elbowed him to the ground with a very forceful blow.

When Napoleon landed, Mercutio nose-dived toward him. But when he came within range, Napoleon got up and shot Mercutio with a blast that covered his entire body. When he stopped, he looked to see if he was still alive. He found saw him in his second transformation and felt the nose-breaking blow of his diamond on the end of his red wizard staff.

Mercutio combined the Hikulo with his staff to create the Kagi no Hiteshita. He flew toward Napoleon and forcefully stabbed him with it. Napoleon removed it and slapped him in the face with his sword handle. Mercutio grabbed it and sent Napoleon to the ground by swinging it over his head.

With blood overflowing in his mouth, Napoleon slowly walked toward Mercutio, dodging every attack he sent his way. When they met, Mercutio punched; but Napoleon blocked it with his right arm and slapped Mercutio with his left fist. Before he landed on his back, Mercutio forcefully flew into Napoleon and pushed him on the other side of the platform. He held the Kagi no Hiteshita like a missile launcher.

The tip glowed yellow.

"Particle Lava Blast!" he yelled. The lava instantly shot out of the weapon and covered Napoleon. Napoleon burst out of the lava and flew toward him. He grabbed Mercutio's collar, threw him to the ground and got on top of him, punching repeatedly.

Mercutio shot Napoleon from him with a blast from his eyes. Napoleon caught himself; he used his mental powers to create Hito blades fall toward him from the sky. Mercutio dodged every single one he came in contact with. When he reached Napoleon, he punched him in the face, kicked in his right shoulder, which caused him to spiral to the ground. When Napoleon landed, he put his dislocated shoulder back in and used his telekinetic ability to trap Mercutio who was about ten feet away. He formed another Hito blade dagger and threw it at Mercutio. He transformed into his third madrocellular transformation and caught the blade with his thumb and index fingers.

Mercutio broke from Napoleon's mental containment and punched him once into the force field. When he came back, Mercutio uppercut punched him in his chin and sent him flying in the air. Mercutio followed and punched him back to the ground with both fists. He sent out navigational fireballs when he recuperated. Napoleon amazingly dodged all of them on his way toward Mercutio. When he reached him, Napoleon put his hands on his throat and pushed him down to the platform with all the strength in his body.

When Napoleon let go, Mercutio kicked him in the groin, then in his chin. He flipped up and saw Napoleon fall to the ground. Mercutio grabbed his shirt, spun around and threw him into the force field. When he came back to Mercutio, Napoleon's face immediately met with his fist. Napoleon grabbed his wrist, twirled him around and sent him into the ground face first.

While Mercutio was on the ground, he picked up the Kagi no Hiteshita. When Napoleon grabbed his clothes, Mercutio sliced off his hand, then sent an ember into his eyes from his sword. Mercutio spun around, cut his stomach and kicked him in the chin. When Napoleon landed back first, Mercutio sent his sword through his heart, knowing it would do no good.

The sword was ejected from him with a blast of telekinesis, sending Mercutio hurtling in the air. Napoleon shot energy blasts on his way to Mercutio. He shot left and right with good results. The last blast sent Mercutio to the platform.

When Napoleon reached the platform, he took out his sword. Mercutio, still in his third transformation, went to his fourth. He snatched the mask off his face and grasped the Kagi no Hiteshita. The two circled and stared each other down both with frowns on their faces.

"You can do it, Mercutio!" cheered Ginzolo. Mercutio, surprised by his motivation looked at Ginzolo, giving Napoleon the opportunity to punch Mercutio in the face. Mercutio caught himself, then sent a line of fire to surround the villain. He then flew toward him and sliced Napoleon in half.

As Napoleon's bottom half grew from his top half, Mercutio put up his sword and walked. As Napoleon's bottom half fully grew, he stood up and put his sword away.

The two stared each other down for at least two minutes.

"I have completely underestimated your strength," said Mercutio.

Napoleon smirked. "I accept your apology," he said arrogantly. "Shall we continue?"

"Bring it."

Napoleon flew towards him and threw out numerous amounts of punches. After Mercutio dodged them, he punched him in his chin, punched his head down, and then slapped him with his right fist.

"Dead!" yelled Napoleon as he continued to punch him. "You're *dead!*"

Mercutio kicked him three times with his left foot, then flipped and kicked his head with his right. Napoleon came back with another kick, followed by two punches to the ribs. He then spun kicked him in; Mercutio fell to the ground.

Napoleon picked him up and threw him to the ground again. Then he did it again.

Then again.

And again.

And again.

And again.

Mercutio stood up; Napoleon head-putted him with a skull-crushing force. He grabbed his shoulders, kicked his ribs in, kicked him in the groin twice and kicked him in his left side with extreme force.

It sent him to the other side of the platform.

Napoleon smiled.

Mercutio was almost lifeless on the ground. Napoleon slowly walked toward him.

"That was a nice warm-up," he said. Mercutio started to shake.

Uh-oh.

"It's time to end this," he said. He made Mercutio faced him and saw that his eyes were orange-like yellow. Napoleon was shocked. He saw all of the wounds *instantly* disappear.

"What magic is this?!" yelled Napoleon.

"It is no magic," yelled Sistro. "It is the Fox Phoenix and the Mighty Spirit of Fire summoning your demise!"

Napoleon ignored Sistro and looked at Mercutio. A fiery telekinetic blast separated Napoleon and Mercutio. Mercutio floated to the middle of the room and the Fox Phoenix exited his body, followed by the Mighty Spirit of Fire. The two fused and formed a mightier version of Mercutio's first madrocellular transformation. It screeched so loud, it woke every animal on the planet. Napoleon heard dragons roar and other animals of fire as they entered the tunnel.

Dragons of all species entered the fiery being. After the dragons, every animal of fire entered the being. Once the last creature entered, the being entered Mercutio's. He hollered in pain as his body started to glow orange. Once he stopped yelling, the blast entered his body; fire blasts exited Mercutio's body and filled the platform.

The arena was a Hell on earth.

After Napoleon and the others got used to the heat and light, he saw a man in orange, yellow and red armor. Spikes came out of his sides. His boots and gloves were long and had claws attached to them. His helmet showed a face that was definitely not Mercutio's. Behind the helmet was a long amount of black hair – permed and ended at his torso.

"He did it," said Sistro. "His final madrocellular transformation. Genesis Fire."

Napoleon looked at the completed Mercutio in the blazing inferno. He stood and gazed at Mercutio, doubting his senses a second time. Mercutio walked through his flames he had spawned from his transformation. The fire and Mercutio were in sync. The flames didn't move without Mercutio's movement or command. Napoleon felt an emotion he was commanded never to feel.

He felt fear.

And why shouldn't he? Here was a being that controlled every single fire source on earth. Even though he still didn't equal Napoleon's power, Napoleon was frightened out of his mind.

It *didn't* equal Napoleon's power.

It *exceeded* it four hundred folds.

Napoleon pulled out his sword and grasped it tight. Mercutio held out his left hand and fire from the inferno created a new sword in his hand.

"Like you said before," said Mercutio as he grasped his new sword with his left hand and took out Hikulo with his right. "It's time to end this."

Mercutio took one step and a geyser of lava erupted from the platform. He took another and fireballs shot around the room randomly. By the time Mercutio made it to Napoleon, he had performed an entire melee of attacks by stepping on the ground. Napoleon attacked with a swipe of his sword. Mercutio spun, wrapped in a cyclone of fire and sprayed Napoleon. Even though somewhat ineffective, Napoleon reacted because it came so fast he didn't feel anything until it landed on him.

Napoleon attempted to punch him in the face. Mercutio moved his head to the right. A wave of fire come that direction as Napoleon entered his fist inside of the flame. As soon as Napoleon retreated his hand, Mercutio sent a single bladed sword through Napoleon's Adam's apple. He quickly took it out and kicked Napoleon in the ribs. Mercutio flew backwards in the air. While in the air, he sent two fire blasts from both swords Napoleon's way.

Napoleon side-flipped to his left, dodging the blast from Hikulo. He then back flipped dodging the blast from the fire-made weapon. After landing, Napoleon pushed off his feet and flew toward Mercutio, but Napoleon met his feet. Mercutio back flipped, kicking Napoleon in the chin. After Napoleon lost his flight temporarily, Mercutio caught his legs and threw him face first into the flaming ground.

Within two minutes, Napoleon stood up. The complete left side of his face – gone. His skull, the naked left eye, his teeth and a flowing stream of blood showed.

This was worse than getting his head chopped off, which happened once.

Napoleon ran toward the completed Mercutio yelling and tightening the grip on his sword.

When they met, he tried to slice him vertically. Mercutio blocked the blade with his right arm.

His *arm?!*

Napoleon tried to attack his left side. Mercutio twirled and blocked the blade with his right index finger. Then his uppercut punched him in the chin with his left index finger. It lifted Napoleon in the air, and he didn't fall until Mercutio punched him in the rib cages with a force as strong as Goddum!

Napoleon once again bounced off the force field. He landed in Mercutio's right hand – headfirst. His armored nails dug into his flesh, picked him up and threw him to the fiery ground. As Napoleon got up he looked at Mercutio and spit. He saw the saliva put out a flame on the floor. He looked at Mercutio again. He put up his sword – put his hands close together for an energy attack.

"Hydro Blast!" yelled Napoleon after a blue crystal energy source appeared in his hands. When he shot it, the entire room was engulfed by water, quickly catching up to Mercutio.

His eyes widened.

When the water hit Mercutio, it filled up the entire volume of the room to where the force field ended. After all of the bubbles cleared, Mercutio was gone. Napoleon was puzzled. Then he felt a tap on his right shoulder. He turned around to see Mercutio frowning at him.

Mercutio ignited a fire in his right hand. The water evaporated to water was half of an inch. Mercutio grabbed the flame; it turned to smoke.

He looked at Napoleon.

"I-it's not possible!" he said as he slowly backed away from him with every step Mercutio took. "You're supposed to be *dead!* That attack was *more* than enough to kill you!"

"He is now invulnerable to water, Napoleon," yelled Sistro. "He is complete, and *you* are about to die!"

"The man has a point, my friend," Mercutio said. "This is your last minute of life."

"I am a perfect immortal!" yelled Napoleon. "You cannot kill me!"

"Oh, really?" said Mercutio. "We shall see."

Mercutio once again set the entire arena on fire with the snap of his fingers.

"That's better," he said. Napoleon was scared out of his mind.

"Y-you haven't seen the last of me."

"It's over," said Mercutio. "This *is* the last."

With a tilt of his head, Mercutio said,

"Goodbye forever, Napoleon."

Sistro's ability of speaking things into existence immediately took its place.

"Death by Fire!" yelled Mercutio. With a push of his hands, every single flame in the room gathered on Napoleon. He hollered as the flames surrounded his body, eating his flesh.

This was the first death.

"Death by Smoke!" yelled Mercutio. He once again waved his hand. The flames came off the half-burned Napoleon. The flames turned to smoke. It entered Napoleon's body and he started to suffocate.

This was the second death.

"Death by Injection!" yelled Mercutio. As the smoke continued to suffocate Napoleon's badly burned body, Mercutio plunged his right hand through his stomach. The spikes ejected a black liquid that poisoned Napoleon's surviving body parts and inner muscles.

This was the third death.

"Death by Light!" yelled Mercutio. He placed his right hand in Napoleon's face, palm up, and sent a blinding white, red and yellow light. Napoleon, still being affected by the smoke and poison, screamed in pain as the blinding light literally fried his eyeballs.

This was the fourth death.

"Death by Release!" yelled Mercutio. With a tug of his hands, Mercutio telekinetically pulled the vortex powers from his blood, until every single cell was out of his body. Napoleon once again screamed in pain and horror. He felt every vein in his body rupture as his powers from the crystal Goddum and Ginzolo left his body. The powers transferred to the owners. The Vortex powers formed the missing piece of Yamalu's Vortex Crystal.

This was the fifth death.

"Death by Mortality!" yelled Mercutio. He formed a giant sword with a burst of fire and grasped it with both hands. Napoleon, burned badly, blinded, poisoned, and taken of his immortality, stood weak, unknowing and unaware of what was happening. Mercutio sliced him in half at the waist. Napoleon's top half slid off and fell to the floor followed by his bottom half.

This was the sixth death.

Mercutio looked over the face of Napoleon, to make sure he was the last person he saw before he died.

If he could see him.

Napoleon took his last breath – the endless force field suddenly disappeared. Both halves of his body turned into a hardened shell. The others were freed, and a sudden wind came and destroyed Napoleon's body. It carried his ashes through the tunnel.

Napoleon was dead.

Mercutio transformed back to himself and looked at the water remains; he bent his knees and swiped some up with his right fingers.

Nothing happened.

He stood and looked at the others.

"And so ends the saga of Napoleon," Sistro said where Napoleon's body once laid. Then he looked at Mercutio and nodded.

"It is done, then."

Mercutio looked at Eviana, who was walking toward him. She put her arms around his neck and laid her head on his chest.

"It's over," she said. "It's finally over."

"Over?" said Mercutio sounding surprised. "This was just the stepping stone of our journey," he said. "This was just the beginning."

"And what a beginning it was," said Sistro. "Napoleon is dead, Ginzolo and Goddum's powers have been fully restored and we have a chip of the Vortex Crystal."

Mercutio looked at the piece he held in his hand. It was hard to believe that little piece gave him all that power. But as he looked at the piece, he saw his fingers, still wet with water.

Then he looked at Eviana.

"I thirst," he said.

"But you'll die!"

"Do it, Eviana," insisted Endstra. "You cannot hurt him anymore." After looking at Endstra, Eviana faced Mercutio. She formed a small fountain from her fingers.

Mercutio, for the first time in his life, drank water.

It was cold, crisp and refreshing. He had never tasted anything so cool not since he first kissed Eviana at Camenstra. It was pure and clean. Never tampered with. The way it felt on his skin made it all worth. God became his only fear. No longer did he have to become paranoid when he smelled water.

He *loved* it, now.

When Mercutio had his fill, he signaled to stop by gently kissing Eviana. She stopped her fountain of nourishment and wrapped her hands around him. Ginzolo smirked at the sight, and was not envious. He suddenly knew that they were meant for each other and that his day would come.

It *had* to.

"We're almost near the exit," alerted Goddum after the lovers stopped kissing.

"Which way?" asked Mercutio.

"Northeast," Goddum pointed. "Just down that way."

Mercutio nodded. "Let's go," he said. The six left the platform and flew northeast. On the platform, Napoleon's crest of his father's kingdom was left on the ground.

The wind came back, and it too, turned to ash.

Napoleon is dead.

Napoleon is finally dead.

Some people were relieved that Napoleon would no longer pose a threat to them or anyone else for that matter. But one could not believe that he was dead. One couldn't believe that he died that easily after all he had done to cripple the Chosen.

That person was Yamalu.

He did not eat that evening. What is the point of eating if you're immortal, anyway? This was not normal for the likes of Yamalu. He never grieved over anyone besides his parents. Not even a mere *mortal* felt the way Yamalu felt now.

That was because he saw the whole thing.

Yamalu was telepathically connected to Napoleon after he accepted the battle with Mercutio. He could see the results for himself. He witnessed Mercutio slice through Napoleon's roughly burned flesh like butter. His heart literally stopped.

It wasn't until Napoleon's body dissolved in the wind. It actually started up again.

He was sitting on his throne when Mascool entered the throne room. He noticed Yamalu's mood and started to feel something in him.

It was remorse.

Half of this was his fault. He kept pulling Napoleon until he ended up killing him. He wanted to make it up to his master but couldn't think of what to do. Then he looked at his master's face a little more closely.

A tear rolled down his right cheek.

"You were right, Mascool," he said. "You were right about everything. I can't control fate. No matter how powerful I am."

"It isn't the end of the world, my lord," Mascool immediately responded. "So an attempt to kill the infidels failed. So what? We can still beat them through time and planning. They're only a few continents away from us. We have plenty of time. Napoleon-"

"Napoleon," said Yamalu as he stood up, "was my son. He may not have been my *blood* relative, but I accepted him as mine. The last time I saw him physically, I sent him out for the Chosen's heads. I never hugged or comforted him, or did anything that equals the word 'father'."

He cried streams.

"I loved him!" he yelled. "Just as you love me! If I can't control destiny then what *can* I control?! Nothing! No one! No alien species, no animal on this earth, not even this goddamn *planet!*"

Mascool was the culprit for the death of so many souls. The death of Napoleon, the deterioration of Yamalu's, even the slow killing of his own. As he thought about how to pass the blame, four words came out of his mouth.

"The Chosen must die."

Yamalu looked at Mascool with big bright eyes. His mouth slightly hung open as he heard those words come out of Mascool's mouth.

"You dare mention their names in my presence?"

"Like you said before," said Mascool with an evil grin on his face. "The enslavement of men and the world is only *part* of your vengeance."

Yamalu remembered saying that. He thought he was by himself that day.

He was doing it again.

"What must I do?" asked Yamalu.

"Find a being on this earth that is stronger than the fire controller," he said. He put his hands on Yamalu's shoulders. "Control it," he continued, "and have your vengeance on the culprit who killed your *son*."

"But what creature can kill a fire devinit that's immune to water?" Yamalu asked.

Mascool grinned with an evil look.

"You know whom I speak of," he said. Yamalu's eyes once again brightened as he looked at Mascool's face. He hugged him suddenly and rested his head on his left shoulder. He burst into tears.

Mascool patted him on the back. "There, there," he comforted. "I will help you look for it." Yamalu breathed heavily.

"No more trials for my suffering," said Yamalu, still hugging Mascool. "The Chosen shall feel our wrath and die under our might!"

Mascool was suddenly silent.

He just said *our*.

Twice!

Mascool responded, *also* in a hug and tears. They even started to sway little.

This is all Mascool ever wanted.

"I am yours," Mascool cried. "Whether at the gates of Heaven or the bowels of *Hell,* I am yours *forever!*"

Then, they continued their bonding.

As brother and brother.

As father and son.

Napoleon was only a memory.

The Chosen walked down the tunnel that led to North Africa. The new feeling that consumed them was positive and filled with hope. Now that Napoleon was finally dead, they each had a new perspective about the way that life should be lived.

Goddum found out that friendship could go a long way. The way you treasure it and carry it with you, determines your soul. If you consider someone your brother and they do the same with you, then there will be a trust in that bond that will never die, no matter how old it is.

Mercutio and he shared this bond.

Ever since the beginning, they had stuck their neck out for each other through thick and thin. It didn't matter if he was the leader. That gave more reason to trust.

Trust went a long way with Goddum.

Mercutio found the revelation of the same moral, but it wasn't toward Goddum.

It was toward Eviana.

She still stood by Mercutio, besides the fact that she could kill him. The trust was strong between these two. Only a *true* love's spirit gave them the trust to stay loyal to one another.

To stay truthful to one another.

As Mercutio thought about it, he learned that no matter what it is, you must always follow your destined path.

Ginzolo learned all of this and more. His lack of trust caused him to endure all that he went through since the beginning of this great journey. He also tried to run away from his destiny, just like Jonah tried to run away from his calling. But the main lesson that he learned was to never hate anyone, regardless of what has happened in the past. We go through things in life so we can know *our* place and where *we* belong. Even though he still sought revenge, his attitude was completely different.

Because for the first time, he felt *love* in his heart.

The way the Chosen were now was what they should've been since the beginning. Their teamwork was their new strength, and with that, they *had* no weaknesses. Their spirits were renewed, their oaths revised, and their heads held high.

You see, before all this, there *was* no Chosen. It wasn't until they saw past the end of their own noses – they saw the truth.

This was the Chosen.

Ginzolo saw an open hole in the far distance of the tunnel. It showed something that was all too familiar, yet it was something they haven't seen in a very long time.

It was the sky."

"We're almost there!" shouted Ginzolo.

"Good," said Goddum. "Any more of this scenery and I'll go crazy!" Mercutio and Eviana laughed at Goddum's facial expression. Ginzolo looked at Goddum and laughed, too.

They were finally a family.

Sistro and Endstra transformed into owls and flew out into the night air. Mercutio and Eviana soon followed and looked around. Goddum stretched as soon as he stepped on the fresh ground. Then he yawned like he just fell asleep on the world. Ginzolo grabbed the sides of the tunnel and pulled himself out. Sistro and Endstra transformed into their human selves. The Chosen and they noticed that they were on the outskirts of a beach.

"Beautiful night for a swim," Mercutio said with pride. He grabbed Eviana on her left side. But suddenly, he heard an all too familiar sound coming from behind the tunnel exit. He turned around, and saw *another* army of tiger Trimals.

"Oh, no," he said, getting the other's attention. "Not these guys, again!"

They snarled and roared as usual, but this time the Chosen weren't on a schedule. Mercutio took out Hikulo and smirked.

"Ready, Chosen?" he said. The others quickly and stylishly pulled out their weapons, ending up in a pose, saying ready.

"Let's go!" yelled Mercutio. They charged through the sea of Trimals and attacked.

Mercutio transformed into his fifth transformation and just ran. The Trimal forces were burned from the speed of was running, not counting the slices from Hikulo. Suddenly, he formed the fire cyclone and destroyed half of the army. Mercutio in a stand-up pose tilted his hand as he held Hikulo.

"Your move."

Eviana in her second transformation combined her sword and the Hydroscepter to create a key weapon. She flipped and froze Trimals that ganged up on her. She flew and unleashed a giant blizzard that immediately killed any Trimal in her range. With a flip landing, she pushed one of the frozen Trimals and it crumble when it hit the ground.

"Now that's cold."

Goddum took out Grodera and started hitting with it. With a spin, he instantly transformed to his first transformation and sent at least fifty into the ocean. With a flip and a swing of the Grodera, he transformed to his second transformation. This time he sent one hundred into the ocean. He put up Grodera, grabbed the ground, pulled it from under them, making Trimals fall, and slammed it over them.

"That's taking out the trash."

Goddum started to spin at the speed of sound, making him look like a spiral of yellow light. When he instantly stopped, the speed of his wind sent the Trimals in the area flying over water. Ginzolo turned to his second transformation, flew toward them and performed his Thunder Rage attack. Even though it killed every Trimal he faced, the attack landed in the water. During the explosion, Ginzolo stood in a pose facing the opposite direction, smiling.

"Shocking."

Mercutio transformed into himself and challenged every Trimal to a brawl. It was him against twenty. He knocked them out one by one, and didn't even use his fire ability. Sistro suddenly joined the battle. He was more of a fighter than he was a wizard.

"You fight by the book," said Sistro. "I guess it runs in the family."

Mercutio suddenly stopped fighting and stared at Sistro.

"What did you say?"

Suddenly a large-sized tiger Trimal grabbed Mercutio and continued to beat him senseless. After it looked like Mercutio was unconscious, it put him on his shoulder.

"No!" yelled Goddum. He flew toward the beast, but was suddenly knocked unconscious with one punch of another large-sized tiger Trimal.

Sistro looked at Goddum, who was on the ground and instantly transformed back to his regular form. The other tiger Trimal picked him up and put him over his shoulder, just like the other one. Endstra went to his brother and Eviana went to Ginzolo.

"C'mon!" they told each other. "We have to leave now!"

"What about the others?"

"They can take care of themselves," they told them. "Mercutio and Goddum will come through and catch up."

They ran about five miles until the large tiger Trimals caught up with them.

With an extreme force, one of them slapped Eviana and Ginzolo in the Southern direction.

"They can take care of themselves!" told Endstra. "We won't be any good if we're captured, too!"

Sistro knew he was right.

In the nick of time, Sistro and Endstra flew Southeast in a surprising speed before they were captured, also, leaving Mercutio and Goddum to fend for themselves.

The tiger Trimals stopped running, and joined the fifty other survivors of the Chosen's elemental massacre.

The two dropped the hostages on the ground and had the others gather around.

"THESE TWO ARE ALL YOU COULD GATHER?" one yelled. "THE MASTER SAID ALL OF THEM!"

"WELL, WE WOULD'VE HAD FOUR IF SOMEONE DIDN'T SLAP TWO OF THEM AWAY!"

The smallest large one started choking the other one.

"THEY WERE IN MY WAY!" it yelled in its ear. "WE HAD TO GET THOSE MAGIC FREAKS, TOO, YOU KNOW!"

One of the regular ones looked at Mercutio and smiled.

"THIS ONE LOOKS SATISFYING," he said with a sensual grin. The largest one grabbed his armor.

"THEY ARE NOT FOR ANY OF YOUR SEXUAL DESIRES WHATSOEVER," he yelled, "YOU SICK FREAK!"

He threw him back to the ground.

As the perverted one snarled, the smallest large one yelled, "ENOUGH!"

They all stopped talking and moving.

"WE TAKE THESE TWO TO MASTER YAMALU," he said. "UNTOUCHED AND UNSPOILED." Then he looked at the perverted one. "OR PENETRATED."

It snarled.

"ONCE THEY ARE ABLE TO WALK," the other continued, "WE WILL PUT THESE CUFFS ON THEM."

He showed the cuffs.

They were purple and had spikes on the end of them.

Go figure.

"THESE'LL STOP 'EM FROM ESCAPING WHEN THEY AWAKE," he continued. "UNTIL THEN, ME AND MY OTHER WILL CARRY 'EM. NOW MOVE!"

The tigers gathered in a cluttered line with the two giants in the front carrying two of the heroes on their shoulders. They headed southwest very steadily and slowly.

Eviana and Ginzolo started heading south after they recuperated from that blow.

Sistro and Endstra headed where they were destined to go.

Cavirielta O' Zulu; the Cave of Light.

And they were separated; away from each other physically. No contact whatsoever. Something that would always be the Chosen's greatest fear.

No matter *what* they accomplish.

LEGACY OF THE DARK WORLD

As the world winds in insanity, sinister songs sing soprano.
The music of darkness plays pleasantly over the earth,
Sending its seductive ways into the innocent's merciful mind.
But the warriors of obscurity oppose the invitation.
They carry powers of unbelievable universes,
Seasonable sorcery,
Love and passion,
Pain and pleasure.
The sins of all abort their offspring,
In hopes that it would continue to prevail in its wicked deeds.
Can the earth be forgiven?
Can we escape the jaws of the genesis of fire?
Only time can tell.

Sing the song of the earth.
Create the harmonies of the purified blessed.
Play the game of the saint's arrival,
In hopes of finally having peace.
Give the question of the population that is;
Why support the chaos?
As the beast within us ejects our souls, be gladdened.
For will begin the rest of your lives,
And end the legacy of the dark world.

The Chosen shall return, bringing forth Trials & Tribulations…

Printed in the United States
53281LVS00005B/181-279